THE FUTILITY EXP RTS

A NOVEL

MARGARET BROUCEK

schaffner press

Tucson, Arizona

First edition
Trade Paperback Original

Cover design: Brian McMullen
Interior design: Darci Slaten

ISBN: 978-1-943156-49-8 (Paperback)
ISBN: 978-1-943156-50-4 (PDF)
ISBN: 978-1-943156-51-1 (EPub)
ISBN: 978-1-943156-52-8 (Mobipocket)

For Library of Congress Cataloguing-in-Publication
Information, Contact the Publisher

Printed in the United States

This is a work of fiction. While real businesses,
institutions, and professional groups are mentioned,
the characters and stories are imaginary.

Advance Praise for *The Futility Experts*

"The Futility Experts starts with a bang and only gets more explosive from there, laughs and satisfying plot twists, a kooky cast, including dogs that only a mother could love. I flipped pages till the night was dawn, dying to figure out how Margaret Broucek would bring all the threads together. A self-invented sniper, a Sasquatch-loving scientist, a raucous neighbor (complete with contested real estate), a struggling family man, where's it all going to end? In a great reading experience, that's where, and an auspicious debut for this talented new voice."

~Bill Roorbach, author of *Life Among Giants,*
The Remedy for Love, and *The Girl of the Lake*

"Margaret Broucek's The Futility Experts makes hilarious art out of disaster. The characters herein might be failures, but they are inspired failures, and Broucek treats them so humanely that the reader can't help but root for them. An extravagantly comic, strangely moving novel. I loved it."

~Brock Clarke, author of *An Arsonist's Guide*
to Writers' Homes in New England

"Broucek's prose is stunning. Terrific turns of phrase, technicolor images, and a linguistic sensibility left-of-center enough to please and amuse without ever becoming gaudy or otherwise drawing undue attention to itself."

~Ron Currie, Jr., author of *The One-Eyed Man, God Is Dead*

"What Kris Kristofferson said when he discovered John Prine is what comic writers are going to say about Margaret Broucek. She's so good that we'll have to break her thumbs."

~David Carkeet, author of *The Full Catastrophe*

For Mom and Tracy

THE
FUTILITY
EXP RTS

A NOVEL

MARGARET
BROUCEK

TIM

Perhaps only people who are very clear on the facts of who they are—their gross weight, the coolness of their marriage, their insignificance at work—can take such flights of imagination as Tim Turner did, daily, in the cab of his pickup, trips fueled by the heroic marches of Sousa, of Fillmore, of the great Karl King. On this particular day it was King's "The Melody Shop" that animated Tim's commute through Boston, sent him rocketing over the blushing leaves on the wet parkway. As the euphoniums worked through their crazed, breathless lines, Tim became a Marine hurrying home at Thanksgiving, a sniper who'd seen too much carnage, thinking now only of his buxom, young, sex-starved lover opening the door for him and pulling him inside as the cymbals clapped the band into a frenzy. He rocked in the cab, bellowing bass notes, urging the truck to leave the ground.

When he pulled into the driveway across from his house in Malden, Tim waited while the cassette spun onto the next march. He reached for the miraculous book on the seat beside him—a guide, he'd come to think of it, to what really matters in the world. *Into the Lion's Mouth: The Ferocious Battle at Ganjgal.* Tim sat for a time just looking at the cover, at the photo of the exhausted Marine in green camo in a strange, treeless landscape, his hand on the rifle grip, daring the photographer to take one second longer. He was unambiguous, this brute. There weren't a million lousy choices for the guy. It was shoot or be killed.

Tim claimed the book against his chest and closed his eyes for the rest of "The Hometown Boy" before accepting the ensuing silence at the end of the tape and shambling toward the house.

Tim's house was a narrow brown clapboard two-story that stood one and a half feet apart from its twin, which had been foreclosed upon and was now abandoned. Both homes were boxed in by brick warehouses. His house had no driveway. (His father-in-law informed everyone of this fact.) But the twin house did have a driveway—a coveted, two-car-length strip across the street, behind a bar, beside the dumpsters, where Tim had just parked. On his way to the door, he heard his wife's plodding piano chords and the thin, reedy tones of young "mea culpa" Bridget O'Connor, who ended every song with "That was so horrible."

This was the first season in the past ten that Tim's wife, Mona, hadn't been picked up for the opera's chorus, so she'd had to spread the word about lessons. Of course, as both he and she knew, the only part of giving lessons that a musician enjoys is the part where she is modeling how to sing or play a piece, not the much larger part of hearing the unimaginable coming back at you.

Tim stuffed the paperback into his sweatshirt pocket as he entered the house. There was no formal entry, you barged right into the living room, where Bridget—eyes bulging, straight-armed in musical terror—flanked Mona at the piano, with Tim's six-foot-long son, Miles, sprawled on the floor nearby, headphones clamped to ears, those ropy arms holding the video controller high above his concave chest like an old man with a menu.

When she saw Tim, Mona's hands went limp over the keys. "Were they in our space?" Bridget's note bent quickly downward and ended in a throat clearing.

"*I'm* in our space," Tim said.

"They were in it this morning after you left, and they stayed all day. Poor Bridget had to park a mile away." She explained the mess to Bridget one more time. "Those bar owners—two brothers, big, big goons—they park in our driveway whenever they feel like it."

"It's not our driveway, Mona, for the fifty thousandth time." Tim headed for the kitchen.

Mona called after him, "You need to tell them that we are the ones who have the permission! I'm telling you, it was *all day*!"

Tim pulled a beer from the fridge.

"And they moved the concrete curbs from one side," Mona shouted. "You know why? Because—"

"Let's talk about it after your lesson." He thought of her as a Chihuahua to his big, tired blob of a hound. So many things appeared to her as potential end-of-the-world causes.

Mona was now filling Bridget in fully. "That bar has changed our lives. The music. We can't sleep! And they pass drugs in the street. It's *all* out in the open. Now they've taken the driveway we've used for years. It's like we don't exist. We'd move, oh, we'd love to move, but we're underwater here. We're drowning."

Bridget hesitated. "Should I start back at the top?"

When Mona began playing again, Bridget could hardly make herself heard over the pounding chords. Tim thought maybe Miles was calling out to him at one point, but he was afraid to make contact. For much of the day, the boy had texted about how Tim forgot to leave money for a paintball party and couldn't he just come back home with it. Tim spun his worn wallet on the countertop as Bridget's notes slid around searching for pitch. The parking, the bar noise, the loans—somehow these indignities seemed all the more so because

Tim had been selected, selected and trained, by the maestro, Herman Gerstein, longest-serving principal tuba for the Boston Symphony Orchestra. Tim had been specially prepared for an elite world of musicians who devoted themselves to the sublime, spent all of their days in a state of bliss. Yet that world had been denied him.

Tim took his beer into the bathroom to wait out the rest of Bridget's lesson. He pulled his sweatshirt off and sat on the john, where he could see his fat face in the mirror above the sink, his staticky hair a crown of rusty wires. Then he soured over his great dragon's egg of a stomach. *Wretched*, that's what his boss, The Publisher, had written on the pages she'd left on his desk the night before, a description fitting more than just his writing. Finally he heard the front door close, then the sounds of Mona snapping up the music and forcing songbooks into the overstuffed piano bench. When he could hear no more of her flittings, he re-slung his pants and stuck his head out the door. No Mona. He heard pots and pans coming out of the cupboard, so he crept to the couch and dumped himself under the enormous, gilt-framed photo of Miles at age two in a double-breasted suit. He nudged the fifteen-year-old Miles with his foot.

"What?" Miles said.

"Did you go to paintball?" he asked.

Miles's thumb tapped so rapidly on the controller it was more like a shiver.

Tim nudged him harder, and the boy ripped off his headphones and said, "You owe Mary Duggin forty-five bucks, and if you don't pay her, I will die."

After pulling his laptop off the side table, Tim clicked on the link for his online piano-tuning class. "I don't suppose the Duggins own a piano." He selected the video for lesson eight in this ten-week, ten-lesson class. He'd finished with the basic tuning concepts (unison tuning, octave tuning, equal temperament, regulating the upright action and the grand action), and now he was learning about minor and major repairs to the fifteen hundred moving pieces of wood or felt—from tightening bench bolts and adjusting the pedals to fixing broken hammers and strings. The course and tools had taken their last seven hundred and fifty bucks, but he was told he could make a hundred and fifty a tuning and do up to three a day if he hustled. Not that he ever hustled.

"How was it, though?" he asked his son, who was now just lying limp.

"You don't get enough second chances," the kid finally confided.

Tim's stomach felt a little sour, so he readjusted his bulk for a lie-down.

Miles continued, "You know, if you pick a bad position, say, you're done for. That's it. In, like, two seconds."

Mona pushed open the swinging kitchen door. "Vinnie's coming for dinner."

"No, no, no!" Tim said. The Sox would be playing the Yankees. "I thought you were gonna see Cher on Monday."

"I don't get you. I really don't," she said. "Do you know how many people would die to have my cousin in the family? Twice he starred in *Temptation's Fate*. Don't pretend that isn't something. So he's coming early! He's visiting friends. Tell your son to clean up."

"Don your finest," Tim said after the kitchen door swung shut.

"Hah," Miles said, and then, after another minute, "seriously, am I supposed to do something?"

"Take a screen break. Walk around a little," Tim said. "Call a girl and remind her who you are." As he spoke, he typed *Ganjgal* into the search box and hit Return. Up came the photo of his forlorn Marine, the hero unable to save those he cared for most. He clicked on the picture and then on Visit Page, to reach the original source, then clicked and clicked anew all over the guy's image but could not bring him closer.

# # #

Beached on his bed, thumbing back through *Into the Lion's Mouth: The Ferocious Battle at Ganjgal*, Tim reviewed the passages he had underlined earlier with a coworker's purple pen:

> A Marine squad is broken down into three four-man fire teams because Marine psychologists long ago determined that while you might join up with the idea of fighting for your country, you will only truly fight for your family, so they give you one...
>
> Every Marine is a rifleman, but one man on each team plans and executes all of the fire team's missions and controls the most powerful weapon. The sniper trains separately, learns to read terrain, to find small movements at great distances.
>
> Each missed shot offers another chance for a rival to erase him; thus the sniper's motto, *Vestri nex est meus vita*, "Your death is my life."

God, these guys were *living*.

"Hello, my dear people!" Cousin Vinnie's game-show-host voice coming from the living room. "Where's my special lady?"

Then the quick clomping of her clogs. "It's the star! The star has arrived!"

"Sorry so late. The star couldn't park. So happy to see you!" Audible kissing. "Lovely as always." His voice dropping on that last line, parodying a Latin lover.

"Look at you! So skinny!" The sound of a spank. "You couldn't park? Tim didn't pull up far enough?"

"Skinny, you say? I'm working on it! Eh? Eh?" Tim figured Vinnie was lifting his shirt for a reveal, and so slid up his own. A blubber hump.

Mona squeaked and fawned, "Oh, I *love* it!"

"Wait, smell it."

Smell what? Tim rolled off the bed and moved to the top of the stairs to see Mona with a glass candleholder clapped to her nose like an oxygen mask.

"Tim!" Vinnie beamed up at him.

"Yo, Vincent."

If Vinnie was a good actor, which Tim felt he couldn't assess, his face wasn't doing him any favors—wide, pockmarked, and it had only one expression, bewildered. "Hey, can I ask you a favor?" The Star dangled a set of keys. "I borrowed a friend's car, but I can't find a place."

On Tim's way down the stairs, Mona told him, "I knew it. They parked you in." Then she pecked her finger toward Vinnie. "They're like Mafia thugs. I'm serious, Vin. Thugs!"

"You want me to talk to them?"

Tim shook his head as he accepted the keys. "Everything's under control."

# # #

Tim's knees were up his nose. The Miata coupe made every man a giant. When he started it, a Streisand-fueled speaker assault drove his head up against a metal rib of the convertible top. He punched off the CD, studied the shifter diagram, got the thing in gear, and then drove around, one hand feeling his scalp for a cut, eyes peeled for a space, until—a mile from home—he finally saw someone pulling out.

Once free of his shell, Tim plodded past apartment block after apartment block, thinking about how he was fat because he wasn't in danger. If only someone wanted to kill him; then he'd be at the peak of fitness. Almost home, he stepped up into the doorway of the neighboring bar, O'Leary's, but stopped at the plywood door. He'd had no desire to enter this bar in the months since they'd opened, and he loved all bars. Time expanded in a bar; stories were trotted out and admired. But he'd watched the rough crowd come and go here. This was no story bar. A small diamond window had been cut into the plywood, just above his eyeline, with the blades of a ceiling fan slicing through the frame. He moved to pull the handle just as one of the brothers was pushing out, the beefier one (and this was a tough call because they were both solid, but this one had no neck, like a trophy tuna in a baseball jacket).

"Oh, hey," Tim said, "I wanted to talk to you about the parking space." One was named Dan, and the other Dave, but Tim didn't trust that he could make the right call.

"I'm outta here right now, man," the guy said, waving him off. "It's been a shitty day."

"I think I may have led you astray as far as parking there." Tim followed him.

"No problem, I'm outta here. And listen," he said, turning back, "I hope we didn't bother you too much with the music last night." *MeeYOUzick*, he'd said. "Was a birthday party, dear-friend kinda thing, so it was a special night."

"Oh, okay," Tim said. "I can understand that if it was a special occasion." He had felt the punching bass in his chest until three a.m. Mona repeatedly worried aloud, "What is happening in our lives?" When the music finally ended, she'd turned to face him. "Whatever this house with no driveway was worth before, now it's half."

When he reentered the house, he found them all seated for

dinner, Vinnie well into a series of anecdotes about interactions with big stars who had seductively bummed a cigarette from him outside a Broadway theater (Miss Winslet) or stopped him because they were both wearing the same big sunglasses (Alan Rickman, who also said to him, and for no clear reason, "You must be very talented."), and because Tim couldn't stand it anymore—this impossibly confident man—he asked Vinnie what had happened with the theater group he started, although Tim had heard it already from Mona.

Vinnie then picked up his fork and devoted himself to his plate. After a while he sniffed and finally said, "You know what? I don't know who they think I am." Then he looked at Miles, tapped Miles's plate with the fork. "I am a founding member, okay? Right from the beginning. So my first show there is *King Lear*, and I'm new, okay? So I'm cast as Knight One, and I know they can't give me a bigger part, because it looks like favoritism to the founders." His hands went up: so be it.

"You don't eat macaroni now?" Mona asked.

"Not so much with the carbs these days. So then they're doing *Streetcar*, Miles, and I am the *prop person?*" He jumped his chair back from the table and flung his arms out. "I should've played Stanley! You go up. You don't go down."

"Down is the wrong direction," Mona agreed.

He reached across to her. "And they acted so shocked when I refused to prop."

"You don't move backwards in life."

"They acted like it was a big insult to *them*! You know what I think? They're not used to artists who have courage."

Then came a long stiff silence before Tim wound him up again with "You know what makes me mad? What makes me really mad is that the Cheesecake Factory would not let you transfer to the New York restaurant when you wanted to move."

Vinnie nodded and appeared to be sucking on something. "I should have made them fire me and taken unemployment. That would have been smart, but I told them, 'Ninety percent of your customers ask for me when they walk in the door. I upsell a hundred and fifty grand worth of avocado eggrolls a year, and you are gonna give that up? In New York?' It's uncanny how stupid people are."

"They're ash-breasted tit-tyrants," Miles said.

"Excuse me?" Mona said.

"Ha! It's a real bird! It's not a cuss."

"Miles, buddy," Vinnie said, turning his chair, "how's school?"

"Fine." Miles's black hair swung into his cheese and stuck.

"Good! You're starting high school? Bottom of the pecking order? Don't forget, we've all been there. But it gets better," Vinnie said, snailing out a bottom lip. "When I was a kid"—he looked up to watch the past—"I was only friends with the girls. The boys were threatened by me. 'Course I didn't know that then! You don't really know the truth until much, much later."

"Miles isn't gay," Tim said.

Vinnie shrugged. "I'm not saying he is—"

"We don't care if he is!" Mona sat up and looked around the table as though someone had disappeared but she didn't know who.

"All I ask, Miles, is, don't ever use the word gay as a slang for something bad," Vinnie said.

"No." Miles gave little head shakes, his hair still attached to the food.

Vinnie eyed the newly reloaded plates of Tim and Miles.

"We've got other things to eat in this house." Mona looked both ways to indicate that food was all around them.

"I had a late lunch." He rubbed his tight stomach. "Tim, how's your work going?"

"If I tell you, will you promise me it gets better?"

"He's on six days a week," Mona said.

"All right, then! They can't do without you! That's good!"

"They can do without me. You know what I did today, on a Saturday, Vinnie? I drove twenty-six miles to that shithole, and I walked into my office and picked up the light bulb my boss had left on my desk, as she does every Friday night, and I screwed it into the desk lamp so she can know I was there. On a Saturday. That's what I did, and I've done it for twelve years."

Vinnie looked surprised.

Tim continued, "Then I rewrote a perfectly good set of product shorts—and by the way, who gives a shit about marching-band helmets? Nobody—but I rewrote them because they had some words in them that she objects to on grounds that no other human can understand."

"The Publisher," Mona explained.

"Well," Vinnie started.

"*Streamlined*—what's wrong with that word, Vinnie? *Streamlined*. How about *gleam*? You got a big problem with *gleam*? Too shiny for you?"

"You know what, Tim?" Vinnie waited for Tim to look up from his plate. "No one thinks they're in charge of their own life anymore. But you are."

"No, Tim is taking charge," Mona said. "He's learning to tune pianos."

"Okay, then! Good!"

"I can make a hundred and fifty bucks a tuning, and a tuning takes an hour and a half, so that's a hundred dollars an hour."

"Lawyer's pay!" Vinnie slapped the table. "Yeah!"

Tim leaned back to reach the fridge handle and yanked the door open just enough to grab another watery beer with the blue mountains on the label. "You know how you figure an annual salary?" He pulled the top and continued, "I know this now. You double the hourly rate and take that times a thousand. So a hundred an hour is equal to two hundred thousand dollars—if you could tune all day, which you can't, but that's the kind of money we're talking about."

Miles said, "No shit?" with his mouth full.

"I'm just saying that Vinnie's right; hourly, it's the same as a lawyer. It's skilled work."

Vinnie conducted with his fork. "The dream's gotta come before the reality. Okay? And this is what you're doing! It's all in that book. You know that book? *The Secret*? Oh, am I gonna buy it for you. It's about the *laws of attraction*! Hey, let's get a piece of paper. You have paper handy?" he asked Mona.

"Just sheets of paper?" She started up.

"I have some," Miles stood, and since he'd been leaning it against the wall, his chair toppled as he loped out of the kitchen.

"He's a good kid," Vinnie announced before Miles returned, ripping pages out of a spiral notebook.

"Everyone gets a sheet," Vinnie said. "Now, what you do is you write on that paper who you wanna be. Visualize your ideal self. Don't show it to anyone. You know, are you a rich man? Are you an opera star? Are you a handsome kid? Some people who are sick write that they're cancer free. You can write anything! But put in as much detail as you can think of. And you can add to this whenever, so just get something down real quick right now. Then you carry it with you, and you look at it. You look at it and, like, believe you already are this person with this certain life. If you believe, *ba boom!* you will receive."

Mona had written straight through Vinnie's directions as though she were taking dictation. Her ideal self had a page full of qualities. Miles was staring blankly at the overhead light, his poised pen never touching the paper. Tim scrawled three short lines in a corner of the page and tore it off:

Rusty Turner
Marine Sniper
21, 6' 2", 9"

# # #

After dinner, Tim sank into the couch to watch the Sox
game, which Mona muted when she and Vinnie joined him.
She lit on the wingback, while Vinnie sat beside him.

Without looking up from the set, Tim said, "I'll draw you
a map to your car."

"I don't have to go right away."

Tim nodded, watching the ump beckon the Yankee's
pitcher over and feel his neck, which had a discolored mark on
it that the pitcher had been swiping his hand over. "You staying
over?"

"Dunno yet."

The ump pulled his hand from a viscous patch on the
pitcher's neck and immediately ejected him.

Tim pointed at the set. "Guy's a rotten cheat. Everybody
knows it."

"Stay here!" Mona demanded of Vinnie.

"Can I?"

"Of course, you can!"

"I'd be very much obliged," said Knight One.

Tim had a sinking feeling, and he sorted all of the things he
wanted to say into cubbyholes of varying appropriateness. He
finally came out with "New York's crazy expensive, huh? What
do you pay in rent down there?"

"You don't wanna know, believe me."

"You behind on the rent?" That one fell out of its cubby.

Vinnie shrugged. "I'll make it up."

"If you are behind, you are behind! These things happen!" Mona karate-chopped the last three words into existence.

Tim turned his whole torso to Vinnie. "You're not planning on living here again." The man had once spent five months in tears on their couch.

"No! God, no. I happen to have an audition here, for a movie."

"What? What is it?" Mona asked dramatically, as if he'd just said he had cancer.

"I didn't want to say anything, but it's a big audition, and you know what? I will get the part."

Then that creepy Dr. Harmon appeared on television in his commercial for testosterone replacement therapy.

"Of course, you'll get the part. That's decided. But what's the movie?"

"...*gently reverses the aging process*," Harmon said from behind a desk in his white lab coat.

"They don't want people to know about it yet, so I can't say anything, but word is that Damon is coming for the auditions. And I will read opposite."

"Matt Damon? Is that who you're saying? Matt Damon?" she asked.

Text of the symptoms of low testosterone popped up on the screen beside the doctor, and Tim counted off on his fingers all of the ones he recognized.

# # #

As soon as Tim got into bed that night—his wife still in the living room making discoveries into the lives of the *Temptation's Fate* stars—his phone buzzed, a Words with Friends prompt. The Publisher had played her word. He pictured her wrapped in a blanket, lying in a lounge chair on the deck of her beach house, looking up at the Milky Way, sloshing a zinfandel down her chin. The Publisher had insisted that Tim get the app. She told him that playing WWF would expand his vocabulary. *Shellac* was her new word, which he had thought had a *k* at the end, so he was already expanded.

Tim played his word, *cops*, which didn't begin to compete with The Publisher's seven-letter triumph, and then he slid the square of torn paper off his nightstand. His ideal self:

Rusty Turner

Marine Sniper

21, 6' 2", 9"

To reinforce this ideal persona, Tim changed his WWF name on the spot to RustySniper21. Then he selected Random Opponent. Instantly the game board appeared with his new name next to TallBlondBabe18 in the scoring section.

TallBlondBabe18 played *cranium* for 22 points, including a triple-letter score.

Tall, blond, and smart? he typed into the message box and sent it over.

He played *rough* for 20 points with a double-word score. Then he wrote another message: **How tall are you?**

World's tallest woman, she messaged.

She played *vine* for nine, then wrote, **So lame.**

He couldn't figure a word to play and was about to resign from the game, when she messaged, **What U looking @ right now?**

Tim set the phone on his nightstand and picked up the sniper book. He heard Mona and Vinnie howl in unison over something funny. There was a section of photos in the middle of the book: shots of members of the sniper's fire team eating MREs off the hood of their Humvee, talking with white-capped Afghans; a few of the ruinous, brown, terraced slopes of Ganjgal; and some of the men at the outpost, snowy mountain peaks behind them.

Tim took up his phone again and messaged her: Hescos & barbed wire.

Then he added, Hescos = big burlap bags filled with dirt. Big as a man. Bullet/shrapnel shields.

Then another bit: Marine outpost in Afghanistan.

And then he thought to add, What U looking at?

She didn't reply right away or play a word. Tim put the phone down on the nightstand and looked again at the now-dead young men grinning.

Then the message came: A one-armed Sasquatch.

Then a follow-up: Envy UR adventure.

Sounds like UR having one, too! What's your name, Blondie?

Megan, she typed. Blondie's better.

DAVIS

Davis Beardsley entered his house to find a great, hairy arm lying in wait upon the floor. To the right of the door, as always, stood Sasquatch, a now-disabled eight-foot taxidermist's creation covered in grizzly fur but looking like a fully upright gorilla with a too-large head and an enormous, humanoid nose. Davis gaped at the woolly appendage and then hoisted the great arm over his shoulder, clasped the leathery hand in his, and carried it to the kitchen counter, where he set it down and stroked it like a sick kitten. His daughter, Megan, had done this, of course, though she would deny it. She had dismembered his most cherished possession in retaliation.

In addition to having a PhD in zoology, Davis was a renowned cryptozoologist, someone who studies animals unknown to science or animals thought to be extinct. He'd led several Sasquatch-hunting expeditions over in Washington state and had purchased the replica from the owner of a truck stop there. The behemoth was the crown jewel of Davis's collection. Now, even if the arm was reattached, it could not be a seamless fix. He would see the repair, a constant reminder that the whole thing was a fake.

That this had happened on the day Davis's new boss was to come see the collection was no coincidence, he was sure. The new department chair, Eric Lindstrom, had asked for a viewing, and what could Davis do but invite him to stay for dinner? His worries about this dinner were lessened by the fact that

Lindstrom had already met Megan. She was taking a college-credit course he offered to high school seniors on Maine flora and fauna. It was one of the ways Lindstrom hoped to boost enrollment in the biology department in coming years. Megan had only wanted in because it got her out of high school two mornings a week.

Davis weighed the downsides of (a) confronting Megan now and possibly sending her into a tailspin or (b) waiting until after Lindstrom's visit. Everything had downsides with Megan. Would he rather she be hateful or flirtatious, as she typically was when adult males came into the house? Megan often put herself right on their laps or, if they were standing, hung from their shoulders or kept an arm around their waist. Megan had been told that if she did this tonight, she would lose her phone forever. Davis was thinking that perhaps it was a mistake not to have given Lindstrom the letter that her other teachers had received, explaining Megan's disorder, but his wife, Jenny, had been afraid it would affect Davis's ability to gain tenure, and she thought she could make Megan understand the importance of keeping her distance. The letter had not changed over the years:

Dear [Teacher's Name],

I am writing this email at the beginning of what will be, unfortunately for you, a long year. Our daughter, Megan, will be in your class this year. Megan has reactive attachment disorder (RAD), not uncommon for Romanian orphans. It helps to understand that the underlying drive for children with RAD is to maintain control over their lives. They never learned that they can trust another person to take good care of them. They have never enjoyed the pleasures of giving themselves up for comfort and protection. They learned manipulation—what they need to do in order to get something from "caregivers" who don't care.

Megan has a form of the disorder that is called disinhibited RAD. As the name implies, she has few natural inhibitions. For instance, she has always been indiscriminately affectionate with strangers. She will come into your classroom as an eager, bright, fun-loving hugger. She will have much to say about your lovely room and your jewelry and the amazing things you know. Then, after a month or two, Megan will become moody and will occasionally be hysterical when she has trouble with some task. She will mumble or slur her words—all of this to draw you away from the others and toward her. At some point she will begin to openly defy you. And if you are missing something, she has taken it…

This letter had grown longer over the years and was now, in its final iteration, up to seven pages, with endless suggestions on how to handle Megan's various attempts at deception.

While Davis pawed through the junk drawer for large safety pins, he pictured Megan letting a finger trail down Lindstrom's cheek, laughing wildly at his jokes, and then he imagined the bachelor Lindstrom blushing and appraising his pursuer, because she was an extremely attractive young woman: a tall, strong Romanian warrior-princess, blond and fair-skinned, with a slight bump on her nose and generous lips. Many found it hard to keep their perspective when she turned on the charm and affection. Imagining her doing to Lindstrom what he'd watched her do to neighbor Tom made Davis's hands shake inside the drawer. He reminded himself to breathe in through the mouth and out through the nose. In through the mouth and out through the nose.

"Megan," Davis called up the stairs, "I have something for

you." He'd decided to present Lindstrom with an angry Megan.

She barreled down the stairs like a kid promised a present and came around the corner, where she saw the arm on the counter. "I didn't do it!" Already the screaming.

"What happened, Megan?" he asked calmly.

"Mom did it! I swear! I swear!"

"Mom did it," he repeated.

"God! I knew you wouldn't believe me! Ask her! Go on, ask her!"

"It's another crazy lie, Megan. She won't cover for you."

"Mom!" Megan called as she thundered across the kitchen, her fury weighing a ton. She tore open the back door. "Mom!"

When Jenny appeared, leaves sticking to her pants, she put it together quickly. "Yes, sorry, Davis, I knocked that off." She was red-faced and a little out of breath from raking. "I'll have it fixed. Professionally."

Megan gave him a self-satisfied look. "See, that's—"

"You may return to your room," he told her.

"Don't you want to apologize?"

"I'd go up to your room right now if I were you."

When the stair-stomping ended, Davis guided Jenny back outside and to a far corner of the yard, where he dropped her arm. "This is the biggest mistake of your life. You cannot cover for her. This erases all of our work."

"I'm not covering!"

"That arm was *ripped* off of him! It's in retaliation for my retrieving her at the fair yesterday. She must have practically hung from the arm to get it off."

"No, it's old, and it fell off. I didn't even bump into it very hard."

"You're going to continue with this?" He reared back. "Knowing the consequences?" Then he flipped one finger out to start the counting. One: "She'll never take ownership of her actions again. Her MO will be to beg someone else to cop to whatever she's done." Two, three, and four: "She'll be fired from jobs, evicted from apartments, living in our house forever."

"I can't believe you think I'd lie." She turned to fetch her rake.

"We need to talk to Peggy about this and also about the phone. I am still against the phone!" He pulled his suit coat tight against the cool wind and marched back across the lawn.

# # #

Sadly, Eric Lindstrom declined an alcoholic drink, and this meant that Jenny, who had salivated for days over the possibility of knocking back a few strong ones in jovial company, was somewhat bitter during the dinner. Davis sat at the other head of the oval table, where he watched her steal sidelong looks at the little bar on wheels she had set up and that held the newly purchased gin and vodka, the sliced limes, the garlic-stuffed olives. Their party life had been over for many years now and would evidently stay that way for some time to come. Davis should have guessed that Lindstrom was too much of a health nut to partake. Late thirties, he was, but still with boyish good looks, fit and trim, and with a crisp wardrobe. Davis's new boss was sitting across from Megan, listing in detail for her the pros and cons, the reasons for and against his making the move up here to "the middle of nowhere" (for God's sake!) and taking on this challenging job "to revive the department," as Lindstrom described it—which task Davis felt he had already accomplished with his infectious interests.

Megan wore a simple sleeveless black dress with a blue silk scarf around her shoulders. Wide-eyed and nodding, she appeared to stay with Lindstrom's every utterance, but Davis knew better. Still, she was tamping her romantic inclinations down nicely and had made only a few exclamations over how smart Lindstrom's thinking was. Davis thought he had recognized a few blushes from Lindstrom, but maybe it was the heat from the prematurely lit fireplace at his back.

"I'd like to say Grace," Jenny announced as soon as Lindstrom had finished speaking. Davis watched them all bow their heads, while he refused. "Bless us, O Lord, and these Thy gifts, which we are about to receive from Thy bounty, through Christ our Lord. And a special thanks today, Lord, for the creation of all of the animals and the livestock. For on the sixth day, God said, 'Let the earth bring forth living creatures of all kinds—cattle, and creeping things, and beasts of the earth: and it was so.' Amen." She looked up brightly.

Davis smiled back at her.

"Amen," said Lindstrom, picking up his fork.

"Cattle," Davis said, after a moment's consideration, "were created by man a little over ten thousand years ago, when they bred aurochs to be smaller and more docile. And aurochs, themselves"—he gave Lindstrom a look of concentration as though they were working this reply out together—"didn't evolve until the global drying and cooling of the Pliocene epoch, when the grasslands greatly expanded. So God didn't create all of the creeping things and the cattle on the same day."

When he first met Jenny, she was not as Catholic as she had become since the troubles began with Megan, and he hoped she would lapse again after Megan went off into the world. Jenny had known he was an atheist from the start and had never pushed him so long as he consented that their children could be raised as Catholics. It was one of the reasons Davis had originally fallen in love with Jenny—because she had let him be, and not just on the religious front. There was no judgment about all of the time he spent researching and hunting his prizes. The woman he had dated before Jenny had finally dubbed him autistic (!) for the intense focus he gave the cryptids. And Jenny didn't insist—as the previous loved one had—that reading was the same as doing nothing. So he had predicted a fulfilling life with such a companion.

"However cattle were created, I'm afraid I don't eat them." Lindstrom forked a green bean into his mouth.

"We never asked? Oh, I'm horrified." Jenny set her utensils down in protest.

"God, Dad," Megan said.

"It's inexcusable," Davis agreed. In the time, long before, when they used to have guests for dinner, no man was a vegetarian. "Please"—he stood to move the large wooden salad bowl next to Lindstrom's plate—"the rest is all yours."

"And it's a beautiful salad, Jenny, so please don't worry," Lindstrom said, taking up the bowl.

"Well, I will! I'm mortified."

"The salad has cheese on it," said Megan. "From a cow."

"Nope"—Lindstrom raised a hand—"cheese is okay. Cheese is A-okay."

As he ate his salad, Lindstrom surveyed the labeled photos on the wall opposite him: *Caspian Horse, Terror Skink, Night Parrot, Armoured Frog*. "Your students must love coming here."

"Well, I'll tell you"—Davis reviewed the gallery with nodding pleasure—"it's great to see an example of a *Lazarus taxon*. Gives everybody hope that other seemingly dead-ended evolutionary lines are actually hiding among us."

"Maybe also hope for the many soon-to-be-extinct species. Which extinct animals would you like to see alive again, Megan?" Lindstrom asked.

She shrugged and faked shyness.

"What about a type of dinosaur? Wouldn't that be amazing?"

"Megan isn't so into animals," Davis admitted.

"Pterodactyls." She flashed Lindstrom a smile.

"Nice choice! Pterodactylus had teeth, you know. Modern birds don't."

"Now, I don't know about that." Davis forced a grin. "Geese have toothlike projections to help them graze."

"They're not teeth, though," Lindstrom said.

"Penguins, too, of course," Davis added. "In a way. They have these spine-covered tongues and upper palates to help them hold on to fish." He made a grasping mouth with his fingers and thumb and moved it out toward Megan.

She jerked away. "Stop it!"

"I heard you have a coelacanth, Davis. Do you think we could display that on accepted-students' day this year?" Lindstrom asked.

"Keep it," said Jenny, waving her fork over her shoulder.

Ignoring her, Davis moved his upturned hands apart, as pans of a scale. "You want the coelacanth, Eric, but you don't want the fur-bearing trout?"

"You should take the merman. He's so creepy!" Megan stuck her tongue out. "Blech. It's like a monkey sewed onto a fish. I think they chopped a monkey in half—"

"Enough, Megan," Jenny patted the tablecloth near her daughter.

"—like with an ax and pulled enough of the guts out—"

"Okay, Megan." Davis's eyes bored into her and then quickly returned to Lindstrom, and he smiled away his frustration before continuing. "A trading post find. Probably a circus thing."

Davis was forever defending his interest in what some called a pseudoscience by noting all of the animals that would have fallen into the same category as Bigfoot in the recent past: the animals pictured on his walls, for instance, along with many others—the megamouth shark, the komodo dragon, the mountain gorilla, and on and on.

"You should vlog about one of your dad's cryptids. That would be a good one," Lindstrom said.

Megan gathered up her hair and slowly coiled it on top of her head. "I already have a vlog topic."

"What's this?" Davis looked from one to the other.

Lindstrom smiled at his student. "Everyone in the class is exploring a Maine animal they don't know anything about and reporting their findings in a video blog called *What's a Blank?*"

"What's your blank, honey?" Jenny pushed her still-empty wineglass away and then slumped back into her chair.

"Secret." Her eyes were locked with Lindstrom's.

Davis immediately dropped his napkin to get a peek at Megan's feet, which were out of theirs shoes but still on her side.

# # #

The display cases along the walls of Davis's den were each seven feet tall, a foot and a half taller than Davis, with fluorescent lights boxed into the tops that illuminated dozens of plaster footprint castings with their little tent labels. Glass shelves allowed the light to filter down through four tiers to the shadowed, least impressive specimens at the bottom. A large map of Maine took up a section of wall, with pushpins of various colors marking cryptid sightings that were explained in a key. But the central feature in the room was in a stand on his desk, a blue sea creature over five feet long. The fish's sheen had faded through the years, and a few of the scales had dropped off, but it was still impressive—like a Frankenstein fish onto which a few extra fins had been haphazardly attached.

"Where do you buy a coelacanth, Davis?" Lindstrom asked with quiet reverence.

Davis placed a proprietary hand on the fish's head. "It

helps to know some of the exotic animal dealers around the Indian Ocean. The taxidermist told me that the brain was quite tiny. All but just a minuscule portion of the braincase was filled with fat; only a small fraction was actual brain tissue."

Megan repeated the family joke: "They're the blondes of the sea."

"Eight fins," Davis lectured, walking around to the other side of the desk. "Two dorsal, two pectoral, two pelvic, one anal, and one caudal. It can move in any direction it wishes, highly maneuverable. They've been seen doing headstands and swimming upside down."

"So, is it that they sort of walk along the bottom with the pectoral and pelvic fins? Has anyone witnessed this?"

"No, no, this fish doesn't actually walk. It's a drift-hunter. But it does belong to the same lobe-finned group as our own ancestors. It's our closest fish relative. And it does move its fins in an alternating pattern, like a four-legged animal." He turned to his daughter. "If you want to know what lobe fins are, Megan, they are fins—"

"I don't."

"—fins that are attached to the rest of the body by a single bone wrapped in muscle and skin, like our limbs." He rubbed the dust off one of the fish's pelvic fins in this performance for Lindstrom. "Most other fish have fins that are just these webbed rays, not a bone covered with muscle and skin. So, our ancestors were like this one, but unlike this fish, they moved into shallow waters and eventually onto land. This is a deep-water fish."

"It was bluer before, almost as blue as your eyes." Megan brushed around the back of Lindstrom to stand at his other side. "And look, Eric, teeth!"

"Real enamel teeth," Davis agreed.

"This one was a girl," she told him. "When they opened her up, they saw that eggs had hatched inside her." Megan turned her wide eyes on Lindstrom. "Already hatched!"

"No kidding?" Lindstrom said.

"Size of swan eggs." Davis found he'd broken out in pinpricks of sweat. "They've been known to have over sixty big eggs in there. This fish was thought to have been extinct for around sixty-five million years until one was dredged up in 1938. Yep, there's a lot more in store for us on this planet."

"Shall we move on to the footprint impressions?" Lindstrom had turned to peer at some plaster casts in a case.

"The yeti prints discovered by Eric Shipton in 1951 while climbing Everest."

"An opposable big toe."

"Right, an ape. Sir Edmund Hillary and Tenzing Norgay said they saw similar footprints on Everest, and Norgay reported that his father had actually laid eyes on a yeti, twice! From tracks we know that yetis are semi-bipedal, sometimes dropping onto all fours. So they're a different species from Bigfoot, who is fully bipedal with more humanlike prints."

Eric shifted over to examine a large footprint cast in the far corner of the same case. "What's this? Three-toed?" He lifted a grin.

"Found in a soybean field in Fouke, Arkansas, 1971. The Fouke Monster, or Southern Sasquatch, they called it. Seven feet tall and weighing up to three hundred pounds. Big red eyes. Attacked a man and a woman one night outside their house. The man had scratches all across his back."

Lindstrom opened his mouth, then closed it, then finally said, "Well, if this print came from a living thing, it would be the only known primate or hominid without five toes. It's a dumb man's fake."

Davis nodded. "It would be unusual. But we ignore strange reports at our peril. Okay, here's a Bigfoot track found in Washington state, 1986." He had moved on to a plaster cast that looked like a giant human footprint, but with relatively shorter toes.

"Dad, take a picture of me and Eric with Sasquatch."

"Well, he's missing an arm right now," Davis said, "but maybe Dr. Lindstrom can stand to cover that side."

"Let's do it!" Lindstrom said, but then Davis stopped the man from following Megan out of the room. "That three-toed footprint, that's just a kitschy thing. I'm not suggesting that was a real animal."

"Oh." Lindstrom smiled and nodded.

"I wouldn't want that to be a strike against me."

"I'm enjoying the tour, Davis. I'm not making judgments."

"Good. Good. 'Cause you know I'm up for tenure. It's up or out now."

"I'm sure your getting tenure or not will have nothing to do with all of this."

"But, well, this—the study of cryptids—this is where all of my research has been, so it has everything to do with it."

Lindstrom rubbed his cheek while resurveying the room, "Well, what was your dissertation on?"

"The legend of the jackalope as explained by the *Shope papilloma* virus."

"I'm sorry?"

"Rabbits with viral warts that looked like antlers. I make a compelling case." Davis then realized he hadn't shown an interest in Lindstrom's work. "What was yours on?"

"Zoological features tending to disprove the theory of evolution."

"Ha ha." Davis grinned. "Wait, is that the real topic?"

Lindstrom's lips disappeared. "Let's not keep Megan waiting."

# # #

That night, Davis toured his collection again, alone, martini in hand. He'd seen his wife go up to bed with her own glass of clear spirits. Tomorrow the booze would have to be discarded for fear it would otherwise go straight down Megan's throat. Davis took tiny steps along the cases and tried to relive the moment he'd first heard of each piece. He replayed the search for the owner and the careful negotiations, the magical arrival, the first touch, the cataloging, the perfect placement. But over time, most of the pieces could no longer render strong emotion. They were nearly thrill-less. Yes, he needed a new one and he needed it now.

TIM

When Tim made it down to the kitchen on Sunday morning, Mona was chopping mushrooms at the table, finishing a thought. "It's a phase, like wearing black."

Vinnie, stoveside in his Gaga T-shirt, whisked eggs in a bowl. "Put your order in to the chef!" he sang.

"What's a phase?" Tim headed for the fridge.

"I'm just talking about Miles."

"Miles is having a phase where he's retreating from the world," Vinnie answered. "But I never did have that phase. I just keep venturing forth. I am an onward person."

Since there were no cooking smells yet, Tim could say it: "I'd better not eat. I'm going to the Olive Garden in a bit."

"Olive Garden?"

"He takes his mother every Sunday." Mona waved the knife.

"They have a lovely *pasta fagioli*." Vinnie said the name of the dish with gusto, like introducing a musical act. "How is the mamma?"

"She's fine."

Mona leaned back to touch Vinnie's furry forearm. "She's been writing a book for women on how to build self-worth through sex."

"No!" Vinnie stopped whisking and gave Tim a shy smile.

"Five years now. Right? She's been writing it five years now?" she asked Tim.

"Is that shredded cheddar? I could have a small omelet." He sat at the Formica table across from his wife and went over the to-do list again in his head. He'd been up most of the night, thinking about becoming Rusty. The sniper was already in him. He just needed to transform his shell—to renew himself. But each time he tried to focus on steps for his renewal and escape, three weights would tug at him: wife, son, mother. He would have to determine plans for setting all three of them to rights. He'd sketched some details on the inside back cover of the Ganjgal book, calling them the *Fire Team Mission*s.

"Get a glass," said Mona, as Tim reached for the juice carton in the middle of the table.

"I was going to."

She slid the sliced mushrooms onto a plate. "Do you know enough about pianos to tell whether one is good or bad?"

Tim shrugged as he pretended to read the back of the OJ carton.

"One of our big opera donors, Sunny Straub, wants someone to look at a used piano she saw at an estate sale."

"Oh, yeah?" He sat up. "Sure, I can make a recommendation. And then she's a lifelong tuning customer. Did she say when?"

She shrugged, "I can call her."

"Let's make it today! Call her today. Let's get going on this thing, Mona. It's the beginning!" *(Fire Team Mission #1: Make Enough Money to Buy Mona the Driveway.)*

# # #

Before Tim left to get his mother, he knocked on his son's door. "Miles."

"Yeah."

Tim pushed in to find him lying in bed with his headphones on. "You're awake!" The boy pulled aside the right ear pad.

"Listen, I want you to leave this room today." *(Fire Team Mission #2: Help Miles Move into the Real World.)*

"Yeah."

"What are you going to do?"

"Dunno."

"Vinnie's making omelets."

"Yeah." The boy barely rolled his head toward Tim, as though he'd suffered grave injuries.

"What're you listening to?"

"Pathogenic."

They were surrounded by Gothic fonts and long-haired, angry fat men on posters for bands named Gorguts and Bolt Thrower. "I don't know how you stand that metal crap."

Miles extended his long arms like Jesus blessing a crowd. "You don't have to like it. You just have to enjoy a balanced diet with fiber and shit."

"Give it to me, I'm going to listen to it on the way to Ma's," Tim said, heading toward the bed.

"It's not a CD."

"Give me the whole setup, the iPod, the headphones."

"Can't drive with headphones. It's most illegal."

Tim sat beside the boy's knees, the unwashed smell of him like a fresh hoagie. "I need to figure out what the ideal me likes to listen to."

Miles offered the gear. "This is the best song."

Tim clapped on the headphones, awaited the song, and jerked at the start of the assault. "It's worse than next door!" he shouted. It was only fifteen seconds before he raked the headphones off. "That's dreadful. How do they get their voices to do that?"

Miles growl-shouted the chorus of the death metal song: "MELANCHOLY IS MY CROSS TO BEAR."

"Ow." Tim grabbed his own throat.

"You keep your larynx down and you don't use your actual vocal chords. You use your fake vocal chords."

"Fake vocal chords. Tell your mother about those." On his way out, Tim looked back at the boneless Miles, who had no ideal self, who had no noticeable desire to join the living. "Whoever you talk to on the phone about all the video games, you should invite him over."

"It's a girl."

"Prove it."

# # #

Tim's mother lived in a Dorchester triple-decker and left it only to walk a block down to Walgreens to buy her food and sundries. Her kitchen counter was loaded with canned goods.

"Who are all the Vienna sausages for?" Tim called out as he waited for her to fix herself up for lunch. "Are you buying the dogs Vienna sausages?" He shook a mutt off his leg. God, the place smelled.

"Do you change the pee pads, Ma?" He suspected the carpets were also now pee pads.

He picked up the dog that wouldn't stop humping him and carried it to the bathroom, where he was going to close it in, but he was instead stopped short by the horror of the walls and floor: tiles chipped to bits, holes punched through backer board, like someone had tried to imprison Bolt Thrower.

"What the hell, Ma?" he said when she came into the hall.

She glanced into the quake zone. "It's something that designer did on HGTV—the Texas woman I told you about."

"It's not your house!" Tim reminded her. *(Fire Team Mission #3: Move His Mother into a Retirement Home.)*

"When I die"—she clutched her shouldered purse strap—"you can reimburse them with the insurance money."

She always said that. She had taken out a dozen policies for accidental death because their premiums were minuscule and she still didn't understand how they worked—that she would not only have to die, but die in an accident.

Tim drove them to the restaurant in his truck, which his mother always acted as though she had never seen before. "It's amazing how small they make trucks now. I once had a male friend who had a truck I could hardly see out of." She slid a hand along the dusty dash. When they reached the restaurant, she crossed the parking lot, spinning around in wonder like a newly released prisoner as Tim held open the front door.

They should have been welcomed like old friends at Olive Garden, but staff turnover was high. On the way to the table, his mother informed the hostess, "I have the calamari appetizer for my whole meal and two glasses of Chianti. And when I say two glasses, I mean two glasses at the same time."

After later repeating her order to the correct authority, Tim's mother filled him in on her Facebook friends, most of whom he didn't know. "Marcy Butts is in Rio. Landed last night. She writes little notes to her granddaughter on the Facebook. Little love notes."

"That's nice."

"Everyone seems to be traveling!"

"Well, those are the ones who have something to post about, maybe."

"I'd like you to show me how to do a video. People are asking for one of the dogs."

He tugged his pant legs down so they weren't so tight in the thigh. "Why?"

"So I can do one of the dogs!"

"No, what do they want to see the dogs doing?"

"Oh, they get into all sorts of naughty things. Tessa sings with the fire engines. Her little mouth gets into the funniest shape, a little *O*, and she sings! Angie Cullen's dog runs around the yard with a barrel over its head, around and around and around, till it runs right into something. I'll show you when we go back." There was always a twenty-minute review of Facebook videos when he took her home.

Tim's mom smiled and waved at a little girl who'd just been put into a high chair by her father at the next table. Then she craned to look behind her for the approach of her wine. "I love the arched doorways, here, don't you?" she said, to cover for all of this twisting about.

"Very Tuscan," he agreed.

"I'm at forty-two thousand words," she then announced, as she did each week.

"Isn't that less than last week?"

"You pay attention! Yes it's gone down. I had to dump a long chapter that was probably before its time, the *woman-as-penetrator* section. I have to be careful not to give the average reader a shock."

When the wineglasses and the spicy calamari arrived, she visibly relaxed. Closed her eyes for the first sip.

Tim unrolled his napkin and said, "You know how we always joke about how you could never go into a retirement community because they don't allow alcohol? Well, some do. Some serve wine with dinner. Did you know that?"

Her eyes narrowed, but the glass was slow to leave her lips. Then she dug a calamari ring around in the parmesan-peppercorn dressing for a while with a look of grave concern. "I'm not interested in communal living."

"No?"

"Were you looking at my bills? Is that what this is? And they don't take dogs, those places."

"Lots of families who have loads of time to play with dogs would love to adopt yours."

She looked away, shaking her head.

"And they'll take your Social Security check and make it work. No more worries. No more bills for me to snoop into."

She chewed brazenly, with her mouth open. Then swallowed hard. "I know you don't want me to pay to have the book published."

"I'd love it if it got published, Ma, but I don't want you to pay one of those vanity publishers. Are you still thinking about that? It's a scam, and you won't have any buyers."

"Thank you."

"You know what I mean. Real publishers promote their books; the scam printers just send them all to you in a box. Or fifty boxes."

"I would promote them on Facebook."

"Okay. Are you really doing this, or are you toying with me, because you are behind on the cable bill, I noticed."

Shaking her head no for a while, she finally said, "Maybe you shouldn't come over anymore." She popped a calamari into her mouth and gave him a bold look. After patiently chewing it down, she said, "I'm not your child, Timmy."

"Okay, yeah."

They concentrated on their meals. Tim was having the shrimp scampi again. All of his shirts had butter stripes from the slinging noodles. His mother took one of his breadsticks, leaned over toward the next table, and began to wave it at the baby girl, shaking it at her like a rattle. The child covered her face and kicked crazily at the high chair until her father turned around and held up his hand to halt all further communication.

Tim's mother snapped away from them.

"Sorry," the man said to Tim.

"It's no problem," Tim told him.

When she finally returned to poking at her food, his mother said, "I think you should try to find your brother. Have you looked on the Internet for a Richard Turner in Florida?"

"No, but you have."

"There are two. One's a psychologist in Winter Park. Isn't that nice? One's a sex offender." She shrugged. "But I'm sure that's not him." Tim's father had left them when Tim was three and had begun another family in Florida.

"Just because Dad had a family after ours doesn't mean his other son and I have anything in common."

"Of course you do! Your father!"

"Yeah, but it's not like I can share anything about my life with Dad."

"Don't be jealous." She slid one empty wineglass aside. "Poor Richard. He could be jealous of you! Maybe he would've loved not to have that father at all."

"The end," Tim said, swiping his fork through the air.

She rocked her head quickly side to side; so be it.

They continued to eat. Tim watched the father feed his child soup at the next table, blowing on each spoonful before delivering it. He started to say something to his mother, but the waiter returned to check on them. "Another glass of wine?"

She covered her current glass as though he intended to pour more into it. "Not today."

When they were alone again, Tim's expression grew pained. "You know, I figured out why I always wanted to be in a big orchestra; it's because Dad loved going to the symphony. I guess I thought maybe he'd see me, see my name on the program, see that we shared something and that I had made it big in a way that he could admire. And then he'd be—"

"He wasn't that into the symphony, Timmy."

Tim set his fork down. "What? What do you mean?"

She brought the napkin halfway up to her lips and stopped. "He loved the Beatles. I remember that."

"He wasn't into the symphony? You used to go on and on

about it after my lessons. The whole ride home! His favorite was Beethoven's Ninth. He used to sing 'Ode to Joy' to you when you drove to Tanglewood with the windows down."

She slumped back, sated. "Okay," she said with a shrug. "Sure, now I remember. He did have a passion for symphonic music."

"Now, no, the way you say that now, I don't believe you!"

"I'm sure if I said it, it was true. I forget things." She wearily waved her napkin.

"*If* you said it? Are you crazy! This was an endless thing you used to tell me."

"I don't think every minute about your father, I'm sorry," she said, rolling her eyes.

Tim dried his flushed face with the napkin.

"When you read my book, I don't want you thinking he inspired the kinds of revelations I've had. He might like to think so, but that wasn't the case."

"No? It was all of the other men you had sex with?"

Quick nods. "That's right."

"Okay, okay." Tim threw his napkin onto the plate. His mother had had an affair with at least one of her cleaning clients. The man must have been home one day and then made it a point to be home on more days. He was a lawyer married to another lawyer. Tim often went out to dinner with his mom and this Ryan Beltzer, and Ryan was always nice to him. They'd go to a place that had a bar on one side and booths on the other. Tim's mom would have whatever soup they were serving, while Tim and Ryan tucked into loaded burgers. She would wear things he hadn't known she had: shawls and clanky bracelets, feather earrings. She thought Ryan was the funniest man in the world—not that she'd laugh at his stories, but after any joke, she'd turn and smile into his face and her hand would move up onto his thigh. Tim would study Ryan's expression then, to see whether his mother was off track, as he often sensed she was. His mother claimed Ryan was going to marry her. And the answer to when was always "Very soon." He knew Ryan gave her money, because sometimes the pressure would lift, great worries would blow out to sea, and the car would be running again or the gushing basement leak would go silent. So Ryan clearly was one of her *practice partners*.

Another likely bedmate would be the jazz drummer who called Tim *Clyde* and always set his leather cap on Tim's head when he came in the door. And Tim could name another few if he had to: the man with the stutter, the guy who bought Tim a lizard, and one she called Mario but later learned was a fake name.

"Not the maestro, though, right?" Tim asked. The principal tuba of the Boston Symphony Orchestra had been his mother's Saturday client. He'd begun teaching young Tim in order to stop him from making a racket around the house. "You didn't have sex with the maestro."

"Sex, sex, sex, is that all you're interested in? You have to let go of your infantile ideas about it, Tim. I'm writing this book for women, to help them appreciate what they contribute to and what they can take away from the practice of mindful coupling."

Tim scooted back from the table and pulled out his wallet, waved it at the server.

"As you know, all copyrights on my writings revert to you upon my death, so I wouldn't let the book languish. You'll need to continue the push."

# # #

That evening, after taking his mother home and enduring another dinner with The Star, Tim shut his bedroom door and cracked the sniper book again.

In a firefight, the key is to keep shooting, even if you cannot place the enemy, because to stop returning fire gives them confidence. Even if you are wounded, especially if you are wounded, you must continue firing.

He could hear his son's voice in the next room: "Wait, you don't know the workaround for that? When you drop objects, they are consolidated into your overall settlement size." The kid's voice had really gone deep this year. It still seemed like some kind of party trick. "Every once in a while, I go and buy out all of a vendor's junk, then drop it and scrap it in the settlement. It means I'm never short on odds and ends like crystals and gears and shit."

Listening to this nonsense made Tim angry. What was this generation going to do for the world? He looked again at the Marine on the book cover, and the Marine looked back with a shared disgust.

When the enemy is well hidden, you look for muzzle flashes, you look for dust curls out there where water is too scarce to wet the ground beneath their guns. When they're far away, you use the detonation flashes of your own shells to adjust your aim. Their bullets snap and crack around you, the pops sometimes coming so close to your ears, you know you have only seconds to interrupt someone else's fine-tuning.

That night, he finished the book. When he finally closed it, his wife was asleep next to him and the house was silent. He dreamed he was up in the gun turret of the lead Humvee in a military caravan, with a relentless wind driving sand into his eyes, and he kept yelling down that he couldn't see, that they had to stop. But the Humvee kept moving.

DAVIS

Because he had decided to send the committee printed tenure documents as well as electronic, Davis was lugging a five-ream package of printer paper up and down the aisles at Staples. No one wanted to read a book-length document on a computer screen, too wearying, perhaps doable for your average supporting docs—much slimmer than his—coming earlier in a career, but in Davis they got a candidate with twenty-seven publications, his field's foundational research. It was not lost on him that Lindstrom had mentioned the present era of widespread extinction during the dinner. Some tried to insinuate that this horrific ongoing event made the practice of looking for cryptids trivial, but in fact it was a great justification for his line of work. Who better to determine whether any complete species wipeout had occurred? Jesus, toner cartridges were always such a pain point here at Staples! The ever-elusive printer model number—2280? 2820? 2840? Neither his wife nor Megan answered her phone. Hadn't he just left them at home? Moving on toward checkout without his ink, he passed the binder area. God, the color choices were blinding! He could imagine some of his students having a field day here—a notebook to match any toenail polish. He had always told his students that binding never made up for bumbling and, therefore, to please not bother.

With five black binders stacked atop his paper, he entered the checkout corral, where he was tenth in line, snaking along beside shelves of chocolate, which he would buy for Megan if she would answer her phone. After Davis looked up to survey the cashier situation, he immediately slapped his phone down atop the binders, spun around, and hustled back up the printer aisle, dumping the paper and binders onto an endcap display and briskly leaving the store. It was Graeme Stoltz at the register. He'd seen Graeme there before. Why hadn't he remembered? And the rageaholic had seen Davis, too, awaited him with nostrils flared. Seeing the poor guy there in action shamed Davis. Watching this fine visual artist slide suckers and paperclip holders across the scanner elicited the same deep shame Davis felt whenever he encountered that Patterson-Gimlin film of the walking Bigfoot (which he could not believe was still allowed to be shown on television). That film was a complete sham, a con, but Davis had been an ardent supporter of it and had helped to spread its lie. It had taken Davis too long to come into line with the majority of the scientific community, admitting that the creature had hairy breasts, unlike any other primate. And the animal's hair, overall, didn't appear to flow naturally, and the buttocks were not distinct enough from each other. But before Davis could see and accept all of this, he and many others had held the film up as a final proof of their religion. They had replayed the footage of the creature looking back at them over his shoulder until they were drunk on it.

Before Megan had branded him a child molester, Graeme—who now performed this part-time work of teenagers as his sole occupation—had been a respected art teacher. Back then, two summers ago, he was a man struggling only with troubles of his own making or of his own nature.

Davis liked to think he would have called out Megan's lie—and he now believed it was a lie—if not for the birthmark. Jenny had come across a drawing in Megan's room of a naked backside with a birthmark like Megan's (a sideways heart–shaped mark) on the small of her back. Megan claimed the drawing came from Graeme's hand. And, in fact, it had, he admitted, but it had been in his zippered portfolio case, he said, and it depicted a model in his live-drawing group. When the detail about the birthmark came out in the press, even Graeme's wife fled the poor man (it wouldn't have been a first affair, Davis guessed). He kept repeating that he hadn't included that birthmark in the drawing, that he'd paid no special attention to Megan at all. The police finally became suspicious when Megan's timelines of the molestations did not match up with Graeme's proven locations, but Davis kept the pressure on. Who remembers times and dates when experiencing unfathomable trauma? Eventually, however, the case was dropped, and Megan moved on to pawing a neighbor man.

Davis watched from the car as Graeme shoved a wastebasket into a too-small plastic bag, his biceps enraged. Soon enough, he knew, Megan would lure a man into trying something that could be proved. She was practicing all the time.

TIM

Rita, The Publisher's gutless secretary, slid a few pages onto Tim's desk and stepped back, frowning. The top sheet displayed a diagram of a football field, with an overlay of dots in the shape of a big head with googly eyes. "She thinks this drill chart was a poor choice," Rita said. "Too offensive to parents."

"Did she do a poll?"

"She did a little poll."

Tim pushed back in frustration, scraping the floor with the thin metal legs of his chair.

"Sorry," Rita said, "everyone agreed." Whenever The Publisher wanted to dump a piece, she got emotional backup by wandering into people's offices and saying, "Can I get your opinion on this? Don't you think this article is pandering/beneath us/offensive to some group/dull/biased/clichéd/run-of-the-mill/etc.?"

"Okay," Tim said. "I'll let the poor guy know that the Simpsons are too controversial." Now he'd have to work overtime to get a new drill selected and described this late in the month. Besides short descriptions of new marching-band products from the advertisers, this was the only other element Tim provided for the magazine: the monthly "Killer Drill," which presented the wet-dream field show of some earnest high school band leader.

"And she'd like to see you in her office right away."

He grabbed his legal pad and followed her. "We were all in over the weekend," he told Rita's withered back. As usual, on Saturday he had screwed in the desk lamp light bulbs for the other editors, Emily and Marcel, so they wouldn't be caught out after The Publisher unscrewed them all on Friday evening.

Usually when he pushed into The Publisher's office, she was concentrating on her iPhone and would remain doing so for an uncomfortable stretch. This time, however, she nearly leapt from her chair to greet him.

"Mr. Turner! Come in, come in!" Then she landed hard, back onto her executive throne.

Something wonderful had happened to her, he thought, already jealous.

"Thanks for taking a moment out."

He lowered himself tentatively into the opposite armchair.

"I've been thinking for quite some time, ever since our first meeting, in fact, since when you first came in for an interview—do you remember that day?" She was breathing hard, actually panting. She was fatter than he was, and inspiration winded her. "I've been thinking about your friend that you mentioned, the band leader for the President's Own."

"Okay…," he said, drawing it out.

"Your old friend."

"Joe Masotta."

"Joe Masotta," she said with an Italian accent, like she was teaching him the proper pronunciation. "Every year since you mentioned him—if you can believe it—every year when I am preparing for my keynote at NMBA, I check the fall concert schedule of the President's Own, hoping beyond hope that they will be playing near where the meeting is held. And now, my dear man, this is the year!" She seal-clapped over her desk. "They're playing in Providence the night before and in Boston that very same night. My keynote is at eleven a.m.! I want to interview Colonel Masotta. Oh, I want this so badly. Just think about it—all of the stories of the inaugurations and the state visits and the presidential funerals. He's got the *history*; he could show *photos*! You know, I watched him in a video interview on the Internet." She reached out to rap her big gold pen against the far edge of her blotter like she was dinging a cymbal. "Fascinating! My God! And he's funny!"

Finally, after twelve years of humiliations, he understood why he'd been hired to do a job he'd been wholly unqualified for: Joe Masotta. "Yeah, he's funny, all right."

"Will you call him?"

"I guess I could see if he'll talk to me."

"Of course, he'll talk to you! Will you try him this afternoon? Pretty please?"

"Sure, but he's busy, of course."

"And if you can arrange this, I want you to know that you will be rewarded with a substantial raise."

"How much?"

"Five thousand." She wagged the thick pen at him. "The title of senior editor and financial remuneration because this— this would be my greatest achievement and a great night for *Bells Up*, a real dream come true."

"Emily's already the senior editor."

"Emily can move over. Emily doesn't come in on Saturdays. Not like you." She was back to her phone, at last. Scrolling.

Oh, God, Tim thought, Emily will quit. She doesn't need the aggravation. "I don't need a new title," he said.

"Well, you'll deserve it if you can make this work."

As he was leaving the office, The Publisher added, "Oh, and Tim, Angela's in the hospital. I'm afraid her cancer is gaining ground. I'll be going over this afternoon, and I'll let you know what I find. Of course, I'm hoping she can still call up at least a few key accounts now it's so late in the month."

"Cancer? I'd heard a rumor, but I just spoke with her on Saturday about a short." Angela was the sales director. In fact, she was the whole sales department.

"You know, I wish I knew where to find twelve more of her," The Publisher said and then tucked her throne tightly under the desk, shaking her head and tsking as though Angela were already dead. Before Tim reached the door, she asked, "By the way, Tim?"

He turned back again.

"Do you know what *stellar* means? The word *stellar*?"

"Yes."

"Do you?

"Yes."

"Then don't use it to describe an activity involving middle schoolers."

# # #

When Tim stopped at Emily's door, she was just setting her bag on the desk, her back to him.

"Angela's in the hospital," he told her.

"Oh," she turned, crestfallen. Tim felt off-balance, looking at her. She'd made some kind of transformation. Her face was glowing and she'd straightened her hair or added hair on until it was long enough to tease her clavicles. God, that was sexy. Wow. It was crazy how this small change hit him, full on. Or, no, it was the low-cut blouse, or just the fact that it was a blouse and not a chaste cotton oxford. This blouse was cut low enough to emphasize—the boobs! Those were not Emily's boobs. Emily could not have had those before this moment. "Wow, Emily. You've changed your look." It was as though a showgirl were resting in Emily's office between numbers.

"What's she in for?" She slumped back against the desk.

"Cancer. That's what I heard."

"Shit, shit, shit." She shook the silky hair. Tim wiped the corners of his mouth with a thumb and finger. Emily had gone from being a lilting balletic melody he couldn't get out of his head all the way to *The Firebird*.

She said, "We have to go see her." The new boobs and hair had required a new leather skirt, he now realized, which she smoothed over her ass as she sat down to pull her phone from her purse.

His tongue sloshed in his mouth. "Sure, I can take you."

"We should go some night this week. She has a kid, right?"

Tim began to rapid-swallow all of the saliva, but he lisped anyway: "Two shons. She's my age."

"Those poor kids!"

"Your hair," he managed.

"Yeah, got it done on Saturday. Not sure if I like it." Then she glanced down at her own cleavage.

Tim nipped a tight smile and stood there in her doorway until he realized by her raised eyebrows that she was waiting for him to answer something. "What?"

"I said, how's Wednesday?"

"Let me check," he said, pushing himself away.

# # #

Eyes closed, his fingers resting on the vibrating Selectric keys, Tim went from visualizing Emily's tits to wondering how much they cost to figuring that the senior editor gig must pay a whole hell of a lot more than he made. Maybe he could just ask her, "What do you make here, Emily?" Maybe she would tell him. He palmed his cheeks, but in his mind he was cupping her breasts against his face, so cool, spreading to cover his eyelids, his lips.

It was a no-hope fantasy. She used to go out for a beer with him on Fridays, but she'd turned him down ever since the night of his *perfect performance*, when every story of his had slayed her, the night she'd needed his steady arm as they left the bar. He was high on himself and rightly so, and at the zenith of intoxication, having driven her back to her car in the *Bells Up* lot, he had grasped her head and pulled her lips over from the cheek kiss she was intending to a full-on wet one, and then she'd reared back and fled the vehicle.

He opened his eyes from the tit fantasy onto his forty-pound gray typewriter. All three editors owned such a boulder. The reason computers were not allowed for the editors was that once The Publisher had read any piece and made her notations in pen, she did not want any editing to go on that she could not see. The hard-copy shorts and articles moved back and forth between The Publisher and the editors, growing more and more crazed with inky trailings. Then a person outside the process, someone who could have no motive for changing The Publisher's directions, took the mess and keyed it into an actual computer program. If Tim scored that raise, then he could maybe save enough money to get out of this asylum.

He picked up his cell phone and thumb-typed "Joe Masotta" into the browser search box, thinking five thousand dollars might just be enough to accomplish *Fire Team Mission #1: Make Enough Money to Buy Mona the Driveway*. Joe and Tim had both studied with the maestro and had taken turns playing tuba for the Boston Youth Symphony Orchestra (there was only one tuba position). When they graduated high school, they decided to audition for one of the Marine bands. They figured since Marine musicians also had to go to boot camp, the number of players auditioning would be much lower than for most orchestras. Joe prepped Tim daily, running him through his audition pieces and yelling at him like they imagined the Marines would do at the audition. At the actual event, however, Tim was nicely asked to run through the E scale in two octaves, and he botched it. Then he mooed his way through the Kopprasch #33 and wasn't even asked to do the sight-reading portion. Meanwhile, Joe was a resounding success and entered boot camp alone.

The photo of Joe that came up on Tim's Samsung browser was of a handsome, fit man in uniform, holding a conducting baton, with his arms crossed, eyes leveled at the camera—an accomplished, confident, middle-aged man.

Tim dialed the contact number for the President's Own public affairs office. When a man answered, Tim said, "Hey, how would I contact Joe Masotta, do you think?"

"May I ask who's calling?"

"An old friend, Tim Turner, from a thousand years ago. But he'll know me."

"Let me take your phone number, and I'll see that Colonel Masotta gets it."

Tim gave his number and then sorted through the mail until he found the envelope from KingMar that poor Angela had asked him to look for. After reading the brochure, he typed up Angela's short.

Come Out Ahead with KingMar Plumes
Are Your Plumes Outdated? Have they lost their majesty? Change your image with KingMar Marching Band Plumes, designed to top off the new sleek and fashionable uniforms. Shako, French Upright, and French Fountain plumes are available in a range of heights and thicknesses. Custom colors also available for an extra fee. Look sharp with KingMar.

Majesty might be one of The Publisher's many forbidden

words, so he'd have to check it against his list, and he wasn't sure about the title, either, but plumes did come out of your head. The next brochure that appealed to him was one for batons, since he had just seen Joe's publicity photos. After he wrote each line, he would say to himself, Who gives a shit? He wondered if the phrase *shaft* and *ball* would send The Publisher over the edge. If so, he would have to think of new names for what actually were the shaft and ball of the baton.

Precision Batons for the Most Demanding Performances

Flagship batons in every inch are carefully weighted and manufactured of inflexible, chrome-plated steel, quality engineered for top performance. The sleek, dimpled 3/8-inch shaft and ball are designed to help the discerning director gauge hand placement. All batons have a one-year warranty against factory defects. Champions worldwide use Flagship batons.

Next, Tim reviewed his choices for the replacement Killer Drill. Band directors had recently sent in charts for marching-band shows called The Planets (with simulated planetary collisions), Portrait of a Nation, Pandora's Boom Box, and Fat Bottomed Girls, set to a Queen song of the same name, the last of which would never make it out of the polling committee. Tim often selected the month's Killer Drill at random, mixing up the handful of charts that came in through the mail—just mashing them all over his desk and then picking one up. Then he would call up the band director and talk with him during the man's planning hour or during lunch. The guy was always thrilled to pieces. Tim's first question: "I gotta ask, man, what inspired such an incredible drill?" He'd heard it all: fireworks, *Star Wars*, the Beatles, the butterfly lifecycle, the Columbian

Exchange, the true spirit of Texas. As he slid Portrait of a Nation from the stack, he began to notice sounds rarely heard in the *Bells Up* halls: murmurings, then all-out hall talking, not in hushed tones but like regular people speak. And this made Tim rise from his chair and come to realize that they were free. The Publisher had left the building to go to the hospital to see Angela. For the rest of the afternoon, he and others made the rounds of the building like it was an open house. Even the reclusive accounts payable woman left her station and swaggered around like Hugh Hefner at the mansion.

"If I had The Publisher's money," graphic artist Connie Garvin announced to a clutch of women by the kitchen, "I would act the exact same way. Money turns you into a complete bitch. It's fucker-juice."

Tim moved on to find Marcel Aubert—the senior (and only) editor for the other company magazine, *Lift Your Voices*, for choral directors—sitting on the desk of the finance guy and telling him, "Fat is actually exhaled from your body. That's how it leaves, and now that I'm running, I've exhaled seventeen pounds so far. Think about it. Fat in the air. Fat blowing in the wind."

Tim paused at each clump of coworkers but didn't stay long. He felt out of sync, uninterested in any line of conversation.

From time to time, a phone would ring or the front door would open, and the groups would scatter and the fluorescent-bulb hum would again become discernible until they realized The Publisher was still off premises and they could once again mingle.

He looked into Angela's office. Just last week he had teased her again about it, threatened to strip down to a Speedo for a meeting. Her office had a beachy theme: striped love seat; blue wave-patterned rug; shelves of erotic pink-lipped conch shells; hand-painted quotes on weather-beaten wood ("A goal is a dream with a deadline," with no attribution; "What we dwell on is who we become—Oprah Winfrey"). Her desk chair was thickly cushioned, and from it he studied the photos of her family: a close-up of her tilting her head dreamily toward a man with a porn-star mustache, and another of two boys dressed up, one as a Minecraft character and the other as a ballot box (a box with a slit and the word VOTE on it). Jesus, what boy wants to be a goddamn ballot box for Halloween? But there the kid was, happy, denied nothing—certainly not paintball birthday parties that cost forty-five bucks. In her desk drawer were all of the Certificates of Excellence that The Publisher awarded instead of bonuses and a composition book that was her sales notebook.

Tim's phone buzzed with a Words with Friends prompt. The Publisher had played her word, *quibble* (24 points). He pictured her sitting in Angela's hospital room, shoving peanut M&M's into her face funnel with one hand and sliding tiles into place with the stubby index finger of the other, all while Angela was gasping for air.

Tim went back to his game with TallBlondBabe18 and played *bad*. Instantly he got a message.

O I like bad.

This was a jolt to him. He rubbed his chest with his left hand, thinking how to reply. Then Mike, the muscle-bound shipping guy, came in and leaned against a filing cabinet. "False alarm. Her car's not back." In his tight Lycra shirt, Mike's nipple jewelry looked like ringworm.

"Yeah, she's still there, playing Words with Friends from the hospital room. Hey, what was going on out in the parking lot this morning?"

"Did you see that shit? She calls me out there to diddle around with the seat belt mechanism. She wants a knot tied in there so the belt will not feed out too far in a crash, which it won't, because that's how belts are designed, that's the whole purpose of a belt, but she doesn't trust it."

"I'm playing a game against someone named Tall Blond Babe."

Mike came over to look at the phone. "What game?"

"Words with Friends."

"Don't get to see her?"

"No."

"Ask for a picture."

"I just started playing with her."

"All right then." Mike hovered a little while longer, but Tim was focused on the phone. "Did I tell you The Troll's got me going up to Kennebunkport on the weekends, now? Do some handyman shit around the beach house? Like I don't already do forty hours' worth of weird shit for her here." Tim frowned at his little game screen, wanting Mike gone.

"Thinking of taking a girl up there next time," Mike continued, but he got no response. "Chaining her to the bed as my slave." After another silent moment, Mike shrugged his bulbous delts. "Guess I'll get back to it."

As he left, Tim messaged, I can be bad if you'll let me. After five minutes with no reply, he put the phone on Angela's desk and looked through her sales notebook. Each page listed a month's sales, steady through the years, the same players returning again and again, until the last few months, when their regular buys grew larger and she'd also landed new companies. As she was shrinking, her income was bulging.

Then the message came: Ur just who I been looking for.

# # #

It was seven-thirty when Tim pulled up to the auction house. The old man who owned it was standing behind the glass door, staring out onto the parking lot. He'd held the place open just for them. Sunny Straub, a sharp-featured woman in early old age, rose from a chair by the door and bustled ahead of Tim through the maze of antique furniture to the grand piano in question, whose closed lid edge she grasped, grinning like a child claiming a toy. As Tim sat on the bench of Sunny's intended purchase, mostly he noticed that its white finish was flawless. He knocked on the cabinet and gave an impressed nod, depressed a few keys, and told her, "Isn't this fine!"

"It is?" she asked, as though he'd confirmed the unimaginable.

"Oh, sure!"

"What about the name?" They looked together at the name over the keyboard.

"It's a good name."

"See, I hadn't heard of it," she worried.

"You can't go wrong with a Klopotek," he said, though he had no idea. Then he ran a scale on it and discovered it was crazily out of tune, but he didn't want to change his mind in front of her, and he remembered the tuning lesson that week, which was about wrapping loose pins with cardboard and hammering them back in so any pin can be set to hold a tuning. "This is good wood, Mrs. Straub," he said. "Buy this, and I will tune it."

# # #

When he got home at nine, the house was dark except for the television glow in the living room, where Miles had assumed the gaming position. Tim found leftover macaroni in the fridge, nuked it, and carried it out on his way to bed. "You need to do other things," he bellowed to penetrate his son's ear pads.

With his long, sticklike limbs, Miles looked like a praying mantis on its back. "I know," he said, then tucked his avatar behind a ruined wall, laid his controller on the carpet, and arpeggioed the air to free up his fingers.

Tim turned back toward him from the bottom of the stairs. "Maybe you should go into the military."

Miles let out a puff of air. "Ha."

"Women love a Marine."

"Why didn't *you* do it?"

"I tried."

"Ha."

"Ha," Tim mocked him as he continued up to his bedroom, where he slipped out of his shoes and lay on the bed with the macaroni in the crook of his arm and the sniper book propped on his belly. He was going to reread it.

He had left both his work and home numbers for Joe Masotta, but the phone by the bed wasn't blinking about a voice mail. He thought he'd open the discussion by catching Joe up on the old gang and what everyone was doing. He would tell him that Maggie was a pharmacist. No surprise. She was always practical, as clarinetists are. He'd also seen Patty. He and Joe used to say that the best thing about their enormous instruments was that they could hide a boner, which they got often over Patty Papadopoulos when she sat her lovely ass in the folding chair in front of them and greased her French horn slides. "Patty's a cop," he'd tell Joe. He'd seen her on traffic detail once.

When he made it up to the point in the book where the hero is told that another sniper will be replacing him on his fire team for a dangerous detail, Tim heard a key in the front door and then Mona saying, "That was fantastic!" followed by a thud like she had thrown herself against a wall.

"I told you you should've come!" Vinnie chastised Miles.

"Just the costumes, Miles!"

"Dressed to kill. How many outfits? I cannot say." Vinnie sounded like a commentator.

"You would have hated it, but it was fabulous. A spectacle." Vinnie sang, "'If I could turn back ti-ime!' Yo!"

"I'm glad it was good," Miles exhaled.

"That woman is seventy," Vinnie informed him. "So I am not old. Okay? Seventy! And the midsection on her? You know what, Miles? I am just a baby."

"Tim," Mona shouted. "I've got good news for you."

Tim set his book on the floor and padded out into the hall.

"She has fabulous news." Vinnie beamed up at him.

Mona clapped at the sight of him. "Daddy's gonna pay for the parking space. He told me today! He'll pay up to fifteen thousand. Now all you have to do is get them to sell it."

"Wow. That's very nice."

"He doesn't know why you ever bought this house with no space."

"And Cher was good?" The quick deflection.

"In-cred-i-ble." Vinnie said like it was four words.

"Not to be matched," Mona added on her way to the bathroom. "I'm gonna potty and then we're gonna get the ball rolling."

Ironically, what Tim had first liked about Mona was her strong sense of self. Even as a teenager, when everyone else was trying on personality hats, Mona didn't seek or need anyone's approval. His friend Joe had met her when the Boston Children's Chorus had sung Handel's Messiah with the Youth Symphony and she'd come around to the back row and wanted to talk tuba. Why did Joe play it? Did it make his lips fuller? Then Joe started bringing her along when he and Tim went anywhere, and it became an automatic threesome, understood that if one of them went anywhere, the other two would join, even skinny-dipping in a pool where Mona was house-sitting. Unabashed, she was an exotic to the teen boys. The threesome did not extend to sex, however. She was Joe's lover only. When Tim heard that Joe had made the Marine band, he wondered how Joe's absence could play out for him and Mona. The very first night they went out after Joe left for boot camp, Tim and Mona worked each other up on the bench of a picnic table.

"Okay," she said, stepping out of her skirt at the foot of the bed, "call Andy and see if he'll sell the spot. It's only nine o'clock in California." Andy Paik was the strip-mall dentist who, along with his ex-wife, Phyllis, owned the coveted parking spot. He'd moved to San Diego after the house next door had been foreclosed on. "We can't miss out on this." She was wild-eyed, like God had appeared to her in the john.

When Andy Paik answered, he seemed genuinely pleased to hear from Tim. "How are you and Mona and Miles? I miss seeing you!"

"We're good! How's California?"

"Well, what can I say? It's magical! It's so much more relaxed here. What were we all killing ourselves for back East? You know? And people are more social here. Of course I miss Phyllis. I really loved her—such a beautiful woman." Tim pictured Andy's wide Korean face falling.

"How's my old house?" Andy asked, suddenly rejuvenated.

"Kind of falling apart, really."

"Oh, really? Oh, that breaks my heart. I have so many wonderful memories of that house." Every time Tim had caught sight of Andy, the guy was running away from the place, crossing the street to his car with his hand in the air to forestall any conversation, as he repeated, "I'm late, I'm late!"

"Hey, I wanted to ask you about the driveway. Your old driveway? Do you still own that?"

"Well, it was a separate sale from the house, since the space was carved out of the parking lot across the street."

"Did you pay cash for it?"

"I think so, Tim, but I can't remember how they worked all of that out at the closing."

"We'd love to buy it, Andy. Would you consider selling it if it has clear title?"

Tim could hear him blowing air out of his infinite cheeks. "Well, sure! Why not? I can't use it! But Phyllis is also on the deed, so she'd have to agree. She's down in Mexico! Did you know that? Living in a ghost town!"

"What would you take for it, Andy?"

"Oh, gosh, I don't know. What do you think it's worth?"

"I don't want to mess around on this." Mona nodded in determined agreement as he spoke. "We had a realtor look at it, and he said top dollar was ten thousand, and we'd be happy to give you that." Mona popped two thumbs up.

"Fine! But, listen. Text Phyllis. See if she'll agree. She responds pretty well to texts."

Tim got the woman's phone number and sent her a message about the driveway. Then he fell quickly asleep. He was awakened by the ding.

"What is it?" Mona jerked herself over to face him as he felt around on the floor for the phone and then held it inches from his face.

Hi Tim, Im advtising the space for 25K. Did you see the spot in Back Bay that went fr $560K????

"It's from Phyllis."

The pple who own the bar are interested in it...understandbly. Hwver, I lk you and Mona, wish we we'd been better aquainted.

"What does she say?"
"It's super long. I'll let you read it after me."

Mbe you could've helped me flee Dr. Pain & his secret violence. Should've gvn you clue as to what wnt on inside 105, tho I'm sure you'd have found it impossible to believe tht your jolly sweet neighbor ws Bluebeard.

"Does she agree to the price?"
"Don't think so."

I have nthing now. Mr. Hyde stopped payments on the house long ago WITHOUT MY KNOWLEDGE. I knew nothng. Myopic frm exquisite pain. Curled up in my rm. Now living in Mineral de Pozos, Mexico, in casita can barely afford. I hobble up a mountain every other day for physical therpy.

Gentle Dr. Jekyll whom you waved to as he walked to car must hv pulled you aside on few occasions and shook his head over demented wife he dearly loved. I was recluse out of fear and immobilty! This is why you didnt know me except through his tales, whatever he conjured for you as you passed in the street.

"What does she say?"
"Hang on."

You once saw something. Once you opend your window onto my wrld. Do you recall??? Anyway, 25K will get you the spot.

Kindly,
Phyllis

"She want's twenty-five thousand."

"That's crazy! It's not worth that!"

"Read it." He handed her the phone.

She put her glasses on. "What's this, she's advertising the space? The boys at the bar are interested?"

"That's made up."

Mona continued to read. "Dear God! That man beat her?" Finally she snapped her head to face him. "What did you see, Tim?"

"I don't know."

"You saw something!"

"I don't know!" Tim rolled away. Then he soon rolled back. "It was a night you were performing. I was in bed, and I heard a woman screaming. But when I went and opened the window, Andy was just standing by his car with one of the back doors open—just standing there by himself—and he said, 'Everything's fine. Not to worry.'"

"You should have called the police!"

"You know, I would have, but she was so odd, I didn't know what to think! And he was this mild-mannered guy! And after he said everything was fine, she didn't say anything."

"You should've asked to speak with her."

"Well, yeah, now I can see that. Anyway, it's twenty-five K."

"I cannot live here without that driveway, Tim. My nerves cannot take it."

After many minutes of silence, after he had shimmied back under the comforter and sighed and was just starting to let it all go and drift away, she asked, "Why did you buy this house?"

His eyelids snapped open.

"That house in Medford, with the professionally designed

garden, why didn't you buy that house?" she asked.

"I believe you signed the papers, too." He heaved away from her and packed the pillow over his ear.

DAVIS

Sasquatch is a bastardization of the Halkomelem word *sásq'ets*—Halkomelem being a First Nations language in British Columbia. Many other North American native peoples also had names for a large, hairy hominid, one who typically appeared to them only in times of trouble for their community. But without physical evidence, and because these hominids held a spiritual role in the native populations, scientists determined they were all imagined. Now let's look at a similar story that took place in Indonesia. The only big difference here is actually quite tiny. What I mean to say is that the "imagined" hominids were only three feet tall as adults. According to the stories of the indigenous people living on the Indonesian island of Flores, the *Ebu gogo*, as they called the petite humans (and which loosely translates as "ravenous grandma"), were living among them as late as the sixteenth century, when Portuguese traders first arrived. Still other natives insist that the *Ebu gogo* were seen milling about into the twentieth century. According to legend, the hominids were hairy, with broad, flat noses, enormous mouths, and droopy breasts on the women, from which the "grandma" moniker likely came. They spoke in strange murmurs but could parrot anything said to them in other languages. They stole food from the modern humans and also took children, in hopes that they would teach them to cook. In the local stories, the *Ebu gogo* were so foolish that the children easily escaped and returned home. Eventually, the fed-up modern humans murdered them all, save perhaps a few who survive to this day, according to legend. None of these stories by the indigenous people were believed, of course, and scientists decided that the *Ebu gogo* had been monkeys. End of story. Until, that is, their bones were unearthed in a cave.

# # #

As he reviewed his *Ebu gogo* submission for a cryptozoology anthology, Davis wandered the Indonesian island of Flores in his imagination—the enormous rice paddies, the prehistoric komodo dragons, the volcanic lakes changing colors on a whim, red to blue to green—until he was reluctantly sucked back into his drab kitchen in Greenstown by some utterance of Megan's, who was mooning over her iPhone on the other side of the table.

"What?" he asked her.

"I have almost thirty contacts," she said, twirling a hank of hair around one ear. "I even have Eric's number."

Davis snapped his laptop closed. "Dr. Lindstrom? Why do you have his phone number?"

"He said we could call if we have any questions about the paper."

"Do not call him."

She smiled at the screen.

"Do you hear me?"

The whole cell phone debacle had happened because Jenny

and Dr. Peggy had conspired against Davis. This was what he had decided. He'd replayed the phone conversation many times in his head.

He and Jenny had been on opposite sides of the desk in his office at the college. They always called Dr. Peggy from there so that Megan could not overhear, accidentally or not.

Peggy had told them, "Better if she gets a phone while Mother and Father can help her understand how to use it and how not to use it, I think. Why don't you make learning how to use the phone her special time?" Special time had been Megan's only successful motivator. It was half an hour each evening during which Megan did something—artwork or a craft project or performing a song—and Davis or Jenny paid exclusive attention to her.

"Did Carla have a phone?" Davis asked about Peggy's daughter, now an adult, who also had disinhibited RAD. This was how they and others had found Peggy, through her book, *Dear to Strangers, Deadly at Home*, in which she described how little adopted Carla moved from being a child who ate like a dog, smeared her feces around the house, and repeatedly stabbed her sister to being a fairly normal adult, capable of having healthy relationships with others.

"No, but phones weren't all the rage back then."

"Peggy," Davis said, "I just feel that trying to control her with that phone is going to be—it's going to put me right out of my mind. You know, right now she can use the computer in the kitchen when one of us is in there, but that's it. And believe me, we have to watch. We have to stand there and watch. She had one site up that—"

"Father, will she be living with you and Mother throughout her life?"

"That's what I said!" Jenny agreed.

Davis's voice took on a high, scraping sound. "It's the very last year for us to exert any sort of influence. And I just see her slipping away with a phone before she's ready, before she's mature enough."

"What do you think, Mother?"

"If she can't keep up with the other girls socially, she won't mature at all. That's what I think. If they arrange to go out, they text and all of that, and she won't know."

"They're not texting her!" Davis flashed her a look of disgust.

"That's right! Not without a phone!" Jenny jolted. "That's my point!"

"They *wouldn't* text her. That's what I mean. They *wouldn't* text her."

"Why wouldn't they text her, Father?"

He sighed. "Look, what's your recommendation on this?"

They heard some crunching on the line, like the woman was eating a large nut. "This phone might just be your dream vehicle for behavior modification. It's yours to give and also to take. Use it before she becomes eighteen and leaves. Because then"—the crunching continued.

"I'm sorry, then what, Dr. Peggy?" Jenny cocked her head.

"What?" Peggy asked.

"She's set loose upon the world," Davis answered for her. "Our greatest hope and fear."

Davis now realized he had been ignoring Megan for much of this particular special time. "Do you want to work on Dr. Lindstrom's video blog assignment *What Is Blank?*"

She slid her phone across the table. "I need you to put Snapchat on my phone."

"Is this for class?" He'd recently put Words with Friends on the phone because her English teacher wanted them all to play it.

"No, it's for my friends. You send videos and pictures, but

only to people you know."

"You can do that in email or on Facebook." He slid the phone back to her.

"No, these disappear! As soon as someone looks at it, it disappears."

"I don't know if that's good."

"You always say, don't put anything on the Internet that you don't want a future employer to see, so this is good, 'cause now it disappears!"

"I'll look into it."

"It's free, Dad. Everyone I know uses it. Like, every single person except me."

"Everyone? Even the science nerds?"

"Totally. Everyone."

He picked up her phone, found the app on the app store, and typed in the secret password. "How are your Words with Friends games going?"

"That's boring. Games are boring. I like knowing what people are doing and telling them what I'm doing."

"Don't tell Lindstrom what you're doing. He doesn't care."

She tipped her chair back to lean against the wall, grinning. "Are you jealous of Eric?"

"That's creepy. Don't—"

"Sounds like it."

"Megan, stop it. You're being ridiculous."

Then, leaning a little forward, she let her chair slam back down. Her eyes went dead and her lips thinned to a tight line. "This doesn't feel like special time."

Above her on the kitchen wall hung a poster-size sheet of paper on which one sentence had been written with a large black marker, "I will not steal money from anyone, even if I think they don't care about it," with Megan's big, loopy signature next to it. He'd made this poster the other night after she'd stolen coins from a jar atop his dresser to spend at the county fair. Beside, above, and under this sheet were a dozen others sporting different signed claims.

"Why don't we work together on Lindstrom's assignment? What's your chosen creature?"

"Tonight I have to write a paper for English. It's about this book." She pulled a small blue paperback out of her bag, *The Housekeeper and the Professor*.

"A book report?"

"We have to come up with a thesis and then support it. I want to write, 'In this book nothing happens.'"

"Don't be ridiculous, Megan. What's the book about?"

"An old man can only remember eighty minutes at a time." She riffled the page corners and tapped her feet. "He has this housekeeper who brings her son to work and they talk about baseball."

"Well—"

"And math, he's like a math wizard."

"Who, the old man?"

"Yeah, and the guy is covered in pieces of paper that remind him of things."

"So you need to find a theme in there. Does the author think memory is all-important, or does this old guy still have a decent quality of life with such short-term memory? In a way, he's like a human Snapchat, isn't he? Is there value in not remembering everything? You know, when people have electroshock treatments—and only when people are severely depressed does this happen—it does help many of them and it seems to do this in large part by wiping away memories. Memories can be debilitating. Is this part of what the story is about?"

"How would I know?"

"You try to imagine what the author's purpose was in

telling this story in the way that he or she did."

Her jaw fell slack as she stared at the cover.

"I know that's what's hard for you," said Davis, "imagining what other people think and feel."

"I just don't see what the point is."

"If you want to connect with people, to have a real relationship with anyone, they need to know that you care about how they feel, that you want to know. So, that would be the reason."

Her phone made the *glug, glug, glug* sound that announced a play on Words with Friends and she snatched it up like it offered a portal to a better world.

# # #

Megan feared driving because she had no control of the others on the road. She usually sighed all the way to the college on Tuesday and Thursday mornings when she drove Davis and herself there so she could attend Lindstrom's course. Then at lunchtime, Jenny picked her up and delivered her to the high school. Despite her fear, or maybe because of it, Megan was a pretty good driver, and, unlike most teen girls, she didn't veer off when a squirrel or a bird was in the road. She hit it. Which, Davis had to admit, was the safest thing to do. Because of Megan's typical driving state, Davis didn't think much of it when, halfway to the school, she began emitting a continuous nasal *en*, a mosquito sound that grew in volume until he was forced to burst out with "What?"

"I can't drive! I can't drive!" she yelled, eyes bulging like their car was rolling toward a cliff.

"Pull over," he told her, but she stopped in the middle of the road and began to wail.

"What is it?"

"Oh, my God!" She crammed her eyes shut.

Davis looked right and left. "What's happening?"

"No! I can't talk about it!"

"Fine." He shoved his papers back into his briefcase. "Get in the back seat. I'll drive. Just get in the back." He waved at the young, unkempt couple in the car behind them as he walked around.

After they were both in place, he put the car into drive and eased forward. Her face was contorted in the rearview mirror. "Are you in pain, Megan?"

"I don't want to talk about it!"

"Well, I don't know whether to take you to class or take you home. What shall it be?"

"Home! I'm, like, ripping open!" Her whole head was purpling.

Davis made the next right in order to circle back to the house. "Will you tell Mom where the pain is?"

When he got Megan home, she ran up to her room. Jenny soon followed, and Davis was about to leave again, but instead he crept up to the master bedroom, which shared a wall with Megan's, and listening there, he learned that not only had Megan had an IUD inserted the day before but that Jenny had taken her.

He drove back to work in a fury. He'd been cut out! After all he'd done to make Jenny's ill-conceived, impulsive adoption decision work for her, she'd cut him out of the discussion. Why? Well, clearly she would rather wish Megan's issues away than work to contain them. He imagined, again, having taken another path in life; his mind drifted back to Aletta—his South African beauty, Aletta Van Der Hooft. She'd been teaching at the University of Vermont with him for two whole months before he'd encountered her, which ought to have been inexcusable, but because of widespread fear of then four-year-old Megan, he'd not been invited to Aletta's welcoming party. Early, very early, Megan had injured others; babies especially; she twisted and poked their delicate, malleable bits. And no threat was effective. Put her out of the car? Fine. There she would stand. Spank her? She passed the time. Hurting others was, if not fun, a release of some sort. This behavior signaled the end of Davis and Jenny's friendships with other parents.

Oh Aletta, Aletta! She had been filling in during Karen Smith-Walker's sabbatical, and finally she appeared at his door one afternoon, wearing some kind of lovely, indigenous, fringed poncho. "Well, off course, the reebbits' horns wehr warts, but who could haff eemagined eet?" She sashayed into his office. "I want to know the mehn who could eemagine such creatures and how they came to be, to penetrate your brain." Machine-gun-like speech, with the last T of penetrate sparking in the narrowing space between them.

Davis's office was a miniature version of his home-based crypto museum, with more skulls on shelves, still more display cases lined with plaster footprints, and a wall-mounted rabbit's head with deer horns made by a student in honor of Davis's jackalope-due-to-virus theory.

"Davis Beardsley." He stood and held out his hand for her.

Hours later, Davis found he could hardly see his menu at the dark bar of the Chinese Bistro and it was only three p.m. Aletta hadn't even bothered to open hers and just smiled at him, lips closed, like waiting to tell him he'd won an award. The mirror behind the bottles of booze had Chinese symbols frosted onto it. He saw they had Tanqueray, which he suddenly longed for.

"I believe they have crab Rangoon," Davis announced. "Do you like crab Rangoon?"

She dug a silver cigarette case out of her bag and set it on the bar. "Tell me the eureka moment." Her r's had a slight, thrilling trill. She'd read his whole dissertation. They ordered a few plates from the bartender, and while they awaited their food, she had many questions for him. He was sure she had talked a little of her own work, but mostly she was interested in his. She got him.

Once the barman had delivered the appetizers, Aletta announced, "You are a mehn of great pehssions." Then she moved one of the Rangoons over onto his little plate and reached for her silver case. "Great eensight and great pehssion. Like my father."

He put his hand over hers on the case. "It's not allowed in this country, smoking indoors. We're Puritans, I'm afraid." Then he ordered two more martinis. "I would like to know more about your father."

# # #

He passed by one of her classes the next day and put his face against the narrow glass window in the door. She paced the aisles as she lectured, stopping often to touch a student's arm or shoulder and ask for input. She laughed easily with them, as she had with him. He could tell that her male students craved her.

That evening, as soon as he entered the house, Jenny played a voice mail for him: Aletta purring about how she would adore meeting for "coffee and a ceegarette." Jenny had listened to it often enough that she mouthed the words along with the recording. "Who's that?" she then asked in unobscured terror, and Davis forced himself to study the facts: He was married to a woman who had only ever wished the best for him, who cared for him, and who had placed herself and a troubled little Romanian in his care. So he erased the nascent dream from his mind. He tapped a rolled note into Aletta's box the very next morning, saying he could not meet with her again, ever.

With that excruciating act of loyalty, he could never have imagined fast-forwarding to this betrayal—Megan secretly on birth control!—and now this debacle had made him twenty minutes late to his first class, which, he could see upon entering, was being overseen by Eric Lindstrom.

"And here he is," Lindstrom coolly announced.

"Sorry, family emergency." Davis rushed down the steps of the lecture hall.

"No problem, no problem. I was here to observe and had the pleasure of offering a mini-lesson on invertebrates."

"Thanks, I'm sure you have a class now, too." Davis swung his paper-blooming satchel up onto the desk.

"No, no. I'm here for you. I need to observe your teaching. So without further ado." His hard heels struck a path up to the back.

It was a known part of the tenure review, but Davis was discombobulated. "I'm sorry," he called out to Lindstrom, "but this really isn't a good day. Can we reschedule?"

"Teach, man, teach! I'm invisible!" The seated Lindstrom towered over the wilting students in the back row.

Davis felt an imaginary IUD piercing his insides. He'd forgotten his topic for the day. He couldn't even review the previous topic because he'd forgotten that, too. "Today," he began, finally, "I'd like to introduce you all to cryptozoology." He clasped his hands in front. "'What?'" He fixed an annoyed expression. "'Is this a Halloween thing?' No, it's not about zombie crypts." He pulled out the desk drawer to search for a marker. "The term brings together three Greek words: *kryptos*, which means hidden, *zoon*, which, as you know, means animal, and *logos*, which is discourse. It's the study of hidden animals. Now, when we think of *hidden* in this case, the animals are not hidden from everyone." He gave up looking for a marker and began a ponderous pacing, appearing to be talking loudly to himself. "There have been local sightings. Legends may even have grown up around these animals, but they have remained hidden to the people with the authority to formally identify and catalogue them. How often do you think this has happened, that there are tales of strange animals that are only much later discovered by science?" He stopped before one of the students. He knew her name. "Michelle?"

"Lots."

"Yes, lots and lots." Lindstrom had walked back down to the front to hand him a marker. "Thank you. And cryptozoologists"—Davis moved quickly to write the word on the board—"*cryptozoologists* also are concerned with animals that are reported to be living in areas they have not been known to inhabit. So, basically what we're interested in, then, is the <u>unexpected</u>," noted and underlined. "Like all explorers, we must remain open to the unexpected. Bernard Heuvelmans, who published *On the Track of Unknown Animals*"—Davis wrote the title and his students knew to copy it—"in 1955 and who actually coined the term cryptozoology, explained that this is a study of animals who are 'truly singular, unexpected, paradoxical, striking, emotionally upsetting, and thus capable of mystification.'" He looked about the room. "Any interest in this here? Wouldn't you like to study some emotionally upsetting animals?

"Well, okay, how does a cryptozoologist work?" He went up on his toes as he was asking. "It helps to speak many languages, because you will be reading accounts in local papers around the world." He dug a book out of his satchel and shook it in the air. "And you'll be hunched over tomes in libraries, reading old tales of wondrous sights, examining great artworks in museums for depictions of the exotic; you'll decode DNA and identify bacteria in the lab; you'll examine related species in far-flung zoos." He let his jaw drop and scoped out the class. "Any interest? We're supposed to be whipping up interest in our freshmen, helping to sustain them through their studies. 'Say, Dr. Beardsley?'" he asked himself in an odd little voice, "'is this about Bigfoot and the Loch Ness Monster? Should we be talking about this in a college setting?'" Davis shrugged, twisted the toe of a shoe against the wooden floor. "Well, you tell me. When will we have reached the end of all large-animal zoological discoveries? French naturalist and zoologist Baron Georges Cuvier claimed that that era had ended in 1812. Seven years later, the South American tapir was discovered, a three-hundred-pound animal! The second-largest land mammal on the continent! And, guess what? Last year, just last year, a new species of tapir was identified in Brazil, hidden from science but not from the locals. Perhaps you read in yesterday morning's papers that an Australian expedition has dragged over three hundred previously unknown species out of an ocean abyss during the past month—many were bioluminescent; one species was the headline-grabbing 'faceless fish.' So let's not kid ourselves." He looked squarely at Lindstrom. "Let's not kid ourselves.

"The hoaxes get to us, though, don't they?" He flopped into the desk chair, pulled out some of the flaps of paper emerging from his satchel, and made a neat pile of them. "They bring us down. They limit us. People looking for attention, newspapers looking to sell copies—I'm not going to give them the satisfaction of repeating their stories here. Oh, sure, sometimes it's fun, but a lot of damage has been done by hoaxes." He gave the group a challenging look. "Because of them, some mainstream biologists think this is a pseudoscience."

Lindstrom let his head flop to the side and pursed his lips in displeasure.

"Have you gone on any searches?" a young woman asked.

"I've been up to Washington state as a leader in several field expeditions." He tapped on his desk like he was marking a spot on a map. "Most of the reported Sasquatch encounters have been there, in Pierce County, with the last one being in May. On one expedition, hiking up Mount Rainier with a team of four other scientists, we heard a call that was uncanny, just spooked the heck out of us one morning, coming from very nearby, and it prompted me to grip my Taurus Tracker three fifty-seven, which is really a great option for quick, accurate shooting that can be fatal for a large animal—not that I would ever want to shoot a cryptid, but, of course, that may be the only way to prove the existence of one as shy as Sasquatch. Anyway, it wouldn't show itself on that day. It just wasn't to be." Though he would not admit it here, he knew that if he ever saw the great beast, he would absolutely shoot it. And he would drag the thing down the mountain himself if he had to. The ultimate vindication lying at his feet. This was often what he pictured just before sex.

Lindstrom coughed, and all heads turned toward him as he stood and, after motioning for the students in his row to clear their legs from the passageway, left the room.

TIM

I need a new man.

Tim gaped at the Snapchat photo of the gorgeous blonde, hand on hip, standing next to Chewbacca for the six seconds that it existed. A California girl with attitude. Bit of an Amazon, this one. It was the first Snapchat that Blondie had sent since asking him to download the app. The first photo of *her*. "Wow," he Snapchatted back, "Not sure I'm UR type based on this guy."

Mike from shipping appeared at the door. "You busy?" he asked when Tim finally looked up. "The Troll gave me a big lecture today on not signing for anything."

"Deliveries?"

"Or mail. I'm not to sign for anything. She says if we don't sign for it, then we can say we never got it. I think she was talking about legal things from lawyers or the courts."

"Maybe this is about the ex-boyfriend."

"That's what I wonder." Mike slouched against the doorway. "Her mind's always going. She's always thinking someone's out to get her."

Tim's phone pinged:

Marine is my type.

"Just got an invitation for cybersex," he said, crossing his arms to mask his glee.

Mike whispered, "The Words with Friends girl?"

"Yeah, BlondeBabeWhatever."

"Who are you in this deal?"

Tim hesitated. "Marine sniper in Afghanistan."

"*Into the Lion's Mouth*! Aw, I knew you'd love it. That guy was one hot shit." He leaned out to survey the hall. "I could stand guard."

Tim smirked. "If I want to have sex with a person who won't be touching me, I can do it with my own wife."

"Hey, hey, I told you about The Publisher's big place in Kennebunkport?" Mike asked. "She don't use it now till summertime. I'm staining the deck this weekend, and I'm trying to get a girl up there. Just something about doing a girl in the boss's beach house gets to me, more than normal. I mean, just putting my naked butt down on The Troll's floral sofa gives me a chubby."

Tim's phone rang, and Mike waved off.

"Tim Turner," he answered.

"This is about an interview?" It was Joe. Joe Masotta.

"Christ, Joe, how the hell are ya?" Tim stood up. "It's been a long time, Joe."

"The note says someone wants to interview me?"

"Well, yeah, as I said to your guy earlier—and I left three messages with that guy—but as I told him, I work for a magazine that a lot of marching-band directors read. It's *Bell's Up*, which is what some directors say instead of horns up, I guess."

"Never heard of it."

"Yeah. So my boss, The Publisher, she wants to interview you as the keynote to the big marching-band directors' convention, and it's happening the morning before you perform in Boston." He laughed. "She's been cyberstalking you."

"I'll do it," Joe said.

"You will? Hey, that was easy. I didn't know if after all this time you'd even call me back. Heck." Tim picked up a pen and started to tap dots onto the *Bells Up* cover girl's cheeks, a high school clarinetist. "I can build things up in my imagination, I guess."

Joe wasn't talking.

"I'll tell you, I look at your life, and it's beautiful!"

Finally Joe spoke: "Tell me more about The Publisher. Anything I should watch out for?"

"How much time ya got, Joe? She's a nut job. But there will be a lot of dedicated band directors there who'll really benefit from hearing you talk."

"How's she a nut job?"

Then Tim told Joe all about the forbidden words and the Selectrics and the light bulbs. "And she doesn't even like music. She listens to talk radio."

He heard Joe tapping away on a keyboard. When that stopped, Joe asked, "How's Mona?"

"Mona? Well, she's okay. Sure. But you know, you're better off without Mona, Joe."

"How so?"

He shrugged. "She's punitive." Then he whispered, "She's kind of punitive, Joe. She hangs on to things. And you don't have to be compared to her father over and over again. Hey, can I buy you a beer while you're here? Can we talk old times over a beer?" Tim was tingling. He had really loved this guy, and now they would reconnect.

"Maybe after the interview. Have your publisher send me the time and place. I'll be there."

"Amazing. Amazing, man! Thanks."

Tim was about to end the call, when he heard, "So did you and Mona ever have kids?"

"Yes, we did, Joe. A son, Miles. You're not missing out on that front either, man."

After Joe hung up, Tim thought that it actually could've

gone worse, the call. There was still some residual anger about losing Mona, but the guy was coming to the convention. He wanted to patch things up. Tim punched his wife's digits into the phone.

"Mona. I'm getting a raise. A very good raise. And you know why? Joe Masotta. The Publisher wants to interview him, and I'm delivering the goods."

"Wait, you told her you could get a favor from Joe Masotta?" Her volume moved into the red.

"He already said yes, Mona. I talked to him on the phone just now. He'll do it. He's coming to Boston."

"I don't believe it."

"Believe it." He could hear her clanging around in the cabinet with the pans and bowls.

"He doesn't talk to us for thirty years, and now he wants to help you?"

"And I'm getting a raise."

"It's about time. Listen, I'm making wings for Vinnie. I can't talk now."

She hung up on him, and Tim gave his phone the finger. When did she start to hate him? Like all other trends, he hadn't noticed until it was well established. The phone rang. Mona again.

"Now that you're getting a raise, maybe we can do some things," she said.

"Well I'm thinking of not doing some things. First, I'm gonna drop the piano-tuning plan, which, I gotta tell you, I was not into. That seems like the most boring, tedious work on the planet. Hitting the same note over and over and over again? Jesus! Anyway, now it looks like I don't need it."

"I thought it was lawyer's pay! Now it's not good enough?"

"Would you rather tell people you're married to a piano tuner or a senior editor?"

"Depends. Depends on what you won't screw up. Listen, I want to go to Joe's thing. I want to see him."

"No. Joe and I are going to rekindle our friendship. You were Yoko Ono. Anyway, it's a work thing, Mona. It's not for the public."

"Oh, please. So does this mean we can pay for the whole thing now?"

"Sure. We'd have to borrow the rest of the money from your dad, but now I could actually pay him back." It didn't bother Tim that he had no intention of hanging around to pay the man back. The guy had never been a father to him.

"If we can get that driveway, Tim, I will be so happy. It will mean everything to me to have that for my students, for company, for my father."

"And you know, I think it might be an investment that pays off big for you in the long run. I've heard parking spaces add fifty thousand to the value of a house. This one gives you two spaces back-to-back, Mona. You wouldn't be underwater any more. And it makes sense because they're not making any more land."

"Would you text Phyllis right now? Would you let her know we can buy it?"

"I'm on it." Tim hung up and looked around his cement-walled office, which was also the photo archives room for the company; they'd just shoved a desk in there among the file cabinets for him.

He thumb-typed into his Samsung:

Dear Phyllis,
We are so upset about your situation with Andy!!!
I really haven't stopped thinking about it. Knowing
what you've gone through, we are offering $25K
for your parking spot, we are not dickering. I'll

send a purchase & sale agreement within the next two days to get the ball rolling. Wishing you well in your healing process.

Best,

Tim and Mona

Then Tim fast-walked to The Publisher's office and told her brightening face it was a go.

"Oh!" she squealed.

"No problem, he said it was absolutely no problem."

"You are terrific!"

"He just needs the time and place."

"I can't believe it!"

"Yep. Said he was happy to help an old friend." Tim jutted one hip out, his arms akimbo, still breathing fast from the walk.

"Well, you must have been a very good friend! What a treasure you must be to him." The Publisher leaned over and added, "Now, can I tell you my next idea?"

He shifted onto the other hip.

"A book. A book about the history of the President's Own, the oldest professional musical group in the country. Did you know Thomas Jefferson invited them to perform at his inauguration? Think of all the incredible moments they've accompanied. Joe will have tremendous inside information, not to mention all the historical photos! So we do a book. Something I can sign at events and give away to VIPs. You and Emily can ghostwrite it. You'll have to let her in on this."

"If she's no longer senior editor, she'll quit."

"Well, I just don't believe she works weekends. Not like you! That's when the best work gets done. Anyway, we don't have to tell her she's been demoted. So how many pages do you think it could be?"

He slowly shook his head. "I don't have any idea."

"Select your target, Mr. Turner. First, you must select your target."

"I don't even know if Joe will help us with this."

"Your best friend? You underestimate yourself. It's one of your weaknesses. Let me know tomorrow about the page count; then I can start costing it all out. Now, more ideas for the convention. Let's brainstorm." She swiveled her throne side to side. "What could we do?"

"Music," he said.

A look of pity from her.

"No, really," he maintained. "Wouldn't it be good to hear music at a convention for band directors? And I think they should play it. All these middle-aged guys, they once had a dream of a life in music that did not include babysitting a load of brats. Let's put them back in as players. It'll be a gift."

The Publisher planted her palms on the desk and rose. "The *Bells Up* Band."

"Doesn't the convention start the day after Veterans Day? They could march in the parade."

"Oh, it's too late to get into the parade."

"No it isn't. You just find a branch of the services that doesn't have a band and ask them if we can accompany them. The Massachusetts Air National Guard won't have a band."

"*Bells Up* honors the Massachusetts Air National Guard. I love it. I love it. I'll get NMBA to send all of the attendees a notice."

"Let me write up their instructions once you've got it all set."

"I will. Send Rita in on your way out."

Just as he reached the door, she said, "Angela is definitely dying, by the way."

He turned back with a look of distress.

"I'm afraid so. She's denying it, says it's a bad flu. And she says she doesn't want any visitors, but I think you should go in. Just you and Marcel."

"How long you think she has? I just talked to her on the phone the other day."

"I would go tomorrow. I wouldn't count on talking to her after tomorrow."

#

It dawned on Tim that he needed money not only to make up the difference in what the driveway was going to cost them beyond what his father-in-law might be willing to lend, but also for Rusty, who could not go off into the world penniless, so there had to be an extra and immediate source of income. He stuffed pillows behind his back on the couch as he explored the next online tuning lesson, which concerned pianos you would never want to hire on to tune, because their pins become wobbly as baby teeth and you could never afford all the time it would take to wrap and pound every pin. Klopotek, Sunny Straub's brand, was not mentioned by name.

That night Tim practiced tuning Mona's upright. She didn't play the piano outside of her lessons, and she could really only chunk through the chords to accompany the easier songs, so the tuning needn't be exact. It had been Mona's mother's piano and had been shipped all the way over from Revere. That's how Mona would put it to anyone who admired the thing: "It was my old Italian mother's until she died, and I had it shipped all the way over." A distance of less than four miles.

In between tuning each note, Tim set the lever down and took a break. He could hear his son on the phone upstairs. "In story mode I get precision kill after precision kill. My screen is, like, awash in yellow numbers. But in PVP, I can't get a single fucking body shot. Maybe I'm just bad at it, but that's enough justification for me to hate it."

PVP, Tim knew, meant "player versus player." He could understand the thrill of a game that turned on the actions of other real people, the unpredictability of it. In one particular game Miles was into, Destiny, you chose your sex, race, and class. Sex and race were just window dressing, Miles had brought him to understand, while each class offered a special ability. Miles's class was Warlock. His power was spells, which meant he couldn't be cool even in a game. Tim depressed the E-flat again, still off, but he made no adjustments.

"And in story mode," Miles continued, "it's the same thing every time—deploy ghost, fight hordes, deploy ghost, fight hordes. Don't get me wrong, it's a great game as far as classes, action, and guns go, but talent and gun progression seem linear, and they lack personalization." Tim hoped Miles wasn't talking to a girl.

Eventually Miles finished his telephonic review and lurched downstairs, toward the kitchen.

"Miles," Tim stopped him, "can you pick your age in that game?"

"Destiny? No."

"Everyone's the same age?"

"Yeah, I guess."

"That's nice. That's a beautiful world." He trilled two of the highest keys and then slammed down on the lowest one and engaged the sustain pedal to make it ring, just like he used to as a child in the maestro's house.

DAVIS

Just inside Davis's college office door stood a fully articulated Neanderthal skeleton tethered to a rod on a wooden base. This was a copy of *The Old Man of La Chapelle-aux-Saints* in France. When it was discovered in 1908, it was the first fairly complete Neanderthal skeleton ever found. As he studied it now, from his desk chair, Davis reminded himself that although his copy stood erect, like modern humans, the first reconstruction of these bones, in 1911, showed a stooped, crouching creature to match the brutish Neanderthal stereotype of the time. That posed Neanderthal skeleton was even provided with an opposable big toe, like an ape, demonstrating that scientists are limited by their own preconceptions. Davis tried always to remain open in conceptualizing things, and one of the recent ideas he was especially open to came from researchers who proposed that relict Neanderthal clans may still be making their way around Central Asia and the Pacific Northwest, as evidenced by footprints identical to known Neanderthal prints. Neanderthals may, in fact, be the cryptids of several recent legends starring hirsute humanoids with great craniums, large noses, and superhuman strength. The merely four-thousand-year-old *Epic of Gilgamesh*, for example—

"Hello?" Dr. Peggy finally answered, sounding typically bewildered.

"It's the Beardsleys, Peggy," Davis said, positioning the phone closer to his wife on the far side of the desk. Davis refused to address Peggy as "Doctor." She was not a doctor of any sort. If anyone should be called doctor during their phone calls, it should be him. Peggy called him "the father," however, probably because she had back-to-back therapy calls and couldn't be bothered to remember specific names. (And sometimes she even called him "the mother" because she found his voice a bit on the high side, she said.)

"Oh, hello! Now, didn't I just talk with you?"

Jenny had not removed her jacket and still wore her purse over her shoulder. She had told her school that she was going for a tooth repair.

"Yes," Davis said, "but we have an emergency. I believe Jenny is breaking the authority bond. I think she's covering for Megan, and she also helped her get an IUD." He spanked the desktop.

Long silence. "Was that the father speaking?"

"Yes." Davis sighed.

Jenny bit her lip and stared at the phone.

"Okay. How old is Megan now?"

"Seventeen," Jenny and Davis said at once.

"Okay. At seventeen, she can have an IUD. Are you religious, Father?"

His shoulders crowded both ears. "No, the problem is not that she has an IUD, but rather that I was never part of the decision. Okay, well, maybe the problem is also that she *has* an IUD. Jenny's sending a mixed message here: you are not ready to have sex, and yet here is what you need to have sex."

"Father, birth control is a woman's right, and it is not a decision that involves the father. Let that one go. What's the cover-up issue?"

Jenny positioned her face directly over the speaker phone. "There is no cover-up, Dr. Peggy, I can assure you of that, but Davis does not believe me."

"I can't believe in something that defies logic," Davis said to Jenny. "The Sasquatch arm was installed by a taxidermist, with a sinewy thread. Think of a leather lace. It's not going to break simply because you bump into it. And here's my big puzzlement. Why was it still on the floor? If you had caused it to fall, you would have picked it up. If Megan had done it, however, she'd have left it on the welcome mat like a horse head in the bed."

After a moment, Peggy's voice came from the speaker. "I'm completely lost."

Jenny stared back at Davis. "Davis is suspicious of everyone now, Dr. Peggy. Megan can't even play volleyball, because Davis threatened her coach."

"It was an easy mistake," he said. "They were together at the fair."

"But he had taken the whole team to the fair!" Jenny was too loud, now. Davis had to look pointedly at the office door as a reminder that they were at his place of employment.

"Can I say something here?" Dr. Peggy asked. "When I was raising Carla, she didn't have a father figure, because we divorced when she was only three, and I often wondered how a father, whose main job is protecting, would reconcile her vulnerability with all of the ways that she acted out—inappropriately, as you know. It's like asking someone to protect a young piranha, isn't it?"

Jenny's expression seemed to soften.

"Mother, love the father for all he has done. Forgive him for ruining the volleyball. Forgive him for not believing you."

"I do. Of course I do," said Jenny, who then put a hand on the desktop and slid it across toward Davis's hand.

"Does Megan still have the IUD?" Davis asked Jenny. "Or was it removed? I am out of the loop on this one."

"Get over the IUD, Father. You've got to let that one go."

Davis walked his wife out, uncharacteristically helloing everyone in the halls, and on his return, he passed Lindstrom's door.

"Davis," Lindstrom called out, "come in here a minute, can you?"

But when Davis entered, Lindstrom was concentrating on making notes (with a fountain pen, for God's sake) in his leather-bound notebook. Davis had only once been in the department chair's office. It was before Lindstrom moved in, when Davis had placed a greeting card on Lindstrom's desk— one showing a red lobster boat in a harbor—welcoming him to the department. Now the office was well established, with the canon of great zoological literature filling all shelf space, and framed black-and-white photos of animals from around the world on the walls. Davis slid out of his suit coat and hung it casually over the back of a chair upholstered in an imperial pattern before sitting in it to await his fate.

"I wanted to talk about your Bio 112 lecture," Lindstrom said, finally capping and setting the pen aside. No hair grew out of Lindstrom's face. His skin was pink and smooth as a doll's. It gave him a look of innocence, and when he was angry, the look read as pleading. "At this early stage, you should be covering basic cell structure and function. Shouldn't you?"

"We do. We would have, normally," Davis said. "I think, actually, that lecture was for you. Again, I'm a bit preoccupied with gaining tenure, given my somewhat eccentric focus. But I mean, regardless, you saw how the kids loved it. Some of the upperclassmen even have a crypto club that meets on Thursdays in the cafeteria."

Lindstrom clasped his hands and appeared to be rolling

and squeezing the juice out of a small fruit. "Some of the students do love it. I was reading your evaluations from past years. You're really recruiting for your specialty. But not a small number felt you weren't covering the syllabus well enough, going off book."

"If you could only correlate those negative reviews with the students' grades, I'm sure you'd see a pattern." Davis squinted in distress, revealing his upper incisors.

"Students know a strong teacher even when they aren't strong students. And part of the issue is probably that you are still lecturing. That's a proven failure in education. If students wanted only lectures, I could videotape classes and fire all of the teachers, just show everything online. No, we've moved on now to peer instruction, where the teacher poses questions that the students discuss in pairs or small groups. It's teacher-as-facilitator. I thought everyone was on board with that here."

"Yes, absolutely, and it's what I normally do. It's peers all the way in my classrooms. Look, come again to the class. I wasn't myself that day. Let's do this again, shall we? And it can be a complete surprise." Davis stood and took his jacket from the high-backed chair and struggled to poke his arms back into it. "Any class. Any time."

# # #

When he returned home from work that evening, Davis found Megan and another girl eating chips and swiping oily fingers against the other girl's tablet computer at the kitchen table until Megan quickly shut it off. Squares of darker yellow wall paint revealed where all of the rules posters had once hung. He felt disoriented without them.

"And who's this?" he asked.

"Tara."

"Hi, Mr. Beardsley." She looked normal enough, and she made eye contact, was more confident-seeming than Megan's past recruits.

"Nice to meet you," he said. "What're you two up to today?" Megan had had a few friends in the past, but she'd always either stolen something of theirs or injured them, or she herself had cut off all ties at some imagined slight.

"I'm going to show her your creatures."

"Perfect. What did you think of the one-armed Bigfoot?"

"Awesome!" the girl said, pulling her legs under her in the kitchen chair.

He plugged his cell phone into the kitchen charger and took a root beer into the living room, where he pulled his laptop out of the briefcase. He had just logged into the website of the local paper when great gasps and snortings came from the girls, with Megan loudly announcing, "I'm gonna get one that says, 'Available for parties.'" They laughed into their fists like buzzing horns.

"Two shows a night," Tara added.

"Oh, that's so perfect!" Their chairs were squealing against the floor.

"One girl I saw had *Wrong side up*, like, right here, across her back."

"Wait, at school?"

"Some website."

"If it was Dana's back, it would say, 'Best side up.'"

"Ah!" Someone fell to the floor.

"Hey, girls?" Davis called. "Why don't you play a game?" Silence.

"There are all kinds of games in the hall closet."

"Jackpot," he heard Megan say to her friend after a time.

"Let's send your guy a picture," he heard Tara whisper, "some crazy picture."

Then came an unintelligible response, and they scrambled up the stairs to her room.

Davis moved to the bottom stair and struggled with what to do. This bedlam was what peer instruction led to.

Jenny came in from the deck, lugging a flower box of dead plants. "Could you clear the counter? Did you meet Tara?"

He nodded.

"She asked me to take the charts down for the afternoon. I said it was—"

"It's fine."

"Were you going upstairs?"

"I don't—they're up there—no, I'm not."

"How long you think this one'll last?" she asked, pulling off her gloves.

"Yes, that's what I was wondering. We want to encourage it. She hasn't had a friend since Lisa. Long time." He returned to the living room.

"Dinner will be a little late!" she called out.

Davis was immediately drawn to a photo of a dead animal on the newspaper's main page, some mystery creature that had been run over by a car.

Legendary Beast Hit by Car

GLENWOOD, Maine—Could an animal found dead on the roadside Wednesday morning be the monster of local legend?

Mary Bartlett found the beast lying near the power lines on Howland Rd., having apparently been killed by a car. "It weighed about 50 pounds," Bartlett figured. "It was black and had fangs curling over its lips, like something Stephen King would come up with," she said. Bartlett was struck by the appearance of the carcass. "So evil-looking," she said. "And stunk to high heaven." Before being taken away by the highway department, the animal's remains were photographed and examined by several local people, none of whom could readily identify its species.

Todd Gardner of Howe Hill Rd. recognized the animal as the same one he had spotted in his yard the previous week. "It's a mutant hybrid something or another, like half-dog half-rodent," he said. "The back sloped way down like a German shepherd. I locked eyes with it for a time and then it plumb took off. I've never seen the likes of it in all my life."

For over ten years, Wexford County residents have reported sightings of a stalking animal with glowing eyes and also monstrous cries in the night. The deaths of a hound dog, a rat terrier, a schnoodle, and countless cats have been blamed on such an animal just over the past few years.

"No one has a clue what it is," Glenwood town manager Sue Noyes, said. "I've heard fisher, coydog, and even a dingo! I hope this one that's been killed is the one done all the damage."

Eric Lindstrom, chair of the biology department at Greenstown College, said that based on his review of the photos, the animal was likely a rare wolf-dog hybrid.

Oh, please! Davis writhed. This was no wolf-dog. God! Look at the photo, why don't you! And why had the writer consulted Lindstrom anyway? That was a bad, bad call. Davis pulled away from the laptop to gain focus. The head was hyena-like in shape. Just so clearly. That and the sloped back and the Mickey Mouse ears all added up to a hyena, not a wolf or dog. He held up his phone and asked Siri to the call the paper, then left a six-minute message for the reporter of the story that ended with "and I'll await your call."

He was reviewing his recorded comments in his head when he heard a thud and a burst of giggles from upstairs. He realized he wasn't at all glad she'd made a friend. No, it actually strengthened his sense of dread.

TIM

Tim's regular doctor had said he wouldn't prescribe it, that Tim wasn't a candidate, that his testosterone reading was normal for his age, but the doctor from the TV ad, Dr. Frank Harmon, said Tim was in desperate need of TRT. It was the tiredness, all the fat around the waist, low sex drive, soft testicles—or so they'd seemed to Harmon. Soft and small. Depression, too, but that was inevitable given the other symptoms, Harmon said.

In the bathroom mirror, Tim's torso had a long way to go to resemble Dr. Harmon's, and he hated that he was thinking about Harmon's torso at all, because it had given him the creeps—the hairless, ripped stomach, pecs like omelet pans on an old man. Harmon had taken his shirt off to show Tim how to apply the gel, but the doctor could have demonstrated just as easily with his shirt on.

Tim followed Harmon's method of squeezing half the gel packet onto each forearm, then rubbing his forearms together and against his flanks, where the skin was allegedly thinner. "Don't waste any of that man gel!" Harmon had barked, so Tim rubbed himself like a mad cricket to get it all worked in.

He needed only body rejuvenation. In his mind he was already a young man, with Blondie serving as mental testosterone. For five days, TallBlondBabe18 had been buzzing in and out of Tim's life, asking after him, making some frank and thrilling suggestions. Reading her texts elevated every moment. If he was eating an apple when she made contact, it was the best apple in the world. "Eating an amazing apple," he'd answer her. He'd told her all about his four-man fire team, the jobs they performed when they were in the Humvee. He was stuck in the turret, the only man exposed to fire, he told her. He was the protector. If a fifth man rode with them, he was called a GIB, Guy in Back. Sometimes he imagined her there, he'd said.

She told him about her longing to leave home. It was rough there, she wrote. Her father was controlling. She wondered what part of Rusty she would be looking up at from the back seat. <Licking my lips>

After slathering on the testosterone gel, Tim rifled through his dresser drawers, yelling, "Mona! Where are my sweats?"

She came to the door. "I put 'em in the rag bag."

"Have they been cut up?"

"Maybe. It's a rag bag."

He marched down to the kitchen and snatched the bag from the pantry, where he found them, unscissored.

"What are you going to do?" Mona asked as he tossed the sweats onto the bed.

"Run."

"To the store?"

"No. On the sidewalk. Like a runner."

In midmotion, as she was closing a drawer, she froze. "Take your phone."

"I'm taking my phone."

"Call if you feel arm pains, nine-one-one, any pains, as soon as you feel them."

He returned to the closet to look for shoes. Tomorrow he would buy runner's shoes. He found an old pair of canvas boat shoes that would do for now.

He jerked his sweats up his legs, slipped into the shoes, and descended the stairs, hands on hips, and with less vigor than he'd had going up.

The backs of Tim's thighs trembled as he waved his fingers down around midcalf, straining to touch the cement of his stoop and thinking about a route. Suddenly he heaved off into the fog, walking briskly, his arms swinging out at forty-five degrees, like ropes on a maypole. After three blocks, he thought he should start with the jogging. He had the same thought again after four blocks, and he actually began. His stomach lifted after each push off and slammed upon landing until he grabbed ahold of it. He held it from the sides, like it was something he was planning to hand off. Was he getting enough leg extension? Was he moving forward or just running in place? Then he slid a hand up to pin down his fleshy chest. He needed a video of himself, he decided. He needed a bit of a coach. A block was good for the first stretch of jogging and then a fast walk for a few more blocks and a cool-down on the way home. Of course, new shoes would make a huge difference in his form. No need to video without the new shoes. His phone dinged in his pocket. A text.

Dear Ones,

Among all of my crippling ailments, one is purely psychosocial: I care far too much abt others' opinions! But here you lovly souls recognze my pain and wish to help (HOW CN THAT BE?). Seems impossible after spendng sooo many years in house of pain, walled off and imagining no one wd believe me.

LET'S DO THIS DEAL! Now, you mst realize that your dear man has likely not pd any taxes or fees on that parking spot in ages, as he hadn't for 105. My attentions wer too limitd to turn towards money dealings. How can IRA disappear without my signing anythng at all? IT MUST BE PART OF THE AGREEMENT THAT HE PAYS ALL TAXES AND FEES!

I believe your silent witnessing on that late summer night emboldened him, catalyzed worst of the torture.

Yours,

Phyllis

Tim tried to block out the images of Andy Paik beating his small, frail wife. So hard to believe that one of the few seemingly happy men Tim knew was a horrible brute. Then again, though, she could be psychotic. Maybe Andy was just trying to get her to leave the car and come inside that night but she was having a psychotic breakdown in the back seat. Still, visions of him pounding on her returned and returned, and Tim just couldn't shake them.

# # #

That night in bed, his pillows propped behind him, Tim held his cell phone to one ear and used his other hand to dangle the last chicken wing before Mona's eyes until she raised her book as a barrier.

"The unpaid taxes on the driveway plus the fines for not paying them add up to five forty-five," he told Andy before sucking the meat off the wing.

"You know, I just had so much going on, I let that slip," Andy said. "I can pay it, no problem. Do you think they let you pay by phone?"

"Prolly." Tim slurped. "I'm writing up the purchase-and-sale and I'll email it to you. I have to write in that you'll pay the taxes and fees. Phyllis wants it in the agreement. Could you sign and email it right back to me?"

"I'm sorry you're having to be the go-between, Tim. But I'm happy to do what I can to move this along."

"Hey, you know, she did you a favor by upping the price!" Tim topped off the mound of carnage on his snack plate with the final bone.

"Oh, sure. I guess. I don't know if it's worth that amount, but it's up to you. Can I fax the form back to you?"

Tim gave him his work fax number.

"I hope you're having a lovely fall in Malden," Andy said.

"You, too." Tim punched the red button and put the plate on the floor. "You know"—he wrenched himself over to Mona—"I think Phyllis is whacked. Andy is so amenable, so mild-mannered."

She held up a finger. "When they sign the form, I want you to show it to the brothers."

"Okay." He heaved his body back over to lie on his other side. "What do you think? You think he beat her?"

She lowered her book. "The first time I met her—I told you, right?—she had locked herself out, and I was teaching a lesson? She wanted to wait here for him to get home. So fine, but do you know she stood over us at the piano and sang along?"

"Right, you mentioned that."

"Who does that?"

He rolled back toward her. "There are things about her that make it hard to picture her as a victim. I mean, she seems pretty pushy in a way—singing along in the lesson, and now she raises the price of the space."

"It would be very surprising to me if he could hurt her."

"Well, the deal is done anyway, as long as she actually signs the thing."

"I want you to put a placard up saying cars will be towed."

"Cars will be towed," he said. "Grenades will be launched."

"I'm with you, though, Tim. I think this is a fabulous investment. For one thing, eventually the bar might want an outdoor beer garden"—she rose up on her elbows—"only if we moved, of course. Or what if a developer wanted to put condos on the parking lot right next to it and they needed the extra square footage? You've heard of that kind of thing, right? Someone's house is in the middle of where they want to put a big thing?"

"Oh, sure," he agreed. Somehow that little piece of tarmac had signaled a great change in fortune for her. He was glad of it, felt magnanimous.

"Hey, you never told me. Who is your ideal self?" he asked.

"That thing we wrote down?"

"Yeah."

She lowered herself back down onto her pillow and laid the open book on her chest. "They're doing *The Barber of Seville* next year. I will be Rosina."

"Oh, okay," he said. "It's funny, though, after you made me give all that up." Over a span of fifteen years, until he was thirty-five, Tim had auditioned for nearly every major symphony in the US. Only once did he make it past the first round, but that one near-miss had sustained him. (It had been quite a tough decision, they assured him.) Mona finally told him she couldn't back him up in his quest any longer. They had a kid, needed more money, a house.

Tim waited for her to answer him, but she didn't say a word.

# # #

As he crossed the park by the football stadium toward the pull-up bars, Tim tugged on his old leather gloves and shouted back to Miles, "Feels good, doesn't it? This afternoon we'll get proper gear."

"Huh?" Miles honked.

Under the shorter pull-up bar, Tim leaned against an upright. He punched his own palm. "We're training for the Marine physical fitness test," he told the still-plodding Miles. "It includes three exercises: dead-hang pull-ups, sit-ups, and a three-mile run."

Miles swung his long hair out of his face and looked back to see if anyone else was about.

"The perfect score is three hundred: that's twenty pull-ups for a hundred points, a hundred sit-ups in two minutes for another hundred points, and a three-mile run in eighteen minutes for a hundred. Anything under three hundred is not an ideal Marine."

Miles drooped like hanging from a hook. "I don't think you can be a Marine. There's an age limit."

"I'm challenging myself."

"I'm not doing it."

"What did I say? Am I asking you to do this? I need a drill instructor. We're already here."

Miles looked toward the stadium again.

"Drill instructors count the reps," Tim told him. "That's all you gotta do. Stand on that side of the bar."

The boy shuffled over.

"Face me, Miles."

Miles looked pained.

"The recruit comes to the position of attention in front of the bar." Tim stood at attention. "Now you say, 'Mount the bar and come to a complete dead hang.'"

"Mount the bar?" Miles mugged.

"'Mount the bar and come to a complete dead hang.' That's all I need you to say."

"Mount the bar and come to a complete dead hang." Miles had the slow, deep voice of a hypnotist.

"Aye, sir!" Tim shouted and leapt for the bar, grasping it and settling like a bag of cannonballs. "Say, 'Begin.'"

"Begin."

Tim strained. "Hold my legs a little bit; take some weight off."

Miles bent and wrapped his long arms around his father's knees.

"You're pulling! Lift! Lift!"

Tim managed to clear the bar twice and then let go and fell onto Miles, taking him down.

"You need to count them off each time."

"Two," the boy said, propped up on his elbows.

Tim flopped onto his back and let his arms and legs splay. His chest heaved like a felled horse. "I only need to get ten times better. You think you can beat two? Why don't you see?"

"Not interested, I told you."

"Okay, sit-ups." Tim remained inert. "In Marine sit-ups, you cross your arms over your chest, sit up until your elbows touch your thighs, then lower yourself until your shoulder blades touch the ground. You count off."

"You're gonna need me to hold your feet."

"Yeah?"

"Trust me."

"Just to start." He bent his knees, and Miles knelt on his shoes. Tim gutted it, heaved himself up for one, then dropped back down and that was it.

"One!" Miles shouted.

"I'm done."

"Good. You're not gonna run around the football field now. There's kids out there."

"No. Let me just run back to the car. Better yet, you drive

a few blocks away first."

"By myself?" He only had his learner's permit.

"Just a few blocks."

Miles strolled off toward the car.

"I'll wait to start running till I see you pull out. Turn right and go a few blocks—five or six blocks." The kid lifted a hand. Tim shouted, "Tomorrow we'll get backpacks and gear to weigh 'em down."

"I'm not interested!"

Finally, Tim reared back and then set off. His stomach bounced as he jogged, like a turkey was taped to his front. He made it to the street and then walked, rubbernecking for the car. After a block, he took up jogging again. He pictured himself running over to help Blondie, who was being dragged out of a car by her father, and he picked up speed so he could nail the guy and—*ow*! Maybe he should try landing on his toes so the impact wasn't so jarring. He walked the next block backwards, hands on hips. No Miles. Tim took off a shoe at the corner and peered into it. Finally Miles drove up from behind and honked.

"I said to go this way!" Tim pointed the shoe in the right direction. "Did you turn the wrong way? I wasn't quite done," Tim panted as he opened the passenger door and lowered himself in, "but this shoe isn't right. Tomorrow I'll have another new pair and we'll stretch out the distance."

"There's probably an app that helps you learn to run and shit."

Tim looked at him. "I need a drill instructor, Miles. I need yelling and threats and disparagements against my mother. Can you do that?"

"Take me to the gun range every day that we do this, and I'll agree."

Tim flicked his hands in a forward direction to get the boy to pull out. Then he clicked on the FM classical station, which was playing the hard-hitting, triumphant brass and timpani fanfare of Janáček's *Sinfonietta*, classical music's Death Metal.

# # #

Since Tim had known him, Marcel Aubert had always sported a weirdly thin mustache, but today, as he drove Tim to the hospital to see Angela, the few whiskers had been waxed up into a threadlike smile.

"Don't get me wrong," he told Tim, "Lesley is a great school and all, but when Rachel graduates and works as a teacher, how's she going to pay off all the loans? She'll be so overburdened. That's what concerns me."

Tim wondered why the man didn't help his daughter with the tuition rather than buy this new Camaro they were riding in.

"Yeah, well, I won't have to worry about anything like that. Miles will be the doofus you call when your Internet conks. The kid who tells you to turn it off and back on again."

Tim and Marcel had waited days to visit Angela, hoping she would be truly past the talking stage. If they could have come to the hospital with some women, they would have been more comfortable. Men don't have any idea what to do with a dying person unless they need to be carried somewhere or their doctor needs telling off.

"I just had the cable company out to my new place. I told you I'm on my own now?"

"Aw, hell, you're separated?"

"Yeah, but it's good. I'm getting to know myself again." A double smile, one beneath the other. "You really don't know how much you've compromised away until you're on your own again, Tim. For instance, I like decorating my own space. Seriously. I love selecting the furniture and the art. I just bought an enormous old highway sign telling you to come visit the Esther Williams Living Pool—it's a seven-foot-long blue sign. My wife would've hated that thing. I love it! I mean how evocative can you get? The pool is alive! Or maybe Esther is alive. I'm alive, I can tell you that."

Tim was fully informed as to the extent of his marital compromises. He'd had to endure the continual presence of Mona's family members, none of whom he would ever choose to be around. He had to care about bar noise, parking spaces, home values. He lived in fear of the future, whereas for a sniper, now is the only time. The sound of the wind, the bobbing of bushes, birds lifting off a roof.

"You waited for your daughter to leave the house?" Tim asked.

"Yeah, but then when she found out, she said she wished we'd done it long before. You know, the fights and everything." Tim rocked in agreement.

When they could see the hospital on the corner, Marcel said, "Hope she'll still be there." The report from Angela's husband was that she was out of it, and it wouldn't be long.

Dread, dread, dread, as the men emerged from the car in the parking lot. They moved like woozy bears just out of hibernation, lumbering in a zigzag, trying to figure out which hospital door was the right entrance. Then they asked about the room number and had to find the elevator, and they deliberately made slow progress—because they knew when they got to that room, their lives would never be the same. They jockeyed for the rear position as they walked down the final hallway. If she was awake and aware, she would hate that they were there. She had asked that no one come. Screw it. Tim went in first. "Hey, guys!" he whisper-shouted to her husband and sons.

Handshakes all around, but the boys' were just limp. Fourteen and twelve years old, they told him when asked.

The younger one had been the ballot box, Tim recognized, as he watched the boy return to his mother's side and rest his hand on the top of her head. At the kid's silent urging, Tim and Marcel finally really looked at her. Gaunt—her face just hollows and bones, her jaw slack but teeth bared, her eyes stuck open, although they did not follow. She suddenly thrashed to one side, grabbing for the bar, but her grasp fell short. When she tried again, Marcel and Tim both rushed in to help her turn herself, but the husband shook his head, "She does that all day. If you move her onto her side, she falls back, and it's all day long." They stared until they couldn't. Then they backed into the walls.

"You were a ballot box for Halloween once," Tim said to the younger boy, who gave a quick nod.

After a while, the husband said, "Tim, she took a call on Monday if you can believe it. Said to ask you for a piece on Trembone Slide Oil."

"Tremblay," said the younger boy. "Tremblay; that's the brand, but it's for trombones."

At that, Angela lurched again for the railing.

Tim winced. "Sure, no problem."

"And she was worried her commissions wouldn't come through to us. After the fact," the man said.

"Oh, they'll come through." Tim put a stop to this concern with his hand. "I'll make sure they all come through. That's taken care of."

They held up the walls until Angela's sisters swooped in. The women sucked right to her, fondled her feet, and carried on about trifles and fussed with the bedding. Tim was glad her sons would have so many others to mourn with. When his father left them for Florida, Tim was the sole mourner. He thought he saw Angela nod to the younger kid in answer to his question—nod that, yes, she would like a sip of orange juice—but then she didn't suck on the straw even though the boy waited an eternity. Was she in there? In the silence, they heard the new age music from the television, and it seemed the perfect soundtrack for Angela's scary mask, a body on interminable hold.

DAVIS

D avis sniffed the envelope again. Not too bad. Certainly not the proper way to send a biological sample, but the lab wasn't so far away, after all. He'd purchased the entire creature's carcass, which was now in one of the department refrigeration units. The highway worker had been an easy mark, even though he'd said he knew it would be worth something and had kept it in his family's freezer. Davis would have paid triple the agreed-upon hundred. That would be a good story for later. And Davis knew of a miraculous taxidermist, a real genius who could make the animal's shape conform to drawings that Davis would provide, but first he'd wait for the lab results. His job now was to get his theory out there before the DNA analysis was completed so his authority could be established once and for all. Toward this end, he turned back to writing in the comments section of the online article, since the reporter had not yet returned his call.

> As past president of the International Association
> of Cryptozoologists, I would like to comment on
> one possible, and I would even add probable,
> identification of the Glenwood Monster. I have
> studied the photos that accompany this article,
> and it is readily apparent to a trained eye that the
> creature is a hyena. Hyena, you say? There are no
> wild hyenas in this entire country! Well, we actually
> have proof in the fossil record that doglike hyenas

did colonize North America, and though they have been considered extinct for quite some time, there are still reports of hyena-like animals occurring throughout the U.S. The Ioway Indians knew the beast well and called it the *shunka warak'in*. The fur is most often reported as being black with a shaggy ridge along the spine. The animal is described as having a higher front half and walking with the neck in a downward curve. Ears stand up, but are rounder than a dog's. One of the

The text box would take no more letters. He had to hit Submit and then continue in a new box.

Well, I evidently reached the character limit for the comments box, so here I will continue my thoughts: One of the interesting things about the hyena is that while many of its behaviors are similar to those of canids (such as the fact that they are cursorial hunters, meaning they are built to be on the run; they use their teeth rather than their claws to grasp their prey; they are hurried eaters; and their paws have blunt, nonretractable nails well suited to agile running), they are actually more closely related to cats (they groom themselves with their tongues; they purr; they don't mark their territory with urine; nor do they lift their legs to urinate, among other things). Despite all of this, however, hyenas don't share enough genetic material to mate with dogs or cats. And the females have such complicated genitalia that it is not likely any other animal could

Next comment:

> Now, again, I was stopped from typing. (I would
> look closely at the character limit in this field if
> I were employed by the Greenstown Daily News.)
> Let me close here with my prediction for this poor
> creature who has met his demise. The animal will
> be found to be a hyena. I am in possession of the
> animal's carcass and will be sending a sample to
> the lab for DNA analysis. Stay tuned!

As he clicked again on Submit, he relaxed a bit and began
to hear Dr. Lindstrom in the adjoining office, not Lindstrom's
words, but their cadence and tone, which seemed urgent. Was
he badgering someone? It was a girl who answered, mewling.
Davis rose and stood near the wall but got no more clarity. He
decided to go out into the hall to see if perhaps Lindstrom's
door was open or if the gaps around it allowed some of the
higher wavelengths through.

The department bulletin board next to Lindstrom's door
provided a plausible reason for Davis's loitering while he tuned
in to the sounds. And then, quite clearly, came his daughter's
voice, unmistakable in its unmodulated pitch and volume. "I
just don't want it to happen again," she blurted, followed by
Lindstrom's calming murmurs.

Davis reached for the doorknob, but he decided instead to
simply remain in the hall where he would be seen by both of
them when Megan left. If Lindstrom was the perpetrator of
whatever Megan didn't want to happen again, his expression
would give him away. Otherwise it was some Megan shenanigan,
as usual.

While he waited, no further sounds emerged. He pulled the
pin from a card on the board that asked for a ride to Portland,

and he held it toward the light, which forced a move even closer to the door. Cooings. Was that what it was? Deep, male cooings. Perhaps Lindstrom had cornered her on the sofa, his finger lifting her chin to meet his approaching lips—

Then the door was yanked open from the inside, and Lindstrom sprang back in apparent alarm at the sight of Davis in the doorway.

"Oh, Megan!" Davis said, leaning in to find her behind Lindstrom. "I was clearing off the board and I thought I heard you in there. These offices have just the thinnest paper walls, don't you find, Dr. Lindstrom?"

"No, I don't hear anything," Lindstrom said, almost to himself.

#

Jenny never wanted the little amuse-bouche Brant set before them when they sat at the sushi bar. She always slid it over to Davis, who then had to pretend to relish two servings of the oddity while Brant watched, smiling and nodding. They didn't know how the sushi chef's name was spelled, but they thought he had pronounced it *Brant* when they'd asked for the third or fourth time, and it finally stuck with them. This was once-a-week date night for Davis and Jenny, as mandated by Dr. Peggy. For the past months, they had left Megan alone at home, but up until then, their neighbor, who had an autistic grandchild and was used to a challenge, would come over to stay with Megan. Jenny had been appalled at his request, but Davis had asked the woman to read and sign the ever-growing lists of behaviors Megan was not to engage in. They were paying her, he'd argued, so they could ask her to train. Still, when Davis and Jenny returned from their date, they usually had to pull Megan away from an inappropriate movie or, more often, the computer, or after getting back in the car, they'd find her along the roadside on her way to pick something up at the store, supposedly. Now, she was on her own at the house, and that unsettled Davis even more than the rubbery, tentacled amuse-bouche.

They were typically nontalkers on a date, except they always had a great deal to say to Brant (though how much he understood, they couldn't fathom). If the television had a sports game on, Davis would bray over some play and ask Brant, "Did you see that? Dear God!" If the news was on, Jenny might carry on about a social issue and beg Brant's opinion, which was always an agreeable, grinning bow. Too much attention was afforded the sushi chef in order to compensate for the paucity shared between them. But on this evening, Davis opened with a line directed toward his wife. "So I've been worried about the tenure thing, you know."

"Oh?"

"Yes. I'm surprised you haven't picked up on it."

"But you haven't said anything."

"Well, I've been nervous, and now I'm feeling less so because I've made a discovery, soon to be published."

"Davis! How wonderful! Shall we get some champagne?" She quickly looked around for the waiter.

"Did you see a price?" He put a hand on the menu.

"We can just get two glasses."

"Sure, then." He signaled to the waiter and ordered them.

"Fun!" Jenny said, bouncing her clasped hands on the bar top.

"It's the identity of the Glenwood Monster—did you read about that?"

"No…" She let the word trail upward.

"Killed by a car recently. A true cryptid in North America, a hyena." He leaned back to give his pronouncement room.

"It was a hyena? Had it escaped from a zoo?"

"No, I don't think so," he said, shaking his head. "None of Maine's little zoos have a hyena, but they may be living among us."

"Hyenas?"

"People have reported seeing them around for a very long time."

"But who are these people?"

It amazed Davis that Jenny could believe in the biblical tales and yet not in contemporary eyewitness accounts.

She unwrapped her chopsticks and then twisted back to Davis. "So, you've tested something and it came back that it was a hyena?" She sounded a bit panicked.

"The testing is going on now."

Brant set their sushi plates on top of the glass case and fashioned a big, toothy smile, as though the meal were a surprise gift.

"Thank you, Brant!" Davis said too loudly. He retrieved Jenny's plate and set it before her. "I sent a biological sample to the lab, but I already published my identification so that it's clear the ID came from my experience and knowledge, not from a blanket DNA search." He switched the soy sauce bottles so that the white, low-sodium one was near her. "Do you know that they asked Lindstrom to ID the thing? Someone at the paper needs a bit of an education on *expertise*."

"What did he say it was?"

"A wolf-dog hybrid. And Jenny, if you saw the pictures of that head, the round ears?" He took his own plate down from the case, smiling again at Brant. "Lindstrom's off his game."

"How long does the testing take?" She still had not broken her chopsticks apart.

"Two weeks, minimum. I'm saving some money by having it tested at a place that does dog-breed IDs for your pet. Then when they say it isn't any breed of dog, I'll pay for the further testing."

"So, if it is a dog, what will happen to the journal that's publishing your piece?"

"No, it's in the paper." He pushed one piece of a maki roll into his mouth and then talked around it: "Don't worry. It's a hyena."

"The *Greenstown Daily News?*"

"Comments section for now, just so I could get a record made."

Jenny relaxed a bit and poured the lite soy sauce into her bowl. The tenure committee wouldn't be reading comments sections. "What do you think she's doing right now?" she asked him.

He picked up another piece, dipped it in the sauce, and pondered the ceiling. "Taking nude photos of herself and sending them to prisoners."

Jenny wobbled her head. "Yeah, could be."

While Dr. Peggy's husband had abandoned their family over the difficulties with Carla, Davis often felt that Megan's troubles—their dealings with Megan—were the only thing keeping him and Jenny together. Who else would have either one of them with Megan as a part of the deal, a part of the shared life? And with Megan, they had something strong in common, something all-consuming.

When they first met, in their midtwenties, Davis and Jenny had had nothing in common. They'd merely sat next to each other at a Boston College football game to which Davis had been dragged by a friend and Jenny by her sister. Jenny kept asking him what was going on in the game. "No clue," he said again and again until, tipsy, she asked him what the heck he had a clue about.

"Animals, ask me anything about animals."

"What animal do I look like?" she demanded, and then turned her face in profile.

That was a surprise question, but after only a moment, he answered, "I guess I'm going to say puma."

She opened her mouth in delight. "I love them! I have a sweater made out of one!"

He tucked chin to chest and peered up at her. "It's a cat."

"The puma!" She sat up straight. "Yes. Got it. So that's what I look like?"

"I was picturing the dove-gray eyes and the long, shallow nose ending in a pink tip. Of course, the brown hair. Puma."

Leaning in, she asked, "Am I dangerous?"

"Pumas have been said to have quite an affinity for mankind…" Davis continued telling a puma story that was swallowed by the commotion over a touchdown. Still, at the end of it, she announced, "You're cute!"

When she next tired of the football game, she turned to him. "Would you like to come over to dinner sometime?"

Around Jenny, Davis felt like a man, which wasn't something he had especially noticed feeling before. She touched him when she spoke to him; she deferred to him along the typical lines— she had him drive her car when they used it, asked him to select a computer for her, let him order the wine. He'd not experienced this treatment from any woman before. Certainly no female zoologist would enjoy playing up to a man. Davis thought that, in return, he allowed her to be wildly flirtatious without the consequence of reckless, unmarried sex, in which she was too Catholic to indulge. She kept asking him to do things with her, and he kept doing them, until they were solidly on a path. Then he finally made the big commitment to her when he put that note in Aletta Van Der Hooft's box. That's how he saw it. Marriage itself was not the truest act of commitment. No, the truest act was turning away from a lovely woman whose ardor had put a match to your crumpled paper soul.

"The best ever," Jenny said to Brant, tapping the front of

the glass counter with her chopsticks as he was reaching in to select a fish. "You are a complete genius," which made him shyly smile at her from within the glass enclosure, like a happy flounder.

# # #

Davis and Jenny arrived home to the smell of brownies, which were cooling on a rack.

"Yum," Davis said loudly enough to reach wherever Megan might be. She soon bounded down, shrieking that they were not to be touched!

"I believe we bought these brownies," Davis said.

"They're for *school.*"

"Maybe for a boy at school?" Jenny asked.

"Shut up!"

"Enough, Megan." Davis put his brownie back and looked around for any evidence of misbehavior. Then he went up to bed, where he started to read and fell asleep, only to be awakened by Jenny, asking, "Davis, what are you doing with these?" and holding up a pair of striped underwear.

"I was asleep."

"These were peeking out from under your pillow."

He twisted to look back at the pillow.

Jenny said, "They're Megan's underwear."

"Right, she put them there while we were out."

Jenny carefully turned back the blankets and the top sheet as though she might unveil a cache of bras and panties. "Well that's strange."

They stared at each other until Davis said, "If you think I'm doing anything inappropriate with Megan, you're very wrong."

"No, no, I just was concerned. I mean it's very strange."

"Stop saying that." And then he sat up and lifted his pillow for another look. "Were you sorting laundry on the bed?"

"No."

"It was Megan or static cling," he announced before lying back down for another attempt at sleep.

TIM

He waited for her in his socks on the wet cement floor of the dark basement, between Miles's mountain bike with the rusted gears and a molding tower of boxed-up Christmas crap. Someone turned the water on upstairs, so the water meter in the corner lightly chugged, like the motor of an antique riverboat. Tim was on a trip of sorts down there, just waiting for his fellow passenger. He looked at his phone again. They had decided to text at eight p.m. Maine time/five-thirty a.m. Afghanistan time, or pretend Afghan time. And sure enough:

GIB here, hon. How was Ur night?

Hi Blondie. Not good, friend in hospital.

O no! How Bad?

Not looking good. IED. Unseen bomb. Our Hummer just missed hitting it. Next vehicle didn't miss. Was just giving him shit the day before. I should've seen it in the road.

O Rusty! Not UR fault! If you'd been looking down, someone would've shot from above. How hell works. Can I send something to the hospital over there? Can I send you something?

Don't send anything.

WANT to.

"Oh, shit," Tim said to his phone and looked up at the sound of footfalls in the kitchen.

It's complicated.

K, give me the steps.

Just send whatever it is to my dad. He was a Marine. He knows the channels.

Tim sent her the address and name of Rusty's father, Tim Turner. She texted back.

If only I cd hold you right now.

Tim put his left arm across his chest and pressed it there as he typed.

How's ur dad treating you?

Mom found my underwear on his side of the bed.

???? Call the police on him!
Do it now!

The basement door opened, and Tim looked up from the phone to see Mona's sour face. "What are you doing down there?" Then his phone pinged again.

Wish you could come get me.

"Looking for my hammer, then I got a work text."

"Vinnie needs you to move your truck." She reshut the door.

Blondie, I'm in Afghanistan. You need to call the police.

When she didn't text back, he wrote again:

Give me your address, I want to send something, too.

# # #

As he entered through shipping on this Friday morning, Tim found Mike inserting NMBA flyers into each October issue of *Bells Up*. He Frisbeed a flyer across the room to Tim. The cover was of a teenage girl playing the French horn with her sad eyes rolled upward toward a practice-session egg timer on a shelf. "*There's still time to register!*"

Tim opened it to find glossy photos of Joe Masotta and The Publisher side by side. She didn't waste any time. On the back, she'd put out a call for anyone wishing to march in a band directors' band in the Veterans Day parade. *Blow Your Own Horn, Again!* she'd titled the piece. Nice.

"Went to see Angela yesterday," he told Mike. "Most terrifying sight I've ever seen."

"Oh, real sick, huh?" He stopped the stuffing.

"She told her husband she was worried about them getting her last paycheck. Know what I think? I think she's right.

There'll be some mistakes made on that check."

Mike scratched a biceps. "Really?"

Tim's next stop was Angela's office. Her sales notebook was still there, and Tim stuck it up under his shirt. At his own desk, he had a look at her previous month's sales. "That's a hell of a month," he said aloud. It would come to about twelve thousand dollars' commission.

"Hey, listen." Mike had appeared in the doorway and was reaching up to set his fingertips on the doorframe for a pull-up, as was his habit. "I didn't want to say anything earlier, but I thought you might be interested in a recent discovery."

"Not really. No offense but—" Tim made a ta-da gesture toward his paperwork.

"It's about Emily's new additions, the bazingas." He lifted himself half a foot and hung there. "I saw them online."

"Sure you did."

Mike dropped and stepped in closer. "I got a site I go to; you rate chicks' racks." He raised his hands in surrender. "Hey, the girls put the pictures up themselves. They don't show their faces. Well, some do. Anyway, yesterday's pick had this little freckle triangle right here"—he traced one over a clavicle—"just like our Emily." He sat in the guest chair.

"I can't listen to this," Tim told him. "I'm working."

"Now that she's all about the cleavage shirts, I am very familiar with the triangle."

"Get the fuck out," Tim said, which blew Mike's head back.

"Whoa. Kill the messenger, why don't you."

It was ridiculous, Mike's inane fantasy. Mike didn't know Emily. She was actually *afraid* of male attention. Flaunting herself on a website for masturbators? Never. Would not happen. When Tim heard the door to shipping slam shut, he Googled the racks website. The current day's rack was a pair of tubular sandbags with nipples the size of coasters, Tim scrolled down to the one Mike would have seen the day before: pale, lovely breasts. The freckles did look a little like Emily's triangle, but there were billions of women in the world. The shot was taken in a bathroom that had a shower curtain covered in big blue polka dots. Tim looked at the comments section—disgusting suggestions about what men wanted to do with the boobs, invitations to email more naked photos. Then Tim noticed the comment from MikeyLikes, which was particularly crass, about shooting his wad all over the breasts, and which at the end said, "Love the little freckle triangle, reminds me of someone I know."

Would Emily subject herself to this while a kiss from Tim was out of the question? No way, it wasn't her. He uncapped a pen and drew the configuration of the girl's freckle points onto the torn corner of an envelope for live comparison.

# # #

"So we're supposed to try to write a book together for The Publisher to stick her name on," Tim told Emily, dumping himself into her guest chair. Today's top was a purply, silky thing, undone an extra button. She lifted both hands to her hair, and her heavy silver bracelets collided, clanking down to the elbows and then moving noisily back to the wrists when she rested her arms on her lap, just like the ones in his mom's dating costume.

"God help us," she said. "About what?"

"The President's Own."

"The Marine band?"

"History of the Marine band. She wants a page count today. Yesterday, actually."

"Two pages. Then it goes downhill."

Tim rolled his fingers on his thighs, then slowly moved a

hand up to take the freckle paper out of his pocket.

Emily, oblivious, said, "Let me guess, this gets done on the weekends."

"Well, I know the director of that band, so he can help us."

"Good, *he* can write it. What are you doing?"

Tim lowered the paper. "I can't read my own notes anymore. She wants us to select our target."

"I don't know what you're talking about."

"The page count."

Emily got up and pulled *Spectacle Design for the Nineties* off of the shelf. "I think this was the last book she published." She flipped to the end. "A hundred and seventy-six pages."

"Target selected."

She sat back down. "What else?"

"Nothing. Except I'm taking a bathroom poll. My wife's got me taking a shower in a daisy explosion—giant gerbera daisy heads in colors you should only be able to see on LSD. I think a shower curtain should be clear. Like, a little frosty but clear. What say you?"

"Jesus, Tim, there are people dying on the streets of our cities at the hands of the police and you're having a cow about daisies?"

"Not a cow, just a little preoccupation. Hey," he said, quickly changing direction, "I suggested that for NMBA, we field a marching band in the Veterans Day parade downtown. It's the day before the convention, so we get all the old directors to line up and play."

"Oh, God. Really?" Then her expression metamorphosed into a look of wonder. "I wouldn't mind playing in this band." He figured she imagined it like he did: the gleeful crowds, the mass of skilled players, the pyrotechnic music.

After they went back and forth naming their ideal playlist and the conversation came to a rest, he decided to ask about it.

"So, have you made all of these changes for some new guy?" Tim flapped his hands near his own hair in the hope that she would not think he was referring to the new boobs.

She deadeyed him, "You know when I decided to start saving for a complete makeover, Tim? When you determined that I was at the point where I'd like to have a sweaty, barrel-bellied, married guy my father's age who pays for beer with nickels and dimes he's dug out of his truck as my lover."

Tim smiled quickly, briefly, thinking her comment might be going that way—a joke. Then he looked down at his hands clutching his thighs. Something had really hardened her. She'd had a personality transplant. "I saw Angela yesterday," he finally said. "She's nearly dead."

#

Super Slick Slide Oil
For over 70 years, Tremblay's Slide Oil still wets a slide like no other, providing long-lasting performance of swift and smooth slides. The lubricant that never dries out or sticks. Put some glide in your slide. A favorite of top performers.

The Publisher clacked into Tim's office in her little hard heels and put both hands flat on his desk like she was holding it steady in a gale. "I'd like you to take that bouquet from Lawrence Fife and Drum to Angela's hospital room this afternoon. It doesn't belong in the lobby. It's slowing everyone down. Depressing."

"Do we know if she's still alive?"

"No one has informed us otherwise." She craned herself back up and turned to leave.

"Her husband's worried they won't get her commissions,"

Tim told her.

She looked back at him, stricken. An accomplished faker.

"I told him that of course they will," Tim said.

"Yes, of course! Why would he even wonder about that?"

"I guess she was worried about it."

"Angela?"

He nodded.

"This makes no sense to me." She took a few steps toward the hall, then turned back. "I've already taken her notebook out of her office, and I'll match her list to any sales that come in. I'm not going to short a dying woman!"

Tim wanted to yank open his desk drawer and throw Angela's sales notebook at The Publisher's mock-suffering face.

She huffed a hot breath. "How her husband can talk about it, and so greedily! It's astonishing! While she's lying in the hospital bed!" After a beat, then: "Have you discussed the page count with Emily?"

"Hundred and seventy-six."

"That sounds about right. Have you worked out the table of contents?"

"In the process. You'll have it next week."

"Tim, next week? How long should a TOC take? I'm not saying it has to be the final one, but how did you come up with a page count without doing a TOC?"

"No, we talked about it, but we just didn't finalize anything."

"Sounds like a perfect weekend project. I'll look for it on Monday."

After she left, Tim opened his desk drawer and took out Angela's notebook. Also in the drawer was the slip of paper describing Rusty, his ideal self. He pinched the tiny scrap and moved it up onto his desktop.

Rusty Turner
Marine Sniper
21, 6' 2", 9"

At the bottom, in tiny print, he scrawled, "To happen on" and the next day's date.

# # #

Tim pulled into the driveway behind the BMW belonging to George, the pen salesman. He was sure George had selected Friday evenings for his lesson time so it would seem most like a date, just as Tim had done when he took Emily out for beers.

As though they had awaited him, Mona began playing the easy piano arrangement of Schubert's *The Elf King* as Tim was opening the door. After she rolled out the dramatic bass theme a few times, George sucked a great breath and began singing the narrator's lines—about a father carrying his son on horseback through the night. On key, yes, but overdone, with strain not strength. Still, instead of rushing into the kitchen, Tim remained by the door, watching George tuck chin to neck, eyebrows up and longing for each other as he then sang the father's lines, asking his son what is wrong, above trembling chords. How many high-end gold pens did they have in this house because of George? Tim wondered. The guy had given Mona dozens, enough maybe to pay a month's mortgage.

Now George sang the little boy's reply, telling his father of the Elf King he sees, who is offering him wondrous things. For this, George placed his hands in prayer and stood up on his tasseled toes.

Next, the Elf King's lines, sung tenderly, enticing the boy to leave his father. Mona had to lean away from all of the Teutonic spewing *s*'s.

Look at the guy, Tim told himself. Why had he been so dismissive of this man who was right now feeling a piece of great music, letting it move him? Isn't this what Tim longed to experience? He readied his hands to clap well before the narrator described the boy dead in his father's arms.

"Applause, applause!" Tim clapped above his head. "Fantastic, guys!"

George gave him a little surprised smile.

"Much better," Mona said.

"Very, very nice," Tim agreed, "and I was glad to see your car in the driveway, George."

"But," Mona answered, shutting the fallboard, "they were in it this morning, moving a ton of liquor boxes in and—"

Tim cut her short, pushing into the kitchen and then opening the fridge. When he turned back, George was there. "Can I ask you something, Tim?" The guy was a foot taller, but he stooped to make up for it. "Would you mind if I spoke to the bar owners about the driveway? Ordinarily I wouldn't get involved, because this is completely your area, but Mona just gets so upset, and I hate to see her that way. Tim, last week she cried."

Tim let his beer arm drop. "And what is it you would say to the creeps?"

"I'm sure they're reasonable guys. I'd try to sell them on the idea that if their neighbors are angry with them, then that's bad for business. Their neighbors should be their best customers! Wouldn't you love to go across the street and sit at the bar and watch a game sometime? Have some onion rings? Of course you would, but not now, not with the way you're treated."

"You know what, George? Yes, I think you should do it."

"Is it really okay? For Mona's sake?" The guy was shifting from side to side, preventing Tim from leaving his own kitchen.

"Absolutely."

"Well, that's great!"

"Here's to you." Tim raised his beer in a one-way toast and shepherded George out to the driveway, where Tim would have to back up to free the BMW.

"I have another favor to ask," George said, stopping behind Tim's truck. "I'm a Freemason. I don't know if you knew that. And I would love to invite Miles to some of our youth events. We get the kids involved in doing things for the community. Last year, we painted over all the graffiti on three city blocks. The kids got a lot of donated sports equipment for doing that, but the main thing is that while they're working, we talk to them about life and help them make the right choices. I see Miles is, well, he's in need of something to do. And maybe, eventually, if it all works out, he would ask to be initiated. Wouldn't be the worst thing in the world for the kid. Great contacts there."

"It's too late, George." Tim clapped him on the back. "Kid's already joined the warlocks." Then he dodged the fairy godfather and closed himself into his truck, which, when started, blasted Sousa's *Semper Fidelis*. He drove too slowly around a few blocks so he could hear the complete polyphonic masterpiece, dedicated to Marines everywhere. The tremendous high and low melodies contrasting and commingling made him dizzy with glee, and he nodded to all curious onlookers like he was leading a parade. Of course, when he returned to the driveway, it was plugged up by the bar owners' van.

# # #

"Let the weekend begin," Tim said when he'd shut the front door again. The reason he knew he would transform into Rusty the next day was that he had decided it. He'd just decided it! He had Blondie's address, and he would go and get her. His wife, it was clear, could settle down with Big George once Tim was no more. George could resolve the bad business with the bar *and* take care of buying the parking spots. Problems solved. And Miles would be a Mason.

"Daddy's coming for dinner." Mona came down the stairs in a nice dress. "Can you clean off the table? He's bringing the money for the parking space."

"Does he know the price is twenty-five K?"

"Yes, he does! And let me take care of this. I'm doing the talking."

Tim flopped onto the couch, where he noticed the folded blankets had disappeared. "Is this why Vinnie's gone?"

"He is visiting the Cheesecake Factory, but he should be back soon," she said from the kitchen, but then she came back out and held up her hand in a stop sign. "Don't say anything to him," she said. "He's thinking of moving back here."

"Christ, I knew it!" Tim winced. "I thought he had a boyfriend down there!"

"He did, and then he found out the man is going to marry a woman. That was the man's Miata."

"He stole it?"

"How would I know?" Then from the kitchen, she added, "Am I the gay police?"

"What about the movie? Is there even a movie?" Tim asked the kitchen door.

# # #

Mona's father arrived in a suit coat and fedora. The jacket came from a time when he was thinner, and it could no longer be buttoned. He spent a few moments at the shrine, touching the piano lid—murmuring to the little framed photo of his wife—before taking his habitual place in the armchair in the living room, leaving Tim, Mona, and Vinnie to crowd together on the sofa while Miles hunched on the floor under one of the windows.

"Okay, guys, I like the parking space." He tapped an armrest. "I like it because Mona needs it for her students, and I like it because it makes a good investment. They are not making any new parking lots in this city. So I want to buy it, for Mona, but it will be my property."

"Good," Tim said. "Very nice." He was happily realizing that when his transformation happened the next day, he would never have to endure this man again.

"Daddy"—Mona shot a hand through the air toward her father—"this is not something you can resell whenever you want, unless we move, which right now we cannot do. And we need the parking to be part of any sale of our house. That's how we get above water. They have to be connected."

"But just giving you twenty-five K? What am I supposed to do, give David and Donna also twenty-five? You see what I mean?"

"It's a loan, Daddy. Didn't I tell you? Tim got a raise. He got a nice raise."

"Very good! Congratulations."

Tim gave a monk's nod.

"So he can pay you back. It's not like we can't pay you back. And he's tuning pianos now too!"

"Already?"

"For some people at the opera, Daddy. Some of the big shots," Mona answered, and Tim just offered a big dumb smile.

The man fixed on Tim. "We'll do a payment plan, then," he said.

"Fine. How's five thousand per year? Can we do that?" she asked.

After a few loud nose breaths, he nodded his assent. "Am I having dinner, or what?"

She kissed his bald head on her way out of the room. "You want wings? I got wings! You want meatballs? I got meatballs!"

"What are you doing these days, Miles?" He looked at the boy with great concern.

"Nothing."

"Is that how you answer a person?"

"Huh?"

"You've just murdered the conversation."

"Oh." He let out half a laugh.

"I'm not trying to be funny."

"I'm helping Dad get in shape."

"There you go! That's an answer. What's he getting in shape for?"

"The Marines."

"No," Tim said, "I'm just trying to get healthier."

"You've got a long way to go. What about you, Vinnie? I heard you're on all the shows."

Tim stood and headed for the kitchen, but the older man pinched his sleeve as he passed and pulled him down. "It's you who will pay me the money, once a year on Thanksgiving. This year will be the first year because you are getting the raise and doing all of the tunings. And if you have to sell something, sell something." He then released the sleeve.

# # #

After dinner, Tim slid the twenty-five-thousand-dollar check into his coat. He would take it to the old man's bank the next morning and cash it. He was sticking with the plan of having George buy the driveway for Mona. He only needed to finalize the transaction, so he texted Phyllis:

Don't have your signed P&S yet. Can you scan and

email? Copy Mona? Hope all is well.

That night, late, while Tim scratched at the blister forming on his over-gelled forearm, he doubled down on thoughts of his ideal self in Afghanistan. To have strong, normal thighs again, and ribs he could trace, or that she could, his Girl in Back. The only worries for him now were his mother and Miles, but his mother was never going to agree to get rid of her dogs, so that was futile, and really, what could be done about Miles? No, nothing could be done, even if Tim had more time.

DAVIS

"That's where it was found." Davis pointed out the dark roadside blotch to Megan, who gave the dirt a blank stare while shouldering her pack. He had asked her to come out of habit, called out to her as he left, like for any weekend errand, but this time she'd said yes. He had actually closed the door behind himself before realizing she'd agreed.

A wind gust flipped up his bangs as he made a slow, complete turn, assessing the surrounding hills. "They like to den on high ground, but that won't help us here, I'm afraid. There's high ground in every direction. Let's just head west and look for scat."

He crossed the road and found an opening between the trees. "A clan of hyenas deposit their droppings in one spot, their latrine. So look for a collection of poop that's chalky white, from all of the bones they eat." He could not hear her following. Sure enough, she was still in the road, squinting at the sky.

"How will we get back to the car?"

Knowing that getting lost was for Megan the ultimate loss of control, he tried to be tender: "I have a compass on my phone. So do you." He patted the hard plastic belt clip holding his cell. A holstered gun hung on the other hip. "We may also find pellets on the ground because, like owls, hyenas throw up what they can't digest, hair and hooves and such."

"If I see a thrown-up hoof, I will die."

"Okay, let's go. Come on. And less talking, more listening, would be good for both of us." She followed him in.

"What am I listening for?" she loudly whispered after a while.

Davis stopped and rolled his eyes upward in the listening look. "They can sound like cows lowing." He made the sound. "They can also sound like elephants trumpeting. Also like chimps. It's a wide spectrum of vocalizations. Just listen for anything out of the ordinary." The woods were much easier to traverse in the fall, now that the ferns had collapsed and the leaves were half gone. He held branches up for Megan and helped to steady her on tricky descents or brook crossings. Occasionally they stopped to listen before continuing on again. Davis never imagined he'd have a daughter as an expedition member, but he had imagined his son tramping along—for a few months anyway he had imagined this, but then the boy was lost. An *incompetent cervix*, they'd said, like it was some bumbling birth canal raised in the woods. Jenny's cervix had opened up early and allowed the baby to come down, causing a miscarriage. It wouldn't happen again, they'd promised her. Next time, they'd sew it up, the cervix, and then release the sutures when the baby was ready to be born. But Jenny had said no, or rather she had just continued shaking her head no, which she'd begun when the miscarriage occurred and kept up for quite some time, like a no-tremor. She couldn't face a loss like that again, she'd said.

So that was when adoption was put on the table, not right away, of course. But whenever any world tragedy happened, Jenny wanted to go and save an orphaned baby. Then when *20/20* aired a segment on Romanian orphanages, showing malnourished children tied to stained cots, Jenny's longing hit an all-time high. The segment showed children with no affect, lost. The reporter explained that Ceauşescu's regime, which had outlawed contraception and abortion in order to force women to have more children, had then decided to spend the country's economic resources to settle foreign debt, so there was no money for the orphanages that were bulging with babies. Next, of course, came unregulated adoptions, which in many cases further endangered the children. When Davis and Jenny adopted Megan, there were nearly forty thousand children still waiting in squalor. Each institution had a "baby shop" of those ready for adoption. If he and Jenny had wanted to save some money, they could have purchased a child from any of the dozens of mothers and fathers who approached them on the street. "You here for buying baby?"

Davis and Jenny had walked into only one baby shop, because it would have been impossible to do two. They passed the rusty metal cribs of toddlers who had never toddled, and although the children were clean, they all rocked back and forth, their own soothers. Not one cried. Crying had proven ineffective.

They had decided on a girl (not wanting to see the child as a replacement for the boy), and Jenny finally stopped at one crib, placed her palm on a child's head, and called, "Davis?" She explained that this one seemed to see her, to react to her a little.

And here she was now, a beautiful, strong young woman who could probably carry her father back to the car should he need it. Her misunderstanding of the world, of human nature, of people's intentions, broke his heart. The machinations she felt she had to go through to gain a simple thing—sustenance—devastated him. But pity did her no good.

They stopped at a swift brook and took a break, letting their legs hang over a large flat rock above the water. Davis asked her for a drink. "I've worked up a sweat, have you?"

She looked down at herself and then out at the woods. "No."

"Hyenas can go for long periods without water, so they don't need to live close to it."

After pulling the water from her pack, Megan drank first and then handed him the bottle. He took a few long pulls and swiped at his mouth with the back of a hand. "Another odd thing is that they don't bring food back to the den for their young; they don't regurgitate any meals for them either, which means the young suckle until they are big enough to travel great distances."

After a long moment of just enjoying the scene, Davis said, "I may shoot the hyena if we see it. I'd rather get a photo but—"

"Is it fully loaded?" She reached over and slid her index finger across the textured grip.

"Fully. Seven bullets. It's just that a photo takes more time than we will likely get. That's how the world of science was introduced to the mountain gorilla, someone finally shot one. Can you imagine? Such an incredible beast, and we didn't acknowledge its existence until a dead specimen was brought down out of the mountains in 1902, after nearly forty years of hearing tales about the creature and discounting them."

"You always tell the same story."

"I've told this to you? I didn't realize."

"It's always some story where no one believes people, but then they were right. Like all along they were right." She loved to point out his behaviors. He did have a preoccupation with scientific bigotry. He would give her that. The idea that human beings living closer to nature should be disbelieved about natural things provoked him. He was the native peoples' paladin.

"Dad?" she said after a while, "I have a problem with people touching me."

"Who?" He flashed on a vision of Lindstrom looming over her.

"Just anyone."

"What do you mean?"

"I'm afraid of people touching me. I've been thinking about why, and part of it is seeing them or their hand come closer and closer, and I freak out."

"Whose hand are you picturing?"

"No, it's not one person! It's just touching in general."

"But you're always touching other people."

"It has something to do with seeing them start to touch me, I guess."

"I did not know this. So it's a visual thing, you think?"

"Maybe."

"It's not the actual touch itself?"

"Could we try something? I was going to ask Mom, but…"

"Sure. You can ask me anything."

"Okay, I'll close my eyes, and at some point, not right away, you can tell me you are going to touch me, and then you move your hand toward me—slowly!—and keep telling me, and then you can touch me."

He turned to face her, sitting cross-legged. "Where do you want to be touched?"

"Just, I don't know, on my arm. Okay, I'm closing my eyes."

They listened to the brook for ten seconds, and then Davis said, "I'm going to touch you now." And he reached over and brushed his fingers against her forearm. She flinched.

"How was that? Not so good, huh."

"Not great."

"Let's try again. Close your eyes. Okay. I'm coming in for the touch." He floated a finger through the air. "Get ready. You can handle this. Remember, I've touched you many times before. Closer, closer."

"Stop!" she jerked away.

"I'm not so sure it's the visual, Megan. I think it's the actual feeling."

"Yeah. Never mind. I don't want you to tell Mom about this."

"No. We can have our own secret things."

#

On the way home, Davis stopped at a convenience store for fountain drinks. As he waited to pay, he looked out at Megan in the car, her face still and expressionless. She seemed to power down when no one was around; she didn't listen to music or read. It was as though the only reason to engage was to affect or manipulate another person.

When he opened the driver's door, she woke to him. "Did they have Cherry Coke?"

"Just regular." He sat and handed her the drink. Then something made him think of his wallet, and he patted the side pockets of his cargo pants, but it wasn't in either one. "Oh, dear," he said.

"What?"

"I left my wallet in the store. I'll be right back."

He jogged back in and interrupted the clerk, who was ripping off a long strip of scratch tickets for a pregnant woman, but the guy said he hadn't seen it. Davis searched the floor on his way out.

"Did you find it?" Megan shouted out of the car window.

He shook his head.

When he reached for the door handle, she wailed, "Dad, did you drop it? Did someone take it off of the counter?" Her cheeks were raw and wet.

"Megan, calm down." He shut himself in.

She continued to bawl. "All your cards and everything's gone!"

"Stop it, Megan! I need to think!" He watched the pregnant lady come out, followed by a hooded teen, who was scratching away at the tickets against his palm and was probably the culprit, Davis thought. Then he mentally went through the process of canceling the credit cards and renewing his library card and his AAA. Had his school ID been in there? All the while, Megan's knees were jumping. Suddenly he got the idea to get out and look beneath the car's undercarriage, and in the process he saw the wallet on the floor, beside his seat. "It's here." He held it up for her. "Okay? Calm down." Dear Lord, what a strange creature she was. How would she ever deal with life's small problems on her own, let alone its calamities? But he only let his mind churn on that worry for a moment before forcing it out of his head. She was not an animal, after all. She would learn.

TIM

When Tim's phone chimed on the nightstand, at five forty-five a.m., and he had to jostle his bulk over to grab it, he realized he had not transformed into Rusty overnight. It was a return text from Phyllis:

> The tinaco is full and life is good. Evry Friday, they pump it full of water frm their truck all the way up to my rooftop. I take a shower during the pumping to squeeze as much as I can from thm. Not as easy to know when they're coming as it is for gas truck, which plays Pop Goes the Weasel while drving down the rd. Anyhow, full of joy now having just left the verdant terrace of Hotel Posada. All around the table--poets, artists, adventurers! Our Friday salon. Then, like dropped into a movie, we hrd first horns of a mariachi band taking to the streets. All the best groups in the country will now descend for the fstival. And for you, Tim, Banda music! Tuba the essential instrument! Come and be impassioned by the alchemy betwn horns & vocals. 20-piece bands! There we sat looking over the jardin with the great aural bounty rising to match the visual (the umber of the casa walls and the impossible sky). Cheap, cheap, cheap lots with views of the infinite high desert. Am now selling real estate. You would be a

king here with your horn!

I cannot sign the P&S. I must insist on gettng full amount, all of it for myself, but Mr. Softy may nt agree. In order fr me to sign any P&S, that stipulation must be in it (PHYLLIS GETS ALL MONIES BECAUSE OF WHAT SHE HAS ENDURED). The funds will help me heal frm my "multiple falls," as I'm sure Dr. Concerned describd to you. Do you recall the wrds I screamed when you opened your window onto my horror? I cannot remember. Wld like to know.

Warmly,

Phyllis

She'd screamed no words, he could tell her that, just a howling cry. Thinking of his inaction that night, years ago, pushed Tim out of bed, and he caught sight of himself in the mirror on the closet door. For Christ's sake, he thought, why was he still fat Tim? Now he had to talk with Vinnie about how this whole becoming-your-ideal-self thing worked.

# # #

The two smoking Asian workers leaning against the bay door of the just-closed Lube Express were grinning away with their brown teeth as Tim rested, huffing, hands on his knees.

Vinnie looked at his watch and too quickly barked again, "Run!"

Tim made a hateful face and launched forward as hard as he could while Vinnie jogged ahead of him, studying his watch. "Now walk," he said after thirty seconds.

They turned a corner, and the setting sun blinded Tim. He had to shade his eyes to see Vinnie's shape up ahead. Again the man yelled, "Run!"

Tim imagined himself running away from a catastrophe, a lava flow or a great wave gaining on him.

"You can do it! Come on! Move it, move it!" Vinnie shouted over his shoulder. "And now...walk!"

His chest heaved out so far, he thought he'd rip his shirt. "How many of these?"

"Couple more."

A young woman yelled, "Shut up!" to someone behind her as she shoved open the door of a two-story brick apartment building. Tim stopped to let her pass, and she scowled at him, hugging more tightly her bucket of spray bottles.

"This is good, Vinnie," Tim said, still standing in place after her car pulled away. "I can feel that this is really—ah—really good. Let's walk and talk now."

"You're done?"

Tim shook his head, hands on hips. "It's just—I need to go over some things with you."

Vinnie walked toward him, and they turned back in the direction they'd come.

"Okay," Tim started, "so I'm doing it. That's the thing. I'm all positivity about making a change."

"Good for you." Vinnie sounded bitter.

"I mean I have absolutely decided my fate, but it's not happening."

"Well, no, of course. God has an appointed time. You can't mess with God's appointed times."

"That's not what you said before. What about all the laws of attraction?"

"That takes a back seat. Look, when you met Mona—" Vinnie swept his hands apart to clear space for what he was about to describe—"that was God's set time for that to happen. And he had to take care of many things in advance: Mona's family had to encourage her singing so she'd be good enough to get into that kids' chorus to meet her boyfriend." One finger went up. "Okay? Then her boyfriend had to get inducted and you get rejected." The second finger popped. "Many, many things go into the set time. When you conceived Miles, that was also God's appointed time. And he had to make sure that a particular sperm was ready and that it beat out all of the other sperms. He does a lot of prep work. You can't rush it, and you can't know when it is. This is what faith is for."

Tim squinted to keep the sweat out of his eyes. "How do you know about this 'appointed times' thing?"

"Joel Osteen. YouTube. That man is a positive thinker, but when even his positive thinking doesn't work, this is why— God's timing."

"For all this supposed planning, God sure comes up with some shitty outcomes."

"Well, maybe you're talking about things he didn't even set up! Maybe you didn't wait for God. You did an end run, and then that's on you.

Tim waved that off like a bad smell, and they continued walking.

"God had someone planned for me," Vinnie said, "but that man went off on his own. He decided to marry a woman. And I told him, 'No, I'm not coming to your wedding! Are you kidding me? You don't jilt a man who has listened to all of your dreams, who has kissed your tears away, and then expect him to throw rice.'"

# # #

The flowers looked too droopy to present, really, and weren't lilies death flowers? Maybe Lawrence Fife and Drum thought she was already dead. Maybe she was. He rode the elevator with a young couple, the man smiling over at him and then whispering to the woman, who kept snorting in laughter. "They're not my flowers," he told them. It was late, nine-thirty. He was supposed to deliver these yesterday. He hoped it was after visiting hours. He wanted to leave the flowers at the nurses' station.

Tim waited a while at the empty station before making the leaden march to her room. Only Angela was in there. He could see from the doorway that she'd pulled her blanket off again. She was the most frightening sight he had ever seen, like someone exhumed. He stared back down the hall toward the station. Shouldn't someone be helping her in some way? Tim set the flowers on the table at the foot of the other bed, the one closer to the door, and turned to leave. Then he thought he heard Angela move. "Do you need anything?" He turned back.

Was someone putting eye drops in the eyes that never closed? "The Lawrence folks sent the flowers," he told her, now taking a few steps back into the center of the room. "That was nice. Everybody's thinking about you."

Her breathing was rough. Where was her husband? Where was ballot-box boy? He inched halfway toward her bedside. "I'm sorry, Angela. I'm sorry this is happening to you. I'm making sure your family gets everything you're due. That's taken care of."

And then her rasp stopped. He waited, watching her still chest. In a moment, he snatched the call button from her bedside and detonated it, then rushed out to the hall. "My friend's not breathing," he told the approaching nurse, and he was surprised to hear himself say the word *friend*. He hadn't had one of those since he screwed Joe Masotta's girl.

# # #

The next morning, Mona pointed out that Tim had a tuning on the calendar, for the opera patron Sunny Straub. "She can help me get Rosina," Mona reminded him.

"Rosina is nineteen years old."

"It's for a coloratura. I am a coloratura. I just need makeup."

#

Sunny and her Klopotek grand piano lived in a big home in Beverly Farms. If you wanted to take a photo of the entire home, you'd have to cross the street and put your back against the home facing it. Sunny's home was Federal-style with wood clapboards and trim that had been left to rot in a few spots around the windows and along the bottoms of the corner boards. She answered the door in a coat and hat, and smiled like Tim had come to gather her for elopement. "Oh, I've just come in myself!" she said. "It's a bit nippy to be in your shirtsleeves."

"I'm pretending I'm in Mexico."

"Well, it's here!" She beamed.

"The Klopotek has landed?" he said, tipping sideways to try to see beyond her into the house.

"It's gorgeous. I can't believe I own it. Listen, I've got just five minutes for lunch now, will you join me?"

"No, I—"

"Chicken salad on iceberg. It's ready right at the moment, so let's have some together."

She unbuttoned her coat, and he helped her off with it. "Whoever invented meat salad gets my vote," he told her.

They dined at the marble island in the kitchen, on blue-and-gold china and with real silverware. Sunny held her Pomeranian on her lap while she ate. Tim had seen three paintings of the Pom just on his way into the kitchen.

"That's a great dog," Tim said because people love to hear how great their dog is. "You lucked out with that dog. Look at her, she adores you!" The dog was staring up at Sunny's chewing mouth.

"Bea's the best dog I've ever had."

"I bet."

"So Mona says you consider yourself a funny guy. Tell me a joke," she insisted and then pertly grinned.

"She said I consider *myself* funny?"

"She thinks you're funny, then." Sunny shrugged.

"She doesn't think I'm funny. Did you know that she's a coloratura?"

"Come on, tell me a joke. I love jokes."

Tim was happy to stop separating the raisins from the salad and set his fork down. "A father sends his son for tuba lessons. After the first lesson, the kid comes home and the father asks, 'How'd it go, son?' 'Yeah, fine,' the boy says. 'I know how to play a C now.'" Tim watched Sunny pull the fork from her mouth, reload it, and slide it into her dog's mouth.

"Then, after the next week's lesson, the father inquires again, 'Did you learn anything new?' 'An E!' the boy answers. "I can play an E!'" Sunny fed herself again from the fork.

"The next week, the father waits and waits, and the child doesn't return from the lesson. All through the afternoon and evening, he's a no-show. Finally, around two a.m., kid walks in with the tuba. 'Where've you been, son?' asks the father. 'I've been worried half to death!' 'Oh,' says the boy, 'sorry, I had a gig.'"

Sunny grinned just as she had during the entire telling and waited to hear more.

"It's about how the tuba only plays a coupla notes in any song."

She cocked her head like a questioning dog.

"Like, if you think of the oompah-pah of a polka, say." Then he held a pretend tuba, rocked, and sang, "Oompah-pah, oompah-pah, oompah-pah, oompah-pah."

"YES! Oh, dear! How funny! Three notes!"

"It's okay."

She scraped up the last of her salad. "Do you know where I was before you arrived? I was at my lawyer's. I'm suing someone."

"Oh!"

"If some people think they can take advantage of an older woman, they guess wrong with me. A man sold me a lemon car."

"What kind is it?"

"Well, it doesn't matter what kind it is. Even if this car is a well-known disaster, I certainly didn't know it, and I trusted the salesman to recommend something to me. This car is what he recommended. Now the engine block is cracked or some such thing."

"A used car."

"Doesn't matter, though, if it's used or not. That's my whole point."

"Right, I was just—"

"I'm suing him for more than the price of the car, for all of my wasted time and anguish." The dog got a last forkful before Sunny changed the topic. "I understand you work at *Bells Up*. I know The Publisher there."

"You know her?"

"We're in some of the same circles. Music lovers."

"I'd appreciate it if you wouldn't mention my piano-tuning work. It's not taking any time away from the magazine, but—"

She put a hand up to stop him. "I am a capitalist all the way, sir. I believe we should be free to make as much money as we can." And with that, she stood up and waited for Tim to do the same; then she led him back through the dining room and foyer and into the grand living room. In every space, Sunny's flowery scent mixed with that of mold and dog. The home had fine furnishings, not a few of which had fallen into disrepair—fraying, splitting, leaning.

The Klopotek claimed the corner of the big room, an ornate beast with a white satin finish. Gilt carvings decorated the sides of the case and rimmed the music stand. Gaudy cartouches had been stuck on where the body met the legs, and then the legs slimmed down and curled out to rest on outturned scrolls.

As Tim set his strap of tuning tools on the floor, Sunny said, "I have to pop out again, over to my dressmaker's."

"Good. Listening to a tuning is an underused torture."

She struggled back into her coat. "I am leaving your check on the credenza, if you could just lock the door behind you." He'd thought a credenza was only an Italian thing, since every one of Mona's relatives made a big point of their credenzas.

When he ran a few scales, he knew he would never be through, but he was determined to remove, wrap, and replace at least one octave's worth of pins that day. He got up to see what the check was made out for. The $250 was what he had expected, and it included his visit to the auction house. He tapped the check but left it there and poured himself a shot of scotch from the glass cabinet. When he shut the door, the whole credenza shuddered and the fine glasses tipped against each other. Near the check was a framed photo of Sunny and her little dog, to whom he raised a toast. Sunny looked a lot younger in this photo, but she still had the same dog, or maybe, he thought, this Bea was one of a series.

He took his scotch out to the kitchen and opened the refrigerator. The stacks of plastic tubs with paper labels intrigued him. He slid out one containing meatballs, and set it on the counter. Four tries for the silverware drawer put him in touch with a fork, and he buried it in a meatball and then walked about the house with the forked ball and his drink. Six more photos and god-awful paintings of the pooch. He discovered her library and scanned the books, all hardcovers of novels that most people bought in paperback and threw out after the vacation, big romances and whole mystery series. He sucked the last bit of meat off the fork while looking out at the green and leafy pool. Did Sunny live here debt free? And what would that be like? This was probably it, he decided, eating a meatball you didn't have to cook while surveying your land.

Then his phone buzzed, and he saw a Snapchat had come through. Tim set the fork on the windowsill and held a finger against the screen to play the video. It opened with some scratchy old LP sound, and there was Blondie, smiling and waving fingers at the camera in slow motion. Then a fast beat, and churning guitars kicked in and the song rocked, and Blondie began running along a beach in a bikini. Summer Footage. What a beauty. And what a song! The energy! And the female singer's voice got inside of him, the chorus: "When I grow up, I'll be stable. When I grow up, I'll turn the tables." Blondie jumped into the waves, and when the foam settled, the camera zoomed in to show her smoothing her hair and opening her incredible eyes. Next she fist-hammered a ball over a net in a sleeveless tee and skimpy shorts, and then other girls patted her ass, and, yes, more leaping, arms overhead, and slow-motion ponytail flicks. When the video ended, he reluctantly pulled his fingertip from the screen. Touching the box next to the message again brought nothing about. That band, that song, Tim decided, that was the music for his ideal self. And that beauty, dear God! That was the ideal self's ideal mate.

Back at the piano, he unfurled the strap holding his tools and began by placing rubber wedges over two of the three strings that play A440. Then he fit the tuning lever over the pin of the third string, rapped the tuning fork on his knee, and struck the A key firmly to compare that tone to the one coming from the fork. The noise startled the dog, who set in to barking from another room, yipping in time with his repeated, upward-bending note. "No, Bea!" he shouted.

Each time he cranked the tuning lever and then released it, it returned, counterclockwise, to its old position. He'd planned for this and had cut small strips from the corrugated cardboard that had separated his wife's china plates. After struggling to get the string off, he unscrewed this first pin, sixty-three turns to remove it. Then he pushed the curled wrapper over it. Then sixty-three turns to reset the pin. Once he'd wrestled the string back on, he struck the note and maneuvered the lever to the perfect spot, but when he let go, it again spun back. Fuck this fuckety-fuck!

If wrapping didn't work, his instructor had whined, then they would need a whole new set of pins, one size larger than the current pins, and they'd need to drill new holes for each of the 230 new pins "and hope to heck you don't crack that pin block, folks!"

Tim hammered at the wrapped pin to try to force it further into the block, and in seconds the little dog was running through the foyer as if borne by a great wind, stopping just behind Tim's right foot, and nipping him in the ankle. Just as Tim wheeled around to find her, she made for the entrance again, where she reset—every muscle coiled for another go. The dog had an underbite and pop eyes and appeared beyond sane. In frustration, Tim managed to overtighten and snap the string. *Oh, hell.* He hoisted his torso over the case to fish it out. Then he moved the mutes and dropped back hard onto the stool to start on the next string. The dog barks made his ears ring. Bea became the embodiment of his difficulty with the pins.

Then the bitch skittered up and nipped his calf. "Damn it!" he cried.

He removed himself to look at the piano from the farthest point in the room while the dog ran tight circles under the Klopotek. He wondered if she was rabid. "Get out!" He rushed her into the dining room.

Back at the piano, he struck the fork on his knee and depressed the A key again, only to hear the fast beat of interference that signifies great discord. It was then that the dog made her last run in their game and needled Tim's Achilles tendon, which made him turn with a start and strike her skull with the tuning fork.

She rag-dolled. The dog was out cold, a tiny floor mat. He cocked her head up and checked for breathing with a finger to her nostrils. Dead.

By the time Tim had closed the piano and returned his tools to the strap, the dog was glassy-eyed and as floppy as a hairy water balloon. Tim carried her through the entire house, until he figured to dump her outside, into the pool, where she floated around the perimeter like a bristly child's boat. With a rag, he wiped the scotch glass and returned it to the case, then took the $250 check and left in its place a note saying that there would be a return visit. Oh, and he had let the dog out. Next he had to drive all the way out to Bells Up to screw in his bulb.

# # #

That night, Tim got a listing from Phyllis for a one-acre Mexican property. In the photo, the view was perfectly framed—a blooming cactus in the foreground giving way to an expanse of dusty-green high desert and a distant mountain range.

This vista can be yours for $26K (CITY SERVICES

NEARBY). Master craftsmn work for $20 a day here. Crying shame but what cn you do? You build over time. One rm to start. Others later, build around a central courtyd. Your tuba ranch, Tim! THIS ONE WILL GO FAST.

When a man has twenty-five K, the world knows. Tim stood at the bedroom window to call Andy in California. It was cold that night, and he watched a man rushing down the street self-hugging.

"Andy Paik," the dentist answered in his jolly voice.

"Andy, Tim Turner here. How are you?"

After a few pleasantries, Tim told him that Phyllis was insisting on getting all of the money from the sale. "She says she needs it all for medical bills, Andy. I guess she's pretty bad off, so do you think you can give it to her? It's not that much, after all." Tim had come to realize that God's appointed time for his becoming Rusty would not arrive until after he finalized the driveway sale for Mona and also made a plan for Miles and his mother. That was what he himself had set up by creating the Fire Team Missions. Why should God not hold him accountable?

After a bit of silence, Andy's sweet voice relented. "Of course! I want her to have it! But this kind of makes me think. You know, she could do something for me, too. It's an odd request, but she never signed our tax return from last year, so I actually had to do a 'married filing singly,' and that really messed up my taxes. So you could say to her that if she'll sign the taxes, then she can have the whole twenty-five thousand."

Tim blew out audibly. "I don't know, Andy, that seems like something that should be worked out between the two of you, don't you think? This kind of thing doesn't go into a purchase-and-sale agreement."

"But she doesn't answer my calls."

"Can't you get a lawyer to deal with this?"

"She's in Mexico. She just doesn't respond. I think she will do this only if she has to sign the tax forms right there at the table before getting the check. Sorry, Tim, but I really think this has to be in the document before I can sign it."

Tim watched one of the brothers lurch out of the bar, yanking a woman along behind him, only half into her coat. He was pulling her faster than she could manage in heels, until one shoe tipped sideways and she dropped onto her bare knees on the cement walk.

"You're a dick," Tim mumbled.

"Well," Andy replied, "you didn't have to live with her."

DAVIS

Finding Megan's cell phone attached to the kitchen charger was like finding a rare bird out in the open, perched just there, beside the banana bread. Davis didn't hesitate. He snatched it up and took it into his den, closing the oak door behind him.

He knew the password. He had set the phone up. He tapped on the Pictures icon and then on Camera Roll. The first item was a video, which he then played.

"Hi, and welcome to *What's Megan*. I'm your host, Megan!" She was out on the back patio, turning in a circle, showing the whole windy, leafy yard behind her. "Megan is a type of creature where the parents travel great distances and leave their young behind. They don't bring any food back for their young; in fact, they don't come back at all. You would think this species would be extinct. But they survive." She brought the phone in to show just her mouth. "They are amazing survivors." Then her whole laughing face was back. "They are devastating creatures, really. They move into the dens of other species and pretend to belong. They suffer the consequences." Now just a single bulging eye took up the screen before it went black.

He placed the phone on his desk and floated his hands away from it, left them hanging in the air for a time. Had she played this in class? For Lindstrom? He felt an instant sense of betrayal, underneath which was the prickly realization that he'd done something very wrong. At some point, he had stopped seeing Megan, assumed she was on an unalterable track. Perhaps along the way, she'd become a regular girl and he'd missed it. For heaven's sake, what kid *didn't* take the parents' loose change? And maybe Jenny really was the Sasquatch arm breaker.

A short time later, Jenny found him at the kitchen counter, mixing up batter with a rubber spatula, the waffle iron out and open beside him.

"I think I have an issue today," Jenny told him.

"I do, too."

"What's yours?"

"When she comes down."

At Dr. Peggy's suggestion, the Beardsleys had instituted an "eggs-and-issues" Sunday breakfast, where anyone could voice his or her feelings about the goings-on in the household in a discussion separate from any heated moment.

The parents sat, utensils in hand, a tower of waffles between them, and listened to Megan's slow descent. When she appeared, she looked sad to Davis. Maybe she had been sad for a while.

"Come on, girl, they're getting cold." Davis said as she swiped her phone off the counter and completed her death march to the table.

Jenny pushed the waffles toward her, and she pinched two off the top and dropped them onto her plate. "No bacon?"

"There wasn't any," Davis said, and he waited for Jenny to locate the smallest waffle for herself. The rules posters were back up on the walls. Above Jenny was a list of apps they had approved for Megan's phone and the rule "No other app is to be downloaded without Dad's approval," which was an unnecessary statement since Megan didn't know the iTunes password.

"Who would like to start?" Davis asked. "Because I have something."

"Mmmph," Megan grunted and surveyed the table like she couldn't recall what butter and syrup looked like.

"I'd like to discuss, in a relaxed way, Megan's future. It's time to really stake out a direction and a bit of a plan for your time beyond 107 Pleasant Street. Now, you're the decider on this, Megan, but you have two good advisers to consult here. What are your current thoughts?"

She let her eyes roll up, lobotomized.

"I think it's still California." Jenny chirped. "Is it still California?"

Megan nodded, two nods.

Davis pushed the butter closer to her. "And I don't even care what you do there, but we do need to make a plan for an approach to this."

Megan shaved a peel of butter off the top of the stick and said, "Tara and I are going."

Another poster read, "No pornography is to be viewed on the phone. If it is discovered that pornography has been viewed on the phone, even by accident, the phone will be confiscated."

"Today, maybe, Tara is going," Davis said. "Things can change. Tell me, what do you envision for yourself in California? What are you planning to do there?"

"That's real syrup, honey," Jenny said. Megan was pouring it in continuous spirals over her waffles.

"Okay," she sighed. "I see myself maybe in a movie." She set the bottle down and raked a curtain of hair behind an ear.

"Acting in a movie," Davis said.

"You're a beautiful girl," Jenny assured her.

Davis frowned. "If you're interested in acting, why haven't you tried out for anything at school?"

"I don't want to be in any of that stupid stuff," she said with a mouthful of waffle.

Davis picked up the now-goopy syrup bottle with his paper

napkin. "So, I see myself as the sort of carrier of reality here. There will be nine thousand somewhat trained actors arriving in Los Angeles the same month as you will. How do you like your odds?"

"Can we help you find a class?" Jenny asked.

The girl let her forearms collapse onto the table. "You think anyone around here knows how to train actors? And what about child actors, Dad? Some children have won Oscars. Where did they train?"

Davis didn't know where to go with what he thought he knew, which was that Megan could no more interpret and model others' feelings than she could build a fusion rocket. Maybe this was wrong, but it was tough to imagine. "What else, if that can't happen? Maybe it's best to start with what you don't want. What are your absolute nos as far as jobs go? I would say working with the public is maybe not so good. And food. I don't see you working with food or the public."

"Teaching volleyball," Jenny suggested and twisted toward her daughter.

"We're starting with things she doesn't want to do," Davis reminded her.

"Why? That's moving in the wrong direction."

"I can walk people's dogs," Megan said. "A lot of people have little dogs out there."

"Do you like dogs?" Davis asked.

Looking only at her plate, her long hair falling forward, walling her off, she said, "You put the leash on and walk them down the street. You're not kissing them. They poop and you put it in a bag. It's just something to do!"

Davis then looked from one chewing woman to the other, neither sharing his gaze. "I'm impressed," he said, "a little. It's a bit of a plan. It sounds workable."

"You could get some referrals by walking dogs around

here," Jenny said.

Davis had a disturbing vision and swallowed a large lump of waffle. "People love their dogs, Megan. Very much."

"I have something to say if that topic has finished," said Jenny. "I'd like to take these posters down."

"Yes!" Megan tensed.

"You've stolen my thunder," he told Jenny. "I was about to make that announcement."

"Oh my God! This is the best day of my life!" Megan yelled at the ceiling. Davis shifted another waffle from the stack onto his plate while the women pulled down the posters and balled them up, laughing, banking them against the table beside him and a few times hitting him directly on the head.

TIM

Hi Phyllis, spoke to Andy. He will give you all monies if you agree to sign last year's tax forms. I'm not comfortable with all of this personal stuff in the P&S and I'm not sure it's even legal, but he wants that bit in there. If you agree, please add the two stipulations to the P&S I emailed you. You can handwrite them in. 1. Andy gives Phyllis all monies from the sale of parking space. 2. Phyllis will sign Andy's taxes at closing. Are you still thinking you can come back here for closing? Is there a day that works best? Thanks for the property listing. It's a shock that such a beautiful place costs the same as this tiny parking spot. – Tim

# # #

The first one he had caught only out of the corner of his eye, but the next mouse Tim saw fully, popping out of a burner on his mother's stove and humping across the counter. "Look at that," he said to Miles, who sat next to him on the couch.

"What?"

"There! There's another one! In front of the oven!"

"Huh," Miles said observing it. "Good thing it got out."

"That oven doesn't work. That's probably their living room. But look at them, in broad daylight."

"Okay, let's go," Tim's mother called as she emerged from her bedroom in a skirt of sneezing, leaping dogs.

"You've got a mouse colony living in your oven." Tim pointed toward the kitchen. "They don't even care that we're right here!"

"You look nice, Grandma," Miles said and rocked up off of the low couch to stand.

"This will be the best lunch yet," she told him.

# # #

She ordered her usual two glasses of wine on the way to being seated at the Olive Garden, ordered them right from the hostess. "I'll have a Coke," Miles joined in. Then, when they were seated and had opened their menus, she told Miles, "*Zuppa* is soup," as though he might get stuck on the word and be unable to continue.

"*Zuppa*," he said with an extra-long Z.

She closed her menu again, quickly, knowing her order, and watched her grandson like he was a pleasing and newly made specimen. "Miles, this is such a treat to have you with us."

"He's gonna fill out an application before we leave," Tim announced.

"Good!" she said, clasping her ropy hands over her chest.

Miles clapped the menu closed. "I'm getting steak."

"Look again," Tim told him.

"He can't get a steak?"

"He wants the lasagna," Tim said.

"With an Italian mother?" she cried. "He's got lasagna coming out his eyelids!"

Miles drummed the silverware on his plate and said, "Do you know how to set a mousetrap, Grandma?"

"Well, I'm not as useless as all that."

Tim added, "I'm sure you can set them, Ma, but you won't. You are an animal lover. Last spring, Miles, she found a rabbit's nest in the backyard over there, and she would—do you remember this, Ma?—you put a metal strainer over the rabbits' den so dogs wouldn't be messing with them. She set her pasta strainer upside down over the den, Miles, and she would take it off at night so the mother could tend to them, but otherwise she trapped those bunnies in there all day long."

"I did not."

"Except when you were pulling them out and hugging them."

"The mother only comes back at night. I read that," she said to Miles.

"And what about the night bird?" Tim squawked. He wanted Miles to understand the kind of attention she needed, because it was his plan to put them on to each other. She would require his help, and helping her would force him to figure out how the world worked.

As she craned around in a quest for her wine, Tim jerked his thumb in her direction. "So she tells me she has a bird trapped in her house. Sees it every night, flying around in her bedroom. Middle of the night every night, right Ma?"

"Oh." Miles smiled apologetically at her. "A bat, huh."

"And I'm supposed to be an expert on bats? It was sleeping in the vent fan!" Then she could see the wine coming and let her shoulders fall. "Do you have a girl, Miles?"

To Tim's astonishment, Miles said yes.

"Tell me about her." She locked onto the stem of one of the glasses.

"She's a girl at school. Her name's Marie. She's wicked smart."

"Well, of course she is! She's got you to keep up with."

"Quick, what's she look like?" Tim asked, while his mother

grasped one of Miles's drumming hands and implored, "Is it too late for the homecoming dance?"

"Yeah," Miles said sadly. "That already happened."

"Unless you can dance to pathogens, Miles doesn't dance," Tim said.

"Ha. Pathogenic."

"Miles, the calamari here is a delight," Grandma said like she was talking to a foreign dignitary.

"I don't like calamari. Tastes like fried rubber bands."

"No, it's tender here. I want you to try it when it comes." Then the waitress arrived, and she repeated her statement: "I want my grandson to try the calamari when it comes," as though the waitress should feed it to him.

After they'd all placed their orders, she said, "Has your father told you about my book?"

"I think so," Miles said.

"It's a book about a woman's gifts."

Miles continued nodding.

"Women have a lot to give, and if you know what they are capable of, you will be more likely to welcome their input. I think if you're going to be coupling with Marie, you should read it. And she should, too."

"How's this lunch going for you, Miles?" Tim asked.

"Your father can print it out."

"Nope, I have a Selectric at work."

"Can you email it to me?" Miles asked.

"Show me how, dear, when we get back. I wish I'd had this book when I first coupled. Would've changed my life. What are you doing to your arm, Tim?"

Both she and Miles gave his arm-scratching their full attention. They were a good pair, Tim realized. They were better together than either one was with him, and if Miles got a job here, they could maybe have free lunches long after Tim was gone.

On the ride home, after dropping his mother off, Tim was appreciating God's restraint regarding his transformation. Tim hadn't yet fully prepared his family for success. And let's face it, he realized, it was Miles that he needed to prepare the most. When they entered the Central Artery Tunnel, Tim put a hand on the kid's shoulder and watched him recoil. "I've been thinking I might be able to teach you how to tell a funny story. It's something I'd like to do for you. It's usually something you pick up on your own, but there are some basic tenets."

"Dad, you're driving, like, five miles an hour."

"First, think of a mortifying event in your life. This is key."

"That'd be right now."

"And it has to be your fault entirely, what's happened. And you really build up to the event in the story, give it some high stakes. Then you end with futility." He regripped the steering wheel. "Always end with futility."

After a minute, Miles said, "I actually told Brianne Mason, 'Tis better to have loved and lost than never to have loved at all.'"

"Wait—" Tim slowed again. "Why?"

"She turned me down to go to this one kid's party. Told me she was moving soon."

"Did you actually say *'tis?*"

"Yeah."

"Were you trying to get her to change her mind? What were you doing?"

"Yeah. Change her mind. Didn't work, though, and then she spread it all around the school, and I got called *Dickspeare*, but it's not even a Shakespeare quote, so I win."

"Miles, God, yes!" Tim punched the roof of the truck cab with his fist and then grappled on to the boy's shoulder again and shook him. "That's what I'm talking about! It's absolutely the right direction. It needs a little more buildup when you tell it to people, like why her, and how long you'd pined for her, but you totally get this."

He accelerated, and they shot out of the tunnel and cruised over the majestic Leonard P. Zakim Bunker Hill Bridge. "And if you wouldn't have said *'tis?* Not nearly as funny. Did you end up going to the party?"

"No."

"Miles, you have to go to the party. For fuck's sake. Go to the goddamn party."

# # #

Your dad's getting a package tomorrow. —Blondie

DAVIS

Davis had been starting all of his classes a little late, in case Lindstrom would be attending. He didn't want the man to come in after the *setting of the scene*. He truly hoped that the visit would take place today, in this class, because it was time for his lecture on the evolution of tetrapods, which was directly related to their discussion of the coelacanth, and he would love to hear how the man could explain the tetrapods without evolution.

When the students had all taken seats and had fully arranged their accoutrements and ended their little, immaterial conversations, Davis could see no way to postpone further, so he wrote *tetrapods* on the board. "From an ancient Greek word meaning 'four-footed.' All mammals, amphibians, reptiles, and birds are tetrapods." And here he paused for a reaction, but none came. "Anything strange in what I just said?"

"I don't know of any four-footed birds," one boy said.

Davis nodded and looked around for any other forthcoming insights. Glancing also again at the door, he asked: "Right, and what about snakes? Hardly four-footed." No, this classification comes not from how the animal moves about today, but rather from how its ancestors moved. *Tetrapods* are all of the organisms that evolved from the lobe-finned fishes that began to walk on land four hundred million years ago. Lobe-fins had fin bones homologous to the bones known as the radius, ulna, and humerus in forelimbs, and to the fibula, tibia, and femur in hind limbs. It is from imprints and the fossil record that we determined that the earliest tetrapods were not terrestrial. Their limbs could never have lifted their midsections high enough to clear the ground, and since we don't see belly tracks in the ancient trackways, we must conclude that they walked in shallow water, which buoyed their midsections.

"So fish developed limbs, but what about the ability to breathe out of water? How did that happen? Well, the evidence suggests that the common ancestor of both ray-finned and lobe-finned fishes had lungs *and* gills. Both. In the ray-fins, the lungs evolved into gas-filled swim bladders useful for buoyancy, since a fish is heavier than water. This meant that they didn't have to constantly swim. But the lobe-fins, some of them, continued to breathe atmospheric air and began to colonize shallow brackish waters and even swamps that periodically dried up. They developed bodies better suited to these environments: flatter bodies, with the eyes moving first to the tops of their heads to see above the water, and then, once they ventured onto land, down again and to the front of what became tall, narrow skulls. They developed necks so they could look around for food. And they grew digits to aid in walking, first eight on each limb, then fewer and fewer until arriving at today's common five, and not all terrestrial animals stayed on land. Whales and dolphins, for instance, had a terrestrial ancestor but returned to the water at some point, still breathing atmospheric air.

"So, adaptation. It's what we do. I've described it here on a large biological scale, but we adapt all day long, to each environment we enter. And I like to think, whenever I'm faced with a very difficult situation, that I'm always adaptable to it. Einstein said, 'The measure of intelligence is the ability to change.'

"Now, what I'd like you to do is choose a partner. Just

turn to the person next to you—your peer—and I want you to discuss and write down what other adaptations the first terrestrial tetrapods likely would have made and why. It's a fun exercise. So you make a list of predictions and then, when you read chapter thirteen, you'll find out how close you were."

He watched the students move from stunned silence to chair scrapings and murmurs, a low conversational drone reverberating while he put on his jacket and sat at his desk. He liked to imagine being among the first terrestrial tetrapods, with no predators and an embarrassment of vegetative riches spreading out from the wetlands. It was no wonder they'd exploded in number and variety. There he was, hunting arthropods among the ferns until the wall clock's minute hand clicked home, and he stood and walked out. When he emerged from the building, it was so foggy, he had to make his car beep in order to find it.

He was halfway to the usual diner, his headlights sculpting cones of light, when his phone rang. Scrabbling around in his pockets, he got the phone out and pressed it to his ear. "Yes? Yes?" he said before remembering to press the answer icon.

"Davis Beardsley?" asked a woman with an accent. Was it Aletta?

"Yes?"

"This is Sheila Dunn at Sunnyside Village; I'm afraid I have some bad news. Your aunt Selma passed away this morning."

"Did she? Oh," he sighed.

"Please accept our condolences. You're the only relative she has on record to call." The woman's voice was attractive. He decided she was British.

"Well, I'm her only nephew. She had no kids, and my mom has passed, too—her sister."

"She left good instructions on what she wanted done. She wanted to be cremated."

"Okay."

"What should we do with her things?"

"What are they?"

"Some artwork and knickknacks, I suppose."

"Well I can't come down to look at them, so you can do what you normally do, I guess."

"We could give them to charity."

Why couldn't he remember Aletta's face? He remembered her body, and her lustrous hair bound up in a chignon, but the face was gone. "Are any of them worth anything?"

"I don't know, I'm afraid."

"Can you have an appraiser come in? Is that a lot of trouble?" That was how the Brits liked to talk, he knew, everything in questions rather than demands.

"I think we could do. Let me check. And shall I give you her lawyer's contact information?"

"Yes. Just a moment while I pull over. You know, I didn't even know she was sick. We exchanged Christmas cards, and she didn't say anything about her health. That was a while ago, of course." Why hadn't he ever called his aunt? Is a phone call so difficult? Could Megan be blamed for this, requiring, as she did, such complete focus? Yes, he decided, yes, she could.

# # #

Even in the dark, Davis could tell that Jenny was nervous with him there in her classroom, sitting in the back on the diorama-laden table. Her voice was thin and high as she described Central Asia using the first of geography's five themes: *Location*. A colored political map filled the big whiteboard once she had launched her presentation. She was using some futuristic application that didn't move from slide to slide but rather worked off a big concept map from which she zoomed in on one section at a time by tapping on the relevant spot and then zoomed away when she tapped elsewhere.

He'd come to tell her about the money he was getting from his aunt, but he'd been locked out of the school building and forced to ring a buzzer and then made to give his driver's license to a woman in the office, who was impatiently paused from some page-counting task. The Pope, hanging above the counter, kindly watched over the driver's license transaction. Davis wondered if other husbands were better known here and were simply beckoned in with a droll comment. He thought he should attempt some light banter: "Good day to be a bank robber." But she simply slid his Visitor sticker across the desk and deepened the frown.

The hall decorations spoke of a schoolwide study of Asia: "Check Out China!" read one banner beneath paper Chinese lanterns dangling from the ceiling. On the wall were illustrations of something called a dragon dance and a photo of a giant panda (past cryptid).

"This region is sometimes called the *stans* because all of the countries share that suffix," Jenny told her students, who were surprisingly still and quiet for fifth graders. Their desks were arranged in groups of four, proving that even Jenny subscribed to the notion of peer study. In the dim room, the many backpacks slung over chairs put Davis in mind of clinging squid.

"Stan means "homeland," so Uzbekistan is the homeland of the Uzbeks. Afghanistan is the homeland of Afghans." She kept her focus on the whiteboard, rarely looking back, probably so as to block Davis out of her mind. Lecturing was his sphere; it was *Davis-stan*. Next screen: *Place, Physical Characteristics* was the heading, and under it was a physical map. "Look at my map here. What do you see, Liam? What's this in the southeast?" She rubbed a palm over the rugged terrain. "Mountains," the boy quickly stated, clearly her Michael Harren (Davis's most ardent crypto-acolyte). "And what about the white areas here?" She flapped her hand near the areas of highest elevation. "It's snow," said a girl. Davis pictured a yeti paradise of jagged crystal peaks. "We learned about glaciers last week," Jenny said. "Could these be glaciers?" She peered closely at the image, the reflected light deepening the fissures around her mouth. In normal lighting conditions, she was still lovely, he thought, her face a little plumper, but still dear.

"These are some of the highest mountains in the world," she told them, pointing generally at the Pamir and the Hindu Kush. "They are part of the Himalayas, like in China and Tibet." Davis smiled at his shoes. They were certainly not the Himalayas, but separate ranges entirely.

With a touch, the map shrank away and a dazzling photo zoomed in, a pile of candy-colored gems with the heading *Human-Environment Interaction.*

Davis could understand that screen-based learning was essential for today's youth, but when had Jenny become a technology wizard?

"That's right, Jamal, gems are minerals," she said. "And what is the main difficulty in getting to those minerals right now in a place like Afghanistan?" Another image swooped onto the screen, a seemingly infinite vista with an armed American soldier in the center, shown from behind as he surveyed the valley.

"You can get really *killed*," a boy said.

"That's an AK-forty-seven," shouted a peer.

"Is it?" Jenny asked, turning toward the child with interest. She was really a lovely person, wanting to encourage. How often had she asked just such a question of Davis when he had made some observation. She then stepped in front of the physical map on the whiteboard and opened her hands over

the vast steppes of Central Asia, as though they'd just popped
out of a hat.

TIM

He'd seen it when he'd driven up to Sunny Straub's house the last time, that same stupid sign from years ago, now disintegrating, barely legible on the big plate-glass window: NORTH SHORE PIANO, WHERE IT'S ALL BLACK AND WHITE. He wondered if Chip deCarlo still worked there. Slowing the truck, he hunted for his beach ball silhouette. Tim and his crew used to move their pianos. This was back when parents bought pianos automatically, like they did encyclopedias. There was constant work then. But it's a younger man's game, piano-hauling. A baby grand starts at five hundred pounds, with a full concert grand going up to thirteen hundred, the weight of a dairy cow. You have to understand balance and inertia to move these giants. You have to wrap them like an egg you're sending off the Empire State Building. And you work for people who don't believe that you and your red-nosed crew can do the job, who grip their cheeks when you tip their treasure onto the dolly and who breathe onto your back as you wheel it over the threshold. Still, he'd done it for years, until he crushed his knees.

"Has someone determined that this is a growth industry?" deCarlo now asked him, examining Tim's new piano-tuning-business card from behind the glass counter where the metronomes were displayed. "I promise you, whatever you charge, I can get a blind guy to do it for less." Why hadn't Tim thought about all of the blind tuners? It was like a cartel. "Two other guys came in just last week. Took some online class. I'm like, are you kidding me with this?"

"Online? Jesus. No, I just thought I'd pop in, say hello," Tim said, repeating his opening line. "I'm kind of surprised you're still open."

"Now till Christmas it's busy." The guy breathed loudly on the intake. "You ever get in with an orchestra?"

"No," Tim said.

"I didn't figure."

"Yeah, no."

"Well, I do need movers. I got a big mama needs to go out this Friday."

Tim looked like he was still waiting for the guy to finish talking. Then he shoved his hands into his anorak pockets and said he'd take a look at where the piano needed to go and see if his old crew was still around. Rusty would still need money when he came into being, and he'd had to put his father-in-law's twenty-five K into their checking, where Mona could see it.

Then he took his time getting back to work, since he'd claimed he was at the dentist.

# # #

Miles was chunking out a few stray chords on his keyboard when Tim opened his bedroom door after work.

"What?" the kid said, collapsing into himself.

"Let's take a trip. C'mon."

"Where?"

"To the moon. C'mon, zip up your pants, let's go."

Miles came out of the house ten minutes later, his hoodie up against the rain, and folded himself into the truck. "Seriously, Dad, where're we going?"

"To see a man about a piano," Tim said. "I thought it'd be good for you to see the outside."

"Ha."

"We're going to see how much of a bitch it will be to move a piano."

"Thought you weren't doing that anymore."

"Just because you declare things doesn't mean they can be so."

"Yeah."

After pulling onto the street, Tim did a double take on Miles's cystic face. "God, your face looks like a hundred-wasp attack. Does it hurt?"

"Huh? No. Not really."

"There's gotta be something you can take, some pill."

"Mum's looking into it."

"Saturday we go to a machine-gun range in New Hampshire."

"No," Miles reverently whispered, checking Tim's expression.

"They have an AK-forty-seven."

Miles pounded his knees. "Ahh! I am literally pooping my pants right now. I wonder if I can even handle a machine gun."

"'Course you can, but listen, before then, I could use some aiming practice on one of your games. I don't wanna waste my money."

"Hells, yeah. I have the best weapons," the boy told him. Then after a minute, he screamed, "This is awesome! I mean, like, I am ripping my tits off!" He grabbed handfuls of his shirt and looked up, grinning, to acknowledge a benevolent God.

#

The house for the piano delivery was a yellow neo-Victorian, with an elaborate roof design, including two Chinese hats over the cylindrical sections, and dormers galore. The load-in looked easy enough—a few steps up from the sidewalk onto the porch and then right into the living room. Two children were clamped onto their mother in the doorway. People bought pianos for their kids because the piano came with an imagined future for the child as a charming adult surrounded by sophisticates. "You're getting a piano!" Tim exclaimed to the frightened boys. "Do you know how special that is?" He told the woman he'd deliver it at six-thirty on Friday. "And not for me, but my guys usually get tipped," he said. "It's work you can only do for so long before having your spine fused."

# # #

"Now we're going to the AOH," he told Miles when he was back in the truck cab. Tim had arranged to meet his old crew at the Ancient Order of Hibernians, although he thought he could probably just show up there any evening and find them.

As they drove alongside a lake with enormous houses across the road, Miles asked, "Why *did* you pick our house?"

"Screw you, Miles. You know why? It was one of only two houses in the whole metro area that we could afford, and the realtor said there'd be condos going in all around us—lofts for young professionals, a Starbucks. He said our house would explode in value."

"That's fucked up."

When they got onto the highway, Tim said, "Hey, what's the song that's, like—" He sang in falsetto, "When I grow up, I'll be stable. When I grow up, I'll turn the tables."

"Really?" Miles asked. "Where'd you hear that?"

"Do you know it, or don't you?"

"There's an app that tells you what a song is if it hears it."

"You got it? Turn it on." Once Miles had his phone positioned, Tim sang the chorus again, tapping a beat on the steering wheel.

Then Miles studied the screen. "No, I guess it has to be the actual band playing. I can look up the words, though."

Tim shook his head. "God, we're dumbbells, aren't we?"

The rain had turned heavy again. "Why do you want to know this song?" Miles asked.

"I don't know." Tim got into the leftmost lane and floored it. "It's the music for my ideal self." He found that he was looking forward to seeing the guys. "You remember Finn, Sandy, and Hal? My old crew? Bunch of gorillas. Once we took a full concert grand up the stairs of the statehouse like it was a box spring. You know the statehouse stairs?"

"Garbage." Miles grinned at him.

"Huh?"

"That's the band name, Garbage."

# # #

Tim had to whip water from his face with his hands before he could make out where the guys were sitting. "Hang out at the bar and order a Coke," he told Miles.

"This'd be a great day to move a piano," he shouted as he approached the old goons in the booth. Jesus, they looked horrible! Finn could barely lift his hand in greeting. He'd lost all color, and one end of his unbuckled belt had flopped down over his thigh. Sandy looked like he'd eaten himself. And Hal was unshaven and glassy-eyed, nervously sliding the salt and pepper shakers around like in a shell game. "You guys look like shit!"

"So don't you," Finn rasped. "Buy us a round, will ya?"

"What the hell happened to you guys? You couldn't move

a girl's tea set!'"

"Screw you." Finn flipped him off.

Sandy pleaded, "You're hurtin' his feelin's, Timmy."

"Well, shit, guys, I can't hire *you*. What're you doing for work?"

"Sandy's bartending over at the Office," Hal said to the shakers.

"Free drinks," said Finn.

"That explains it." Tim waved them off and went to the bar to get four beers. He studied himself in the mirror behind the bottles while the bartender poured. A little jowly, but his hair looked healthy, still ablaze. When he returned, he slid in next to Hal and reviewed their mottled faces, their lopsided postures. "Is this it, guys? Is this the end of your lives?"

"You don't look like Adonis, Tim," Sandy assessed him over the top of his glasses.

"Yet. I'm working on it. You know what our big problem is? Mostly? Testosterone. You've lost a lot of your natural testosterone."

"You ever hear about the woman whose doctor prescribed her testosterone?" Sandy asked. "She told him it was helping her condition, but she was starting to grow hair in new places. 'Well, the benefits outweigh the side effects,' he told her, 'and a little hair won't hurt you. Where's it growing?' And she looks at him and says, 'On my balls!'"

"Ha! Good one," said Finn.

"You know, *I'm* taking testosterone," Tim told them. "It clears your head, revs it all up again."

"Your insurance pay for that?" Sandy had something white and crusty around his lips.

"Yep, well, with a copay."

"Don't let your wife accidently come in contact, she'll grow more than balls, that Mona. She'll have herself a decent-size willy." Hal held a salt shaker horizontal and jiggled it to stand in for the wife's new member.

"Screw you. You know why I wanted it? I want to look ahead in my life and see something coming that I actually welcome. I want to be delighted to get out of bed."

"I'm delighted to get out of bed 'cause my wife's still in it!" Finn grinned around the table.

"See? See what we joke about? It's pathetic! I'm turning back the clock. I ran a mile this morning. Have any of you ever run a mile?"

"Oh, sure, I have," said Finn.

"When did you ever run a mile?"

"I was just gonna make another wife joke."

"Well, don't! Take yourself seriously!"

"You know, *you* can't move a piano anymore either, Tim," Sandy said, again with the over-glasses appraisal.

"Not this instant, but soon I can."

"Well, don't talk about us."

"Look, I'm just at the beginning, but I'm at least trying. You guys make me realize why all this is so important."

"How's Miles doin'?" Finn nodded over to the boy.

"Miles is—I don't know, Miles is Miles. He has no drive. He's not a leader."

"Jesus, Tim, why does everyone have to be all gung ho?"

"I got an answer for you: one life. That's it! Some guys our age are with a beautiful young woman down in Mexico or someplace. They've still got it. The only real impediments to having a truly wonderful life are fear and laziness." He followed Finn's eyes over to Miles, who had his head buried in his arms on the bar top. "I'll have to find another crew for Friday."

"Hell, yeah," Hal said. "Them days are over."

# # #

On the way home, Tim asked Miles, "You interested in hanging out with George and a bunch of his friends doing good works for the town?"

Miles didn't look up from his phone. "I don't understand the question."

"George is worried about you."

"What's his deal? Why's he always trying to hang around after his lesson?"

"Why do you think?"

"Huh? I don't know. Lonely, I guess."

"He's okay to you, though? He hasn't done anything creepy or anything?"

"No. But I'd rather work at the Olive Garden. And that's not saying much. Look, I got Grandma's book." He held up his phone.

"Delete it! I mean it, Miles. She should never have sent that to you. It's her very personal life."

"I'm reading it." The boy pressed himself against the passenger door, as far away as he could get from Tim, and opened the file.

# # #

Almost texting time. Tim had his cell on the kitchen table, next to the curling and dog-eared *Into the Lion's Mouth*. Tim's hero from that book, the sniper—he also sometimes felt deflated, defeated. Tim remembered one spot he had underlined and he looked for it again.

I often felt the outsider. The Ascars routinely went AWOL for a time and even when there, they were on their cells or smoking hash. The Americans weren't much better, with their video games and lack of discipline. It was like we were making a movie about war, with breaks between takes.

Rusty texted Blondie that the thing he missed most over there was a sandwich. A real sandwich with thick bread and mayo squirting out the sides. She wrote that she'd make him one every day in Mexico. Oh, how she loved the look of that property listing he'd sent her! They could run around in shorts and bare feet. They could position their bed to watch the sunset. She was going to start saving the money from her dog-walking business.

I got a dog you can walk.
Says the lonely creep.

I love wiener dogs. So cute.

Hell, no, Great Dane.

Tim popped another one of Blondie's brownies into his mouth. He would grind the rest down in the disposal before Mona could see them. He'd told his wife he was expecting tuning tools from someone on eBay, so the package had not been a big item of interest.

How's Ur friend in hospital?

Don't know. Haven't heard. Cn you resend the video? So beautiful. Crushed me.

Sure!!!! Sending anything you want!

Love Garbage. My favorite.

When Tim heard the front door open and keys landing on the credenza, he came out from the kitchen. "I leave enough space for you?" he asked.

"Yes, very nice," Vinnie said.

"Good, you wanna make a little money? I have a piano-moving job."

"Dear God, a piano?"

"It's easy with enough guys. Two hours, tops, this Friday evening, and I can pay you a hundred."

"Fine. Maybe it'll be my new profession. Today a customer said to me, 'How can you not know if the cheesecake is gluten-free?' She kept saying, 'This is the Cheesecake Factory! This is the Cheesecake Factory!' like I don't fucking know where I am? I said, 'Okay, so what will happen, lady? Are you gonna die? Are you gonna croak from a gluten? Tim, what am I now, a chemist? Should I know all of the properties of all of the world's food items, for fuck sake?'"

"Why are you back there? What happened to *Temptation's Fate* and all that?"

"Well, I used to know a man who came into the restaurant all the time and I think he is the one I am supposed to be with. So at first I was just eating there as a customer every day, but I couldn't afford to do that. Anyway, now he's not coming in. Which I guess I shoulda known. It was a long time ago." He ran the zipper down and up his jacket a few times before pulling out of it in frustration.

"Don't you know anything about him? Where he works?"

"We didn't talk a lot." He took a hanger out of the front closet and fitted it into the shoulders of the jacket. Tim watched him bite down on the hanger's hook, zip up the garment, and then smooth it down with his hands before clearing a large space into which to put it.

"Can you get Miles a job there?" They both looked over at the boy, who was moving his lips in and out while staring at the video game.

"Miles!" Tim shouted, and the kid looked at them out of the corner of his eye.

"Yeah?"

"Tonight's the night I play your game."

# # #

When Tim sat cross-legged next to his son, he felt powerful for the first time in a long time. He could feel his thigh muscles straining against his jeans. Even his hands on the controller appeared veiny and strong. The TRT's results were worth the roar in his ears.

"I thought we were going to do Destiny," Tim said, seeing a cratered moonscape on the screen.

"Destiny's dead. Destiny blows compared to Red Horizon. Want to create your own avatar or play as me?"

"You got decent weapons?"

"Yeah. Duh. What you see here, this is my outpost."

"Creepy."

"Everything's made from refuse left by the creatures who used to live here. We don't know much about them yet, but they appear to all be dead or they left. That's my dog, Simba. He notices things. That's what he's good for. Here's my room."

"What's the sign say?"

"Nice, right? I love the blue swoop on the bottom. Found it in a junk pile. We don't know how to translate all of their symbols, but the second character means female. There's a document with all known translations. I made this whole structure we're in right now. Took me three weeks, mostly just to get enough tin. And see those big fans up there? Those operate on a pulley system."

"That's cool."

"I didn't have enough electrical wiring, so only the first one is electrified. Then it powers the rest. See the bands?"

"Sure."

"The rubber was hard to source. That's Marie there."

"So Marie's fake."

"No, that's her avatar."

"Who are you fighting?"

"Bots. They can repair themselves and build more of themselves and shit. They may have been the demise of their creators."

"I want to shoot them, Miles."

"Okay, let's wake Marie and head out. Marie's the fifth-top destroyer in this game."

Outside the settlement, the road passed the rubble and ruins of places similar to the bombed-out war zones Tim saw on television. They had no transportation, so they kept snug to walls wherever possible. The bots moved fluidly, like living creatures, and shot projectiles right out of their limbs. Marie saved Tim on several occasions, and Tim saved her once, he thought. The bots began reattaching their pieces as soon as they were hit, making the whole exercise, the whole game, futile. Still, Tim found that his reflexes were lightning-quick. It was clear he was as ready as he'd ever be.

DAVIS

When Davis awoke again at five a.m., he realized that his wife had been out of bed for hours. He descended the stairs, listening for her. From the direction of the kitchen he heard the light raining of her fingers on a keyboard.

"Why are you up so early?" he asked.

She shook her head. "Couldn't sleep. Up since three."

"Are you shopping?" He tried to make out what was on her computer screen as he crossed to the refrigerator.

"Looking up some possible vacation spots. Wouldn't it be nice to go someplace warm this winter, now that we can afford it?"

The day before, Davis had announced that he'd inherited fifty-nine thousand dollars from his aunt. He said ten thousand of that could go to helping Megan move and getting her set up in California. He'd been grateful that Jenny hadn't suggested other purchases, because he thought they might need the rest of the money to see him through a period of unemployment.

He took a gallon of milk from the fridge. "Let's not book anything yet. Wait till I hear about tenure. Why couldn't you sleep?"

"Nerves or something."

"You must have picked up on my anxiety."

"It can be my own anxiety, I think."

"Why? The kids? I thought the Good Behavior Game had solved all your problems." Jenny was employing a behavior-management program in her classroom, which put kids into teams, and any individual's bad behavior counted as points against his or her team, possibly preventing them all from winning a prize.

"The kids are fine," she sighed.

"Well, I get being frustrated with the administration. Now we're in the same boat. I actually think Lindstrom has turned the whole group against me. Had my vote come up last year, I'd be in." He selected a box of corn flakes from a cabinet and shook some into his blue bowl.

"I don't know about that. We haven't been invited to their parties in quite a few years."

"Yeah, but that's Megan. That's from her kicking Brian's son's teeth out. And I know we haven't been invited to the adults-only parties either, but it's still the shock of the teeth thing, I think." He set the milk back down without pouring it onto his cereal and opened his laptop as he sat on a stool. More pronouncements from Pope Francis in the news. "Did you hear the Pope says evolution's A-OK? The Big Bang actually happened? Now what will you tell the kids?"

Jenny had always followed her conservative parish priest as far as what science "facts" to teach. Now Davis knew she was worried she'd have to tell the children that she'd made some mistakes. She shut off the desktop computer and rose, already dressed for work.

"You look nice," Davis said. She basically wore the same five outfits every week due to their limited finances, but her Tuesday skirt never failed to move him, the way it hugged her hips.

"You always say that when I wear this skirt."

"I'll stop immediately," he said, returning to the news.

# # #

Davis had decided to do the interview in his office at the college. He did a little rearranging in there so that the photograph hanging directly behind him was the big one of the okapi—another wonderful cryptid, a relative of the giraffe, with zebra-striped legs. Students began gathering in the hall when they saw the lights and the video camera being set up. A production assistant for the news program stood in the doorway and shushed all passers-by just before they began shooting, since closing the door would have made the room a sauna.

The newsman was the one from the six-o'clock news, and this made Davis so nervous he couldn't lower his eyebrows. Then he forgot to listen to the actual question at the end of the intro, so he simply began speaking: "Let's start with my area of specialty as a cryptozoologist. The term brings together three Greek words: *kryptos*, which means hidden; *zoon*, which means animal, and *logos*, which means discourse. So it's the study of hidden animals. And when we think—"

"Hang on a second," the cameraman said. "What's that? Somebody crying?"

They all listened.

"Yes, that's someone in Dr. Lindstrom's office next door," Davis said. It sounded like Megan.

"Can we knock on the wall?" the newsman asked Davis. "Do you mind?"

"I think she'll stop soon," Davis said. And in a matter of a few seconds, she did. Likely some frustration over a grade, he figured.

"Okay, let's start again, Professor. Tell us about your hypothesis."

"Well, in the fieldwork of cryptozoology, we rely heavily on eyewitness accounts, and there were several descriptions by people who had seen the Glenwood animal that just weren't consistent with any dog. The way it moved. The sounds it made." Davis then cleared his throat and made a sort of growling moo that went up in pitch at the end. Then he bared his teeth and did some high chitter-chatter. "And then I saw a photo of an animal with standing rounded ears"—he balled up his hands and placed them on his head—"set fairly wide apart, like so. And then that bone-crushing jaw"—he shook his head in wonder—"it made me recall the very real presence of hyenas in the North American fossil record, and I had to come to that conclusion."

"I think she started up again in the middle of that," the sound recordist said.

Yes, he'd heard it, the sobbing. Davis gripped the edge of his desk and felt ready to hurl it over and march into Lindstrom's office to see what the situation was.

"Let's get this one more time, Professor," the newscaster said. "And I loved the animal sounds. Be sure to do those again. Then I'm going to ask you about the test results, and don't forget to mention that you'll give us an exclusive when they come in."

"Next Thursday."

"Right. Build up some anticipation." The anchorman watched the camera operator, and when he got a nod, he tipped his hand toward Davis. Action.

# # #

Lindstrom's office was open and empty when Davis tore over there after the last video take. He was mortified that he had waited as long as he had. He didn't care if Lindstrom came in while he was looking about for evidence—something having fallen between the couch cushions, perhaps. He tipped the trash can to have a look at the debris. Nothing of Megan's there. No notes from one to the other. No sweet cards left hastily on the desk. What was there, front and center, was the fat, embossed leather notebook that the man lugged around and wrote in during meetings. He was a great one for notating during any conversation. Davis had been surprised when he hadn't brought it out at dinner. He lightly flipped the cover open. And then he turned the first page, and he continued to flip the pages and found on each mere scribbles. Tornado swirls. Triangles. The guy also favored horses' heads. Here on one page was the date of the recent meeting to fund lab equipment requests (at which Davis gave an impassioned argument about the vital place of video and audio recording devices in the modern application of the scientific method). On that date was drawn a full side view of a Shetland pony. There wasn't an English word anywhere in the whole pound of paper. The man was a simpleton. It made complete sense in light of Davis's experiences with university selection processes.

He mentally excoriated himself on his way across campus. He had cared more about his own fame than his daughter's distress. His mood was beyond sour, then, upon arriving at the college's Crypto Club meeting in the newly designed Center for Student Innovation (an oxymoron). The crypto guys—and they were always all guys—were huddled around a laptop in the conference room with its see-through garage door still open to the hallway. (An ironic tip of the hat to the kinds of innovators who actually *dropped out* of school.)

Globsters had been scrawled and underlined at the top of the whiteboard. Right, he remembered, today was Globsters Day; no wonder they were all so titillated.

"Oh, globsters," he said. "What have you got on the screen there?"

Michael Harren, Davis's primary acolyte, whipped oily

packets of hair out of his eyes and slid his laptop slowly toward Davis like presenting proof of a murder. Globsters were always the most frightening of cryptids, mysterious creatures having washed ashore—blobs with teeth or long Nessie-like necks. "This one's no decomposed whale or basking shark," Michael instructed Davis. On the screen was a plump, four-legged creature with the skin of a spit-roasted pig, lying on its side.

"The Montauk monster," Davis said, nodding cursorily. "What do you see there?"

"Well, a clear beak, for one. Bird's head on a mammal's body," Michael announced.

Davis put two fingers over one of his own eyelids and rubbed at the headache beneath it. "You have one photo, one angle. Nothing for size reference there. Is it the size of a mouse or a dog, Michael? What looks like a beak may be exposed cartilage. Decomposition is transformative, guys." The boys looked insulted. Several, together, pulled the laptop back to face them. Had he been looking at a different screen? "This, I'm here to tell you"—Davis snapped a fingernail against the back of the laptop—"is a drowned raccoon." He unstacked the pizza boxes, moved them all so they were side by side and continued: "Evidence: long tail. Evidence: fingers. You see the fingers there? Evidence: long legs, too long for anything in the martin genus." He pulled out a pepperoni slice and took a bite. While chewing, he added, "That's no monster, guys. The only monsters here are us."

# # #

"No, she seemed fine." Jenny looked up at Davis, startled at his question. "She sat right at this table and had a slice of pie, and she seemed just fine." Jenny had been cutting out circles of colored construction paper at the kitchen table and slowly laid her scissors down.

"Okay, but it was definitely her crying. You know it's easily identifiable."

"She was probably late turning in an assignment."

He pulled out the chair next to hers. "I wonder. I really do. Lindstrom is an odd character. I don't think he makes good decisions. He's up here in Maine; he's lonely." He put a hand on her abandoned scissors. "Did she ask you for the IUD?"

"Yes."

"Well, that's something, see? I think we should confront her, and if she admits that he's come onto her, I think we should believe it this time."

"You want to ruin another man's life? Graeme Stoltz ended up divorced. For nothing!" She let her hands flop onto her lap.

"Well, Lindstrom isn't married, so that won't be an issue. And I think, other than taking the change jar, which regular kids even do, Megan has been relatively normal for a little while now. So we should give her the benefit of the doubt." Then he stood like he'd been given an order and walked into the hall to call up the stairs to Megan.

An ominous silence, until finally she answered with an annoyed "What?"

"Just come down, we want to talk to you."

"What?" she asked again as she slumped into the chair beside her mother.

Davis walked to the opposite side of the table and leaned straight-armed against it, "I believe I heard you crying in Dr. Lindstrom's office today. Is that right, honey?"

"No."

"Honey, I know your crying when I hear it."

"It wasn't me!"

"Were you in his office today?"

"No!"

"Let me start this a different way." He found he couldn't look at her and continue, so he looked at the floor and cupped his cheeks and paced a small circle while he put the idea forward. "We're concerned that Dr. Lindstrom may be taking advantage of your affection for him. And if that's the case, then as an authority figure in your life, as your teacher, he is doing something he should never do. And I want you to know that we would believe you if you said he was doing something inappropriate. We would absolutely believe you this time."

"Eric's not the problem." She looked defiant.

"But someone is the problem?" Jenny asked.

"Someone in this room is the problem, but I'm not going to talk about it." She stood and returned to the stairs.

"Megan!" Davis called.

"I'm not talking about it!" And up she flew.

"What was that about, Davis?"

"Who knows?"

"I think we need to talk with Dr. Peggy."

"I guess so."

"Me and Megan. I think just Megan and I should call her."

"Really?"

Jenny was red-faced. "She's not going to talk about anything...sexual. Not with you there."

"All right, but do it soon." Davis retreated to his den, taking the tiny *Ebu gogo* skull from the hall table with him. He shared a look with her as he rocked in his desk chair. He had something in common with this hobbit lady, he knew. He could feel his time also running out.

TIM

Tim entered through the mail room with the intention of asking Mike if he wanted to make a hundred bucks for a couple hours' work on Friday evening.

"Really? Move a piano?" The guy drew the last word out, then made a sour face.

"Yeah, but there's four guys. Piece of cake."

"I dunno, man. I mean, I guess? You're lucky I don't have mah-jongg," Mike said, wagging a paint stick at him from behind the shipping desk. "Hey, you finished *Into the Lion's Mouth?*"

"Oh, God, yes. Twice."

"Okay, that Taliban guy who put an AK in our Marine's face while he was trying to save his friend? And he acted like he was gonna surrender and held one hand up." Mike held the paint stick in the air. "And then with the other hand, he reached down and pulled the trigger on his launcher, shot a grenade straight into the guy's chest, and it blew him—*poom!*—straight backwards. *POOM!*" Mike staggered.

"Then, when the grenade didn't explode, he smashed the guy's face in with a rock."

"Complete devastation." Mike beamed. "That's what I'm talking about."

Then, what the heck, Tim decided to ask Mike out for a beer after work, to try cultivating a friendship with him. They could talk about Marine stuff, and Tim had been dreaming about a long string of beers like he hadn't had in a while.

"What about tonight? You got mah-jongg tonight, or you want a beer?"

"I could use a beer," Mike said. "You know, I'm serious about the mah-jongg thing. I'm very competitive."

# # #

On his way to The Publisher's office, Tim saw the graphic designer, Jan Middleton, emerge from the restroom. He hated to run into Jan because she could never do a simple greeting. She imposed herself. She jammed herself into your earhole possibly forever.

"I'm so depressed about Angela," she said, zombie hands out and threatening to hook him. "I was telling my husband about how she was always so friendly. One example—and I've got a million—but one example is that she used to eat these coffee candies I have in a bowl—and if you haven't tried them, you should stop by. Seriously, take a handful. I'm sure Angela would tell you all about them; God, she loved those candies. You have to order them on Amazon. 'Course one bag was just under the price for the free shipping. That's how they do it. Hello! Jeez, you'd make about a million bucks selling them over the counter at someplace like Walgreens. Angela said whoever was marketing those candies should have been shot. Because you couldn't walk in and get them anywhere! So, then last Christmas…"

Tim imagined himself on an Afghanistan trail, reaching back for a rock, raising it high, and smashing it down on the clattering mouth.

"Angela said she would send me an entire box of them. That's five or so bags! I guess because she felt so guilty always eating them, but I didn't blame her. They were heaven! My husband found them originally—so then, you know, he starts in on me: 'Did Angela replace the candies? Did you ask her? Did you ask her? Did you ask her?'"

"Sorry, Jan, hot memo here." Tim held up his envelope.

"Oh, yes! Go on! Here I am, talking about coffee candy, for God's sake! Can you believe it? Move along, sir! Move along." Then she saluted him as he tripped over himself in his haste.

Tim handed Rita the envelope with both hands. "This was in Angela's office, her sales notebook. I know The Publisher wants it. Tell her everyone's seen it and we're all impressed with Angela's last month's sales."

She looked up at him sympathetically. "I see you think I take orders from anyone."

Jesus, he could kill them all today. "You can have a different life, you know," he told her. "Just write it down, what you want. And then don't give up on it. That's where people go wrong."

She opened her drawer and slipped her hand in for a pad. "Is Clooney with an *e-y* or just a *y?*"

# # #

Tim carried the first mugs to the table with the same tight smile he'd always had with Emily when they used to come here of a Friday night, a smile he couldn't rein in.

Mike met his grin and kicked out the other stool for him.

This bar, Tip Top Taps, had replaced the Brown Street Tavern, which always featured a line of old regulars at the bar, most keeping their jackets or big coats on in winter to falsely signal that they couldn't stay, that they had things to do. Men bought each other drinks, claiming rounds with a finger raised. Now the place was a brew pub, and there was real food, but it was too clean, too bright. They had kids' booster seats stacked up in a corner. It was like a bar at Disneyland. Children negated the main purposes of a bar, like this boy running around their table with his boots untied, snotty face. He would occasionally stop running to grab the edge of their table and wiggle it, forcing the men to keep ahold of their beers. Tim gave an irritated look around the place, trying to share his feelings with the boy's parent.

"I bet that Marine sniper would be great to have a beer with," Mike said. "There are probably a lot of stories he couldn't tell the guy who wrote the book."

With one more shuddering of the table, Tim snatched the kid's elbow and told him to knock it off. This physical contact sucked the child's mother over, and she guided the boy away like a collie, then pointed Tim out to her girlfriends at the bar.

"Okay, I got a story for you," Tim said, as Mike waved at the women. "I helped this rich woman assess a piano, the most ornate grand I've ever seen and with a brand name like an old Russian satellite: Klopotek."

"Hot woman?"

"No, no! An old woman my wife knows."

"Well, they can still be hot. I knew this old lady—"

"Wait, so she buys this thing, and it isn't cheap, and she has it delivered to her big federal mansion up in Beverly Farms. Then she—"

"I bought a snowblower from a guy up there. Didn't run worth shit. Don't buy from rich people."

"Yeah, so then she has me come over to tune the monster, and, well, see, I'm taking these online tuning classes from this pulpy albino guy who looks like he crawled out of a dead cow. And I have almost finished the course, but this is my first real job, so I go over there to tune this barge, and she comes to the door with a little dog in her arms, one of those dogs that if you shaved it, it would be a lizard." He shimmied back onto the stool for the long haul. "She's got paintings of this dog all over, like an art museum from a very bad dream. Thankfully, she leaves the house before I start working. Sets my check on a table. Well, every time I strike a key—"

"Shari Levine, at my mah-jongg. Fifty-seven years old and tits straight out, like on a shelf." He cupped the air.

"No, so every time I strike a key, her little dog comes running over and nips me with her needle teeth. Right in the ankle."

"What'd you do, kill the little fucker?"

Tim narrowed his eyes. "Well, yeah."

"What I'd'a done. We getting sandwiches?"

"I'm not getting a sandwich, no." Tim was angry about the ruination of his great story. It was as though a meal he'd longed for and that was sitting right in front of him had been whisked away before he'd gotten in a single bite.

"Hey, what's happening with Tall Blonde Babe?"

Tim softened. "She's changed my life."

"How so?"

"Blondie's the only one who sees me. She knows what I'm capable of."

"Blondie. That her real name? What if she had a name like Sophia?" He ran his hand along an imagined marquee.

Tim wasn't listening. "It's hard to explain, but you know what? You should text with her. She knows who you are on my fire team."

"I'm a sergeant."

"Right, our Humvee driver. In fact, she's been asking to talk to some of the other guys, so you'd be helping me out. Here's her number." Tim showed him his phone screen.

Mike keyed the number into his contacts. "That was a badass driver in that book, huh? Taking the gunner back in, under fire, over and over again?"

"You would do that."

Mike looked up. "I absolutely would."

"Blondie's living in a very controlling environment."

"She of age?"

"Eighteen. But she doesn't seem eighteen at all when she writes. She was writing the other day about how she thinks the opposite of bravery is conformity. Right? And it is! Does that sound like something a kid would say?"

"It does not."

"No. And she sent me brownies with a little love note."

"Awww. Wait, to Afghanistan?"

"In care of my father, who's me, but she knows me as Rusty."

"You think that's a good idea? At your house?"

"I get packages all the time—tuning tools, piano parts that I buy used. No big deal."

"I hope not. Maybe your wife could smell the brownies. And you didn't share the brownies with your team? I'm gonna tell."

"Had to get rid of them."

"What're you gonna send *her*, rocks?"

"I thought I might get a bullet engraved with our names."

Mike laughed a repeated *sh* into his fist. "What does she think you look like?"

"I look like me, at twenty-one. I'm myself."

"At twenty-one."

"Just my face."

"That's good. You pudgy back then?"

"No."

"That's good. Getting any cybersex?"

"A little. I don't have much time alone. We talked on the phone last night. She likes to put her mouth over my ear and pant."

"Oh, boy!"

"I've always loved that."

"Jeez, who wouldn't?"

"I didn't call her to have phone sex, I wanted to tell her a story. That's my thing, not that you would know. I can walk into any bar with no money and drink all night, that's how good I am."

"You tell her the dead dog story? That's kind of a downer."

"She's got a rough life." Tim drew with his wet finger on the table and pictured the Snapchat photos she'd sent of her family's kitchen. "She feels she needs to leave her family. It's really a bad situation—I mean, her dad's a complete freak. She showed me pictures of this room full of rules on signs that she has to obey." Tim took a long drink and set the mug down. "'Sometimes it takes more strength to let go than to hang on to someone.' That's what she said. Does that sound like an eighteen-year-old?"

"Well, you better get the strength to let go pretty soon, Tim, 'cause you are married."

"Like hell, I am," Tim spat back at him. "And I'm never gonna *be* married. That's a big mistake."

"Well, I'll agree with you there," Mike said slowly. Then he downed the rest of his pint and switched to an upbeat voice. "I will text her as your buddy and tell her how fucking awesome you are."

Tim leaned over the table toward him. "We're stationed at Outpost Monti, like in the book. Every day we either train the Askars how to shoot or we go out in a convoy."

"I'll tell her you have a big dick."

"She already knows. I'm going to text her right now about you."

Tim stood to pull his phone out and then went around to Mike's side so he could see the text.

Hon, Mike our driver wants to meet you. He saves our butts every day and is the bravest of the team, next to me ☺

"Next to *you*?" Mike elbowed him.

"Write something." Tim proudly slid his cell over and watched Mike type.

Hi, Blondie, Mike here. This is gonna be fun.

DAVIS

He could hear the murmurings of his wife and daughter upstairs, while he stared at the white screen of his laptop. "Selma Richardson was born," Davis finally wrote, and then he realized that, while he knew the year of his aunt's birth because she was one year older than his mother, he didn't know the month or day, and he didn't know anyone still alive who would know it. "Selma Richardson (1933-2017) passed away peacefully on Monday, September 29, at her home in Sunnyside Village. She was the daughter of…" And he filled in all of the dead relations and himself. What he remembered of her was all of the weird stuff that kids focus on, like that she grew corn in her front yard, that she forced a second helping of everything on all children, that she was blind as a bat in a swimming pool and would glom onto you as you swam by, not much that belonged in her obituary. He recalled that she attended Marymount College, because his mother used to say it in a mocking, singsongy voice, so he wrote that down. People should write their own obits and keep them with their wills. In his, he would list some of the journals in which he had published and the fact that he was a loving husband and father, and perhaps a grandfather if Megan had children by then and kept them alive. And what if it said that he'd discovered the reappearance of the hyena in North America? That's *New York Times* obit-worthy, my friend. And he would select as its companion the photo of him standing in the drifty snow of

Mt. Rainier in a fur-lined hood with an ice pick in one mitt and a .357 in the other, the very photo he looked at now in its bold frame on his desk.

Mexico? He thought he heard them talking about Mexico up there. Megan had clearly squealed the word. This was upsetting because hadn't he told Jenny that they could not afford a vacation? Not when he might be soon out of work?

# # #

"Permission to come aboard?" he said from the hall outside his daughter's bedroom door.

"Come in!" Jenny called out.

No room for him on the bed with them, so he perched on a corner of Megan's vanity, having to sweep away some of the clunky iron-forged puzzles that Megan collected—those curling, twisting, interlocking pieces that she loved to discover how to separate. "I've been writing Aunt Selma's obit."

Both women frowned. "Was she the sister Grandma hated?" Megan asked.

"Grandma didn't hate anyone," Jenny told her.

"She wasn't in love with Selma," Davis allowed. "I'm finding it hard to figure what would be important to her, which events and accomplishments. It would be best if everyone wrote their own obituaries."

"I know what I would say," Megan said, overloudly.

"Let's find out what Mom would say first," said Davis.

Jenny covered her mouth for a moment, looking right and left, and then removed her hand and began: "Jennifer Beardsley died making squid *pomodoro* and smoking a cigarillo in her tiny kitchen overlooking the turquoise sea...at the age of a hundred and one." She squeezed Megan's thigh. It was nice to see them connecting in the way Jenny had always wanted.

"Sounds delicious," he said. Maybe they *should* all go to Mexico once he got tenure, spend his inheritance on a fun memory before Megan left them. "And what about your major accomplishments?" he asked Jenny.

"That would be the major accomplishment."

Megan then stood, hugged herself, and beamed up at the star-stickered ceiling. "Megan—" she said of herself. "Wait, what's Prince Harry's last name?" she asked her mother.

"Windsor?" Jenny guessed.

Looking up again. "Megan Windsor—"

"So she likes a redhead!" Davis said, fitting himself into the family moment.

"Megan Windsor"—Megan swept up both arms—"died while riding a camel naked through a coconut grove." And the arms floated back down.

"A coconut bonked her on the head?" laughed Jenny.

"No…" The word was drawn out by Megan while she imagined more. "She was shot by her father with a three-fifty-seven."

"Now, wait." Davis pushed his hands out to stop this.

"Which was always loaded. Everyone knew he always wanted to do it." She and Davis dead-eyed each other until Jenny said, "She doesn't mean it."

"I thought I asked you not to wear that sweatshirt," Davis finally said. Megan was wearing the pullover with the University of Vermont logo on it—a *V* with the allegedly extinct catamount leaping through it. That cat had cost him tenure. He wished he'd never seen it in that empty lot by the Citgo, the long, switching tail moving slowly through the tall grass. "Give it to me," he said. He held out a hand to her.

"Okay, but I don't have anything on underneath. You still want it?" She grasped the bottom of the sweatshirt, ready for the reveal.

"I'll get it." Jenny shooed him out. "You go on now."

But he stayed another moment, there on the vanity, shifting a few of the iron puzzles about and remaining in control.

# # #

His Taurus Tracker .357 was still there, holstered in the desk drawer, which Davis had just unlocked and opened in order to release the worry that Megan had taken it. She knew how to fire it. Seven years earlier he had let her shoot this gun while they were visiting the cabin of some friends. They were all shooting it, the adults and some teenagers. A row of bottles had been set up, and while the hosts' children took shots at them, Megan began to ask, then beg, to be given a try. Davis had been showing the other kids how to aim and shoot, and he finally called Megan over—"Come on, Eagle Eye, let's show 'em what you got"—while everyone else returned to the porch. He wrapped her fingers around the grip and explained how the hammer and trigger worked and then cocked it and aimed with her before letting go and stepping back. She stood with the gun straight-armed and squinted mightily, then turned and pointed the gun at the porched watchers, wailing, "I'm afraid! I can't do this!"

Everyone shrieked, "Point the gun down!" "Drop the gun!" All of them ducking behind the railing. Davis lurched up from behind and grabbed her arms, forced them down. "Okay, we're done."

"No, I want to," she whined. "Help me, Daddy! Help me!"

He grinned sheepishly at the audience and shrugged, and again he helped her get into position, and he had just let go of her when she swung the gun once more toward the terrified group.

After prying the revolver from her hands, Davis coolly

said, "Okay, you did what you wanted to do." People always blamed them, Davis and Jenny. Their emotionless attempts to redirect Megan were forever met with raised eyebrows, with people pulling on their lips and shaking their heads.

Davis shut the drawer and locked it. He'd become a globster, a seemingly unknowable creature that was really a common animal whittled away, a swollen, battered, hairless raccoon.

TIM

The M16 was lighter than Tim thought it would be. The gun plus the thirty-round magazine weighed in at just under nine pounds, the instructor said. Tim looped the sling over his shoulder to feel it hanging. "I could carry this on a long hump," he said to the guide, a rangy old man, loose limbed, seeming more relaxed than anyone Tim had ever met. They stood under a canopy at the firing line of a gun range strewn with junk: old swing sets with frying pans hanging off them, rusty propane tanks, pumpkins on stumps. Stop signs had been planted and painted over with their distance from the firing line.

"This is the select-fire version, the military version," the guide said of the M16. "It'll fire semi and full auto. It requires special licensing and is pretty darn expensive." The man laughed after each phrase, a scratchy *heh-heh*.

"I know all about this gun." Tim nodded, as he inserted his earplugs. *Into the Lion's Mouth* had spelled it all out: Marines must pass the marksman test with this weapon in all positions: lying down, sitting, kneeling, and standing, at ranges of two hundred, three hundred, and five hundred yards. Tim snatched it off his back and let one ping off the two-hundred-yard metal sign. The kick had hardly moved him.

"Nice," the instructor yelled.

"Wow, Dad!" shouted Miles, who was still walking along the row of rifles, trying to make a choice.

Then Tim scoped and pinged the three-hundred-yard sign.

He'd been shooting bots in Red Horizon for hours every night. "Can we attack the pumpkins?"

"Everything out there's for you." Which at a hundred and twenty-five bucks per person seemed only right. The M16 ripped the top off a pumpkin, spewing a glob of seedy pulp from the jagged hole.

"Flip it over to the fun switch," the man said, and Tim flipped the switch to full auto. He raked a row of plastic liter bottles, which exploded and sloshed up colored water like a fountain getting started.

"Awesome!" Miles whispered after the echo drifted away.

"You try something," Tim told him, and then turned to the instructor. "Kid's a well-practiced sniper."

"Oh, is he now? I think the most fun gun I have is the Glock nine-millimeter automatic, here, Miles. Want to give that a try?" He slid a clip into the handgun and showed Miles the proper stance.

"You're an inspiration to men everywhere," Tim told the guy. "Right up there with guys running a dive shop on a beach."

"Yeah, well, somebody's gotta do it, heh-heh."

Then Miles drilled holes into a propane tank, which shot out flames.

"Woo!" Tim hollered. Miles giggled and kept giggling while a stack of pumpkins became orange, pulpy carnage.

Tim crossed his arms. "You can empty a magazine in no time, huh?" The price included twenty rounds in each of three guns.

"Sure can. Want to try the Uzi, Tim?"

"No, I'm just doing Marine guns. You said you have the M two-forty-nine?"

"Yep, it's a very light machine gun with a bipod attached. You can lay on this cardboard here. The linked rounds are a hundred dollars for fifty. I told you linked rounds are extra."

"Right." Tim set his stomach down on the cardboard and snugged up to the gun, with the ammo belt trailing off to the left.

"Rotate your selector switch from safe to fire and engage your targets." Tim flipped the switch and smiled up at Miles. The rounds cackled and casings flipped into a pile on the right while glass blasted all over the field. After the last round came a thunder crack and a long, hanging echo. Tim's arms felt tingly.

"That's awesome!" Miles said, hugging his ribs and jumping.

"I'll be surprised if that hemlock's still alive next year," the man said, staring at the lone tree on the range.

"Aw, did I rake it?"

"Shouldn't have been hanging out on a battlefield, heh-heh."

Miles bent his long legs into a crouch and, holding the Uzi chest high, practiced pivoting side to side. Then Tim watched him ding up a bunch of hanging steel plates that rang long afterwards. "There's a sight on that thing, Miles," said Tim. The kid had just sprayed. If he wasn't learning how to shoot from that game, what the hell was the point?

"The Secret Service used to carry Uzis right underneath their jackets," the instructor said. "There was a holster that located the gun right under their left arm, out of sight. When you have the stock folded, it becomes a very small gun." The guy had these tidbits about all of the guns, which made what would have been a very expensive fifteen-minute session stretch out a bit.

The last gun Tim tried was the M9 Beretta, the standard Marine sidearm for use in close, defensive situations. Mona's dad had one and had shown it to him when he and Mona were dating.

"How's that feel in your hand?" the instructor asked him.

"Fits it like a glove. Really feels good."

"Nice grip there."

"Wonderful."

"Now this is a double-action pistol, so the first trigger pull is harder because it pulls the hammer back. The rest are single-action shots with an easier trigger pull. Take the safety off."

Tim arranged his stance and held the gun as the instructor showed him. In that instant, sighting the heart of a man-shaped paper target, he felt changed. He held his breath and thought he could slow his heartbeat until he was stone, moving just the one finger, *ZOT!* right in the heart.

"You're made for this," the guy told him. "See those gongs hanging on the rod? You can play a song with those."

"No way," said Miles.

Tim shot each one of the five cast-iron frying pans so they could hear what the gong notes were. "Miles, you hit the one on the right twice after every note I hit." They took their stances. *Plang plang-plang, plang plang-plang* rang out like the oompah-pah of a tuba until Tim depleted his ammo. "Our first duet," he told the guy.

"I got something else for you, Miles," the man said and grabbed a folding chair on his way out toward a stump with another pumpkin on it. "Sit here and hold this Glock." Miles put himself in the chair, about eight feet from the pumpkin, grinning like a kid on his birthday. "Now try to carve a face into it."

"No way!" he brayed.

"Go ahead. Maybe start with the eyes."

Tim watched his son straight-arm the gun and punch holes into the pumpkin, drumming his boots on the ground between shots, whipping his hair over his shoulder. The gun's nose leapt with each shot, then the *ahh!*—the pop and then the bawl, over and over, as the pumpkin's features ripped into place.

"That was outstanding." Miles inspected the sneering pumpkin on his lap in the truck cab. "I'm gonna set this out on the stoop with a candle. Scary as crap."

"Looks like that pumpkin had a stroke," Tim said. "I'm surprised you didn't have more control given all the hours you practice."

"It's just a video game."

"Bingo." Tim was angry about the money he'd just spent. Highway robbery. Guy sold bullets at jewelry store prices. "Why don't you learn how to program those games, ruin other boy's lives?"

"Way to kill the buzz, Dad."

"Look, Miles—are you listening to me?" The truck swerved a bit in Tim's effort to stare the boy down. "I need you to take on more responsibility, for you and for your mother. You turn sixteen in a month, I want you to have a job."

"What's Mum got to do with it?"

"If something happens to me, you should be ready to help out."

Miles fingered one of the chewed-up pumpkin eyes. "Are you sick?"

"No, I'm not sick, but what the hell's the matter with you, Miles? When I was your age, I had dreams. I wanted to improve myself. You lie around like a walnut! Don't you have any dreams?"

"I'm not you!" Miles flashed him a look of disgust. "I don't know what I want to be, okay? At least I won't be disappointed." The last sentence fogged up the closed window, an aside to himself.

"You think I'm a disappointment?" Tim stomped on the brake, shoving the pumpkin into the dashboard as they skidded to a stop on the gravel road. "I'm a fucking disappointment to you?" Miles avoided eye contact as with a growling dog. Tim dropped both meaty hands into his lap. "All I wanted today was to have a little fun. Hey, be a hero to my son, and now you wanna take me down, too?"

"All's I'm saying is—"

"Aw, screw off. You think you're telling me something new?" Tim opened his door and started it dinging. "I know what shit this all is. My whole life is shit, Miles! You wanna try working for a woman who's got your balls in her desk drawer? You wanna wreck yourself hauling enough pianos to buy something your wife harps about for ages and then have her tell you she never wanted that house? Never wanted it! You wanna have a—a son who resents you because there's never any money, and then you take him to have this impossibly expensive fifteen fucking minutes and he says you're a goddamn disappointment? Gimme that thing!" Tim snatched the pumpkin, swung it over, and dropped it out onto the road. Then he slammed his door, backed up twenty yards to the sound of the engine's high revving, rammed the truck into drive, and peeled out, blasting through the treasure. As he eased up on the gas and settled in for the drive, he said, "Take that, you big creep."

# # #

Today I painted the snack king in his apron, inside his casa whch is ruin of an old bakry, 100s years old. He stood for me, behind his cart topped with paper sacks rolled down at the neck holdng nuts and seeds that he sells in the Jardin and serves in even tinier paper bags topped w/hot sauce. Red and blue finches in cages behind him. Baby Jesus in a glass box. I hadn't seen his wife in a while.

"Better to be alone than in bad company." YES YES! Have to sit to paint or left hip howls in torment. Señor smiley will get gobs of money from the Govt if I sign his form. He now has world-class health insurance! Addition to agreement: PHYLLIS MUST BE ON WORLD CLASS HEATH INSURANCE.

P.S. Saw falcons riding thermals over your future property yesterday. WONDERFLL VIEW LOT WITH POWER! 26K!

# # #

Tim's mother didn't answer his calls, even as he moved farther back into her apartment, her dogs trying to swim up his legs. He wasn't so unhappy to be here, for once; it was good to be out of his own house, crowded with angst. "Knock it off!" he told the dogs as he tried to wade through them to the kitchen. God, that was some awful, acrid smell in there. An upturned plate covered one of the electric stove burners. He raised it to find that the coil had melted. How is it possible to melt a burner coil? On the table lay a note:

Tim,
Here are the policies. I am in the basement.
Love,
Mom

The basement of the triple-decker was where the washers and dryers were, so he left the apartment to help her carry the clothes up. Had they determined that he would review her policies? Flush them, he'd say. Flush them; they're worthless! When he opened the basement door, her legs and feet were in view at the foot of the stairs.

"Ma!" he called, as he jacked down the flight. She was sprawled facedown on the cement. "Ma?" The one eye he could see was open and blinking.

"Can you move at all? Did you break something?" He kneeled and put his cheek against the floor to talk to her. She moaned something.

"What? What did you say?"

"Leave me." There was blood on the floor, spreading out from her head.

"I'm calling an ambulance." He scrambled up and pulled out his phone.

He surveyed her as he waited for someone to answer at 9-1-1, her body like a marionette tossed aside between shows. He'd found her on the floor once before, as a kid. One morning on his way to get his breakfast, she was laid out in the middle of the living room floor. She asked for the neighbor woman. "Call Kathleen," she'd rasped, one hand cupped over an eye. She'd come home the night before with that man whose name was not his real name.

After telling the dispatcher where they were and going back up to prop open the outside door, Tim returned to sit on the stairs beside her feet. "Are you in pain? Looks like it."

She moaned.

"Why would you do this, Ma? Hey, stop moving. They're gonna be here any minute."

Then the phone rumbled in his hand—a Snapchat, he noticed, before sliding the cell back into his pocket. Seconds later he pulled it back out and watched the entire video with the sound off. He knew the Garbage song well enough that it played in his head. He watched, emotionless, as Blondie ran in the surf and then spiked the volleyball and had her ass patted, and when it ended, he set the phone down on the steps and listened for the ambulance. What was wrong with him? he wondered. That girl, Blondie, was a high school kid, someone his son might lust after at a school assembly.

When the EMTs arrived, Tim stood back and watched the guys. One slipped a collar under and around his mother's neck and then held her head while the other laid an orange board beside her. They both grabbed hanks of her clothing and counted to three before rolling her over onto it. They were swift and sure of themselves as only the young can be.

#

The scans showed a fractured hip and collarbone. According to the surgeon, she would be in the hospital for a week after surgery and then in rehab for another month, after which it would be good for her to live with a relative for another five months or so while she received in-home assisted care to reeducate and strengthen her muscles.

"Or maybe it's time to get into an assisted-living situation?" Tim asked the doctor, who was so tiny, she must have needed to stand on a box to operate.

"What about the dogs?" his mother croaked.

"I'm sorry?" asked the doctor.

"She has three dogs. It's not your problem." Tim said.

"If assisted living is everyone's idea of a good move, then that could be where she goes after rehab," the doctor said and breezily left the room.

"I can't take the dogs, Ma."

"It's just for a week." Her facial skin looked nearly worn through in places, like gauze pressed onto raw meat.

"Do you listen? You won't be home for over a month. At best!"

She waved him off, the back of her hand a seabed of loose cables.

"Do you know anyone who would take care of them for you?" Tim knew she had no friends.

"My son."

"If those dogs would pee outside, your son might have a chance at it, but no way. Mona's not gonna allow it." His wife once released a mushroom cloud over a piece of sausage on the carpet, so pee was beyond imagination.

"You'll think of something. And they need to be fed now."

"If you had died, what did you think was going to happen to them?"

"I guess I wouldn't care then."

"Did you get a supplemental health policy like we talked about?"

She stared at the window.

"Then you're going to one hell of a nice rehab place, Ma. It'll make Guantánamo look like Club Med." He fell against the wall and huffed through his nose. "I'm sorry I didn't see you're so unhappy."

She slid a hand down under the blanket to feel her hip.

"How bad does it hurt right now? They've got great drugs here." He plucked the pain-scale card from her tray table. The card had facial expressions to match the numbers on the scale. "Point to one, Ma," he said, holding it up. Ten was "Worst Pain Possible," with the face red and crying. "Is it up near ten? Where is it?"

She glanced at the card then cranked back windowside, tears streaming.

# # #

Tim stepped into the foyer again and closed the front door of the triple-decker his mother lived in, detonating the barking bomb inside her apartment. How could her neighbors have stood this for all these years? After turning the lock of her apartment door, he nudged the thrashing, gasping dogs away with his foot.

"You wanna eat, guys?" They scrabbled toward the kitchen and there began leaping against his legs again, like battling for rebounds.

"Hey, enough!" he said, as he opened a cabinet looking for dog food, but he found instead shelves of unopened boxes from Amazon: an indoor grill, a juicer, a Conair ExtremeSteam clothes steamer. He slid them out and stacked them on the counter. The other cabinets held more sealed treasures—an electric space heater shaped like a grate of coal, a recordable DVR, three glass liquor decanters—but no dog food. "Where's your food, guys?" He knew one's name, but not the other two. In the fridge he found half a can of refried beans and pulled that out, also a few eggs. He would cook them a scramble on one of the working burners and then try to figure out what could be done.

# # #

Sunny took a while to get to her door. Tim kept looking back toward the driveway, at the frenzy in his truck cab, and then trying to peer into Sunny's frosted sidelights. Finally came the blur of a shape in the glass, and when she pulled opened the great door, she was pleased to see him. "Well, howdy-doo!"

"Howdy-doo to you!" he replied. "I'm sorry to show up unexpected."

"No problem at all! I'm anxious to get that piano shipshape." She moved to the side to beckon him in.

"No, it's not the piano today, Sunny. I've come for an odd reason, actually. My mum's in the hospital."

"Oh, no!"

"Yeah, she fell down some stairs and broke her hip and collarbone. It'll be a month before she's back home."

"Well, I'm sorry to hear that! Poor dear."

"Oh, yeah, not good. You know she has these three small dogs"—he stole another glance at the hairy windows of the cab—"and I thought of you because of little Bea. That's her name, right?"

"Oh, Tim, I have to tell you about Bea. She died!"

"What?" He reared back in shock.

"She drowned in the pool! I had a heck of a time finding her, because she was afraid of water. I'd begged her for years to get into that pool. She was trying to please me."

"Never in the pool before that?"

"Not once."

"But you'd always wanted her to swim."

"That's right. And, Tim, she was old, so lord knows what got into her." She seemed a bit pleased. Bit of a smile.

"Wow." He nodded. "Well this makes my reason for stopping by even more appropriate, maybe. My mum has these three little dogs. Cute, cute dogs." He turned aside to face his truck. "And I'm looking for someone who can take them for a month, say. I would take them, but my son's allergic. Swells up." He moved cupped hands around his wincing face, portraying several large growths. "They're in the car. Wanna see 'em?"

"Little doggies?"

"Yep. I'll go get them. Is that okay?" He fast-walked over to his truck like a kid banned from running. He could not open that door fast enough, watching their tongues flash against the windows. At last he freed the three snaggletooths along with a bank of their rotten breath, and he tried to rub loose the back of his neck as they capered about on the stiff brown grass.

"Oh, look at them!" Sunny patted her thighs. "Come here, babies! Come here!"

He could see in her eyes that he was going to be able to leave without them, at least for a day till the shelters reopened.

"I don't have any leashes right now, but I can bring some," he told her.

"Oh, I could open my own leash store," she said. "That one looks quite old," she added, pointing to the one his mother often claimed wouldn't live the night.

"If she dies, don't worry about it," he said. "I'm afraid I don't have dog food either, and now I need to get back to the hospital."

"I'll give this a try." She gave him a strong, quick nod. "A month goes by in a minute.

As soon as he shut the truck door after himself, he felt the dog pee soaking into his pants, which grew colder against his ass during the long drive home.

DAVIS

Stationed again at the kitchen table, attending Megan's special time, Davis should have noticed her texting frenzy, but he was lost in thought over another scientist who had been all too quickly dismissed: Gregor Mendel, the world's first true geneticist. Mendel had published his pea plant crossbreeding discoveries—which would later be presented to all the world's schoolchildren as Mendel's laws of inheritance—in the *Journal of the Brno Natural History Society*, not a career-launching venue, and he was dead sixteen years before his theories were confirmed by peers. At least he'd been able to stake his claim in print, as had Davis in the comments section of the *Greenstown Daily News*, not to mention the spotlight on the evening news. He had on his screen, now, the original newspaper account of the beast, at which he again shook his head over Lindstrom's mistake.

"If you do your ethnographic research," Davis said, mostly to himself, "you know that when the Ioway Indians reported on just such a hyena-like creature, its fur was said to be black." Davis tapped his pointer finger against the screen over the newspaper photo of the black-furred Glenwood monster.

"It's a dog," Megan said, and went back to poking her phone screen.

"Well, you know dogs, I guess, now that you're in the business."

"Yes, I do."

"If I were working for you in your dog-walking business, what are some dos and don'ts for me?" Davis was desperate to make a rules chart for the dog-walking.

"I don't need help. I'll be doing all of the walking."

"I guess you could say, 'Don't yank the dogs. Don't drag them along. Don't swat them or—"

"I know how to walk a dog!"

"You know not to leave them alone, right? If someone steals them, you'll be liable."

Megan screamed, which brought Jenny into the room. "He won't leave me alone!"

"Don't use that tone, honey," Jenny said, taking off her reading glasses. "Would you like some lunch? I bought braunschweiger, Davis."

"I'd love it."

"Can't he make his own sandwich?"

"It's no bother for me." Jenny located and assembled the mustard, cheese, lettuce, onion, and liver sausage on the countertop.

Davis never understood how the girl could get so bent out of shape over his small distresses, like losing his wallet, and then want to deny him a simple pleasure like a sandwich. "It tastes better when it's made by someone else," he said.

"You will want to make some man a sandwich one day," Jenny said, wagging the bread knife at her.

"But it won't be someone like Dad."

"Didn't Daddy say he was giving you a lot of money to get you to California? I think that's worth a sandwich."

This made Megan bolt up and pop off her chair. "Okay! I'll make it!"

"Ah-ha! Better get a video of this!" Davis said.

Jenny grabbed the phone off the counter and started the video going as Megan laid the first slice of rye onto a big white plate and smiled to the camera. "I'll do it like Gina Achillini," she said of the libidinous cooking-show host. Then she slathered a dollop of hearty mustard across the rye, back and forth across the rye, and shook a lettuce leaf of its last clinging droplets before bedding it down with the two rounds of sausage, one resting its pink cheek upon the other. Slowly she peeled back a single slice of Jarlsberg, in a longed-for reveal, and kissed the air after each thin slicing of the glowing red onion. At last, she massaged the bulging delight with the other slice of rye, cut the prize on the diagonal, and thrust the plate out with a saucy look, as if to shove it straight into the lens.

TIM

"The page count is a hundred and ten," Joe Masotta told Tim over the phone. "You know how I know? I already wrote that book! *The President's Own: Standing on Ceremony*. Didn't you guys look this up at all?"

"No kidding? Jeez, congratulations! I had no idea you wrote a book." Tim pulled out a desk drawer, looking for napkins.

"Well, it's out of print now, but it sold pretty well."

"I'm sure it did! Maybe we could buy it from the old publisher, rebrand it or something." He pulled out another drawer. He needed a Kleenex to stuff under his shirt, which was still wet with excess man gel.

"How does this benefit your publisher again?" Joe asked.

Tim sighed. "She wants a book to sign at events, so she does want her name on it, but she'd give you half billing."

"Tim, what is wrong with this woman?"

"How much time do you have?"

"Plenty."

"Okay, last year, at this same convention"—Tim tried to put his feet up on the desk, but the plastic chair wouldn't allow it—"she took me around the big hall and introduced me to some of the band directors, and she's laying it on thick with these guys. This one is 'the absolute future of marching bands.' That one is 'the greatest spectacle director in the U.S. of A.' You get my drift. And the only thing these guys ever asked her for that I remember was that they all wanted to be part of a

DVD that showcased their drills on the field, which she has just said are breathtaking, right? So later, then, at dinner, when it was just her and me, I asked about this DVD and how she saw it going, and do you know what she said? She said she had no intention of making any DVD because they'd all copy it by the *thousands*, these directors, and they would pass the disks around like free candy to all their friends, and it would be a big fat joke at her expense, because—and I quote—'band directors are all thieves, liars and thieves.' Swear to God, Joe. Liars and thieves. But, hey, I don't want to turn you off on this convention talk with her, 'cause you'll be doing that for the directors. Those guys worship you."

There was a long silence before Joe asked, "What else about her?" and Tim told him how he didn't think she was going to pay a dead woman's family all that she had earned.

# # #

After the call with Joe, Mike popped in and hung himself on the wall. "She's nice."

"Who?"

"Blondie."

"Wait. What do you mean?"

"She's—she has a lot of wisdom, like you said." He ran his thumbs up and down his ribs.

"Right, but what—" Tim's cell phone rang and he stood to access his back pocket, saying, "Hang on, my mum's in the hospital."

He watched Mike back out with his hands up in surrender as Sunny began talking, "Tim, are these dogs housebroken? Maybe this is just because of the shock, but they are just going potty potty all over my house!"

"Oh, sure, no, they're housebroken. They lived in an

apartment. I think they're just very sad, very anxious. I mean, they don't know where they are."

"Well…I can try this for another day or two, but if it doesn't improve, you'll have to come get them. How's your mother?"

"It's pretty bad. She's in a lot of pain."

"Oh, the poor thing. But I'm not surprised. I hear it's just desperate pain for months. I'm afraid of falling for that very reason. But then they say the more you fear it, the more likely it is to happen."

"Sure."

"'Cause then you stiffen up."

"That must be what happened."

"I'll bet my eyeteeth, it was. Listen, when are you coming to finish the piano?"

He sidestepped from behind the desk and moved into the center of the windowless, cement-walled room. "Well, the thing I have recently learned is that you need to let a piano acclimate to the new space before tuning it. Otherwise, it's just going to pop right back out of tune. So we should wait another week or two, I think."

"I never heard that."

"Makes two of us."

When they hung up, Tim searched his phone's browser and called the local animal shelter to ask about their intake process. The person who answered had a gender-neutral voice. "We can make an interview appointment for you and your dog where we look over the vet records and give the dog a personality test."

"What's that, Meyers-Briggs? These are extroverts." He smiled up at the dome light.

"There's more than one dog, sir?"

"My mum's in the hospital and can't take care of them. Three of 'em. Their personalities are very doglike."

"They would need to be examined for dental issues. That's

a cost we can't absorb. Do you know of any dental issues?" A husky voice, but he decided it was a woman, a man-hater.

"I'm afraid to stick my fingers in their mouths."

"Guess we don't need the personality test, then, sir. Also, the fact that there are three? I would suggest you try a kill shelter. Our wait for just one *sterling dog* is now six to eight months."

Oh, Christ, it's the rich, he thought. The rich are buying up all of the slots in the shelters. "What kind of donation would get them in this week?"

"Well"—he could hear dogs barking suddenly, like she'd just walked through a door into the kennel area—"our normal intake fee is two hundred dollars per dog, so it would have to be substantially higher than that. And then, still, not if they're aggressive in any way. Kill shelters can usually take them sooner, and I think the fee is around twenty-five dollars."

He spoke more loudly. "If they decide they have to kill a dog, do they let you come get it?"

"I don't believe so, no. I think it's in the contract that you surrender the dog no matter what the consequences." Then she started talking to someone else about getting something cleaned up quickly.

"One of these dogs is old," he interrupted.

"Sorry?"

Louder: "One's very old."

"Yeah, we can't take that dog. I can tell you that right now. We have to give our limited spaces to dogs who stand a chance."

He put a hand on his desk and leaned over his shoes to ease some gas pain. "So what would you do if you were me and had to get rid of three little dogs?"

"I get asked that a lot, sir, and as I always tell people, I would never be you. I would keep the dogs. Like, you know, a lot of people say they are moving to places that don't allow dogs. I would never do that."

"You're better than me. Good for you." And he hung up. Then he stood and pounded down the hall to the mail room. "So you chatted with Blondie?" he asked Mike, red-faced.

Mike swung his feet off the metal desk. "Sure, sure, you said I should. Remember?"

"Okay, but we need to coordinate this. Suppose what you say we're doing over there doesn't jibe with what I say?"

"I just say we drive around all day, looking for IEDs."

"Our mission is to train the Askars, Mike. You read the book. We're not out escorting troops every day. How are the Askars going to learn to shoot?"

"Whoa, man. She's not writing a report on it. And I'm a driver, so what am I doing if we're not going out?"

"Why did you say she's nice?" Tim moved to block Mike's exit from the shipping desk, though he hadn't made any indication of leaving.

"She is nice. She asks how I'm feeling about things."

"You send her a picture?"

"Sure. You told me to do this, remember?"

"How do you send a photo when you don't have a uniform?"

Mike pretended to get back to work, stuffing an envelope for an order.

"Lemme see the picture."

"It's bare-chested"—Mike shrugged—"so no uniform."

Tim pictured it and hoped the nipple rings were offensive to her. "I sent her that necklace," he said to show Mike he'd claimed her. "An engraved, silver-plated, nine-millimeter bullet."

Mike nodded, impressed. "What's it say?"

"'Rusty's GIB forever.' Stands for 'Girl in Back.' Of the Humvee," added Tim. "With the numeral four in forever." He drew the numeral in the air.

"Christ! What are you doing, Tim? You're never going to be with her."

"Rusty's with her."

"Shit, Tim. This is fucked up."

Then the ass buzz and a notification tone. "Blondie," Tim explained after pulling his phone out and looking at it. "A video." He held it up for Mike to see the Snapchat notification.

"Touch it," Mike said.

And then there she was, making the sandwich in slow motion. Tim held the phone out so it came into clear focus for him. "Look at that." They mooned at the screen together.

"I don't care if that's dog shit on the bread," Mike said, "I would eat that sandwich." The lettuce exploded into droplets, the cheese slice peeled slowly from the stack like in some long-awaited final unveiling. When she finally cut the sandwich on the diagonal, they sighed together. And she held the plate out to them with a look of adoration.

"She fucking made you a fucking sandwich," Mike gave him.

# # #

That night around two a.m., still awake because of a testosterone-induced pounding in his ears, Tim heard a woman scream. He shoved the covers off but still lay there listening until he heard her cry, "Stop it! Stop it!"

From the window, he saw only shadows behind the bar, underneath the back stairs.

He raised the sash and shouted, "Hey! Hey there!"

"No!" a man grunted and leaned back into the light to glare up at him. It was one of the brothers. "Go back to bed!"

"What is it?" Mona asked.

"Call nine-one-one," he told her, as he snatched up his

pants and jerked them on. He hooked the long, silver Maglite from beside the television on his way out.

The brother had a woman up against the dumpster. Tim heard grunts and gasps from her as soon as his boots hit the stoop, and he saw the guy's jerky movements. He hid the flashlight behind him as he pounded down the sidewalk. He felt blown toward them. He back-swung the weapon while crossing the street, then stroked it up in a long swing and clubbed the back of the man's head. It was like hitting a stone. The brother crumpled and the woman gaped around, looking to escape.

"You're okay," Tim told her, patting the air. "You're safe."

She knelt, tentatively, eyes on Tim, and placed a hand on the man's bloody hair. "What did you do?" She kept touching him and then looking at her red fingers. Tim watched the man's jacket rise with each breath. "I'm gonna call an ambulance," the woman said slowly and calmly, as though Tim had a gun trained on her. She reached behind her for her purse.

He rubbed at the blood on the flashlight with his thumb. "My wife's called. How bad was he hurting you?" The woman looked much older than the bar owner. She pushed the phone into her hair, yellow as the sodium streetlamp. He heard the short squeal of his bedroom window sash.

"What's going on?" Mona yelled.

"This man may have killed my boyfriend!" the woman said.

"He's breathing! He's fine!" Tim shouted.

"What did you do?" Mona worried.

He stepped out into the circle of the streetlight and looked up at her small silhouette. "I saved her from him. She's gonna be fine now."

DAVIS

Davis had been delighted to hear about the big cookie, not that he was cheap, but it would be an unusual and memorable end to the evening. Nice of the reservations lady to ask about a special occasion and to then offer a festive big cookie on which they would write *Happy Anniversary Jenny and Davis*. All free.

The restaurant was in a former mansion, one of the historic homes on High Street, which was now too heavily trafficked to appeal to any rich homeowner, so the funeral parlor, the big insurance agency, and Le Jardin had taken up residence along the road, installing their spotlighted signs behind the stone walls. The attractive, middle-aged hostess in a black wrap dress shared a secret smile with Davis as she looked up from the reservation sheet before leading them to the table in what had been the home's formal dining room, clad all in walnut and with a view onto the restaurant's garden, now showing gourds and vibrant lime and purple lettuces and a row of big blue-green leafy creatures that he supposed were kale.

"Lovely," Jenny said as she sat.

"Yes, isn't this nice?"

After the hostess left them, Jenny put on her glasses to study the garden. "Look at those blue-bottle sculptures. We should ask where they get all the blue bottles."

"Isn't there a wine called Blue Nun?" Davis asked.

"They look very whimsical. We don't have whimsical things."

"I guess we're not whimsical, then."

"I think I am, though."

Then the waitress came and they ordered champagne—just two glasses, not an entire bottle, which would be ridiculously priced, Davis had assured Jenny in the car as he was suggesting what they should order.

"I'll have the steak, at medium. And my wife would like the salmon, well cooked."

"No, pasta carbonara," she corrected.

"That's highly unusual," Davis said in order to let the waitress know that he hadn't been ordering salmon for no reason.

"Yes, that's what I'd like," she told the waitress.

"Throwing caution to the wind," he said loudly as the girl walked away.

"Most people wait until the drinks have come to order dinner. Did you know that?" she asked him.

"If you know what you want, it's saving the girl a trip."

The champagne soon arrived, and Davis lifted his and waited for Jenny to snap her glasses back into their case before lifting hers to meet it. "To twenty-three years," he said, and they clinked. He took a sip while she set her glass back down.

"Tomorrow's a big day," he said, having sufficiently acknowledged the current special day.

"Oh?"

"Test-results day. And Lindstrom's asked to see me."

"What about?"

Davis shrugged, "Tenure, I suppose."

He looked around to discover whom they were out among. A silver-haired man on the other side of the room slid his wineglass over to a young woman in impossible heels, who then peered into the large red bowl before lifting it for a drink. Davis knew by now that if you wondered whether the girl was a daughter or a date, then she was a date.

"I don't imagine he'll cut me loose if my prediction comes true. Do you?" he asked his wife. "And then there's also that Megan problem that he has. Did you have the call with Peggy yet?"

Jenny nodded.

Davis stopped unfolding his napkin. "What did Megan say? Anything about Lindstrom?"

"No. She said he was the only person she could really talk to."

"Mmm. What does that sound like?"

"I don't—"

"Ma-nip-u-lation, plain and simple. He's going to be sorry he ever took on a class full of under-eighteens, because as a teacher, you see, he is guilty of sexual abuse of a minor."

"Do you enjoy talking about this? Envisioning this?" she hissed.

"No."

"Well, stop it, then."

Davis rotated his champagne glass on the table and watched it. If she thought he was going to drop the matter completely, to let Lindstrom play his games without consequence, she was deeply mistaken. They didn't say another word to each other until the waitress arrived with their meals. After forking a few bites, Davis resettled himself into his chair. "So one of my best memories of our twenty-three years is when we went to the Mount Washington Hotel and sat out on the back veranda and the fireworks went off up on the mountain." He waited, eyebrows lifted, for her most-loved moment, but she only nodded and chewed, looking at the plate.

"What's one of your favorites?"

"Oh, I don't know, Davis."

"Well, I'm very happy to have had all of these years with

you." If she would look up, she would find his soft, loving expression. "Are you happy, Jenny?"

She released her fork loudly onto the side of her plate and pulled down her vest. "No. No, I'm not."

"Why not?" he bleated, astonished.

"I want to feel loved!" she said, too loudly.

"I do love you," he whispered after grinning out at the room.

"I have to feel it. And I don't."

The young woman across the way pulled her hand up to cover her mouth, her wide eyes locked with the old lecher's. Davis refocused on his steak, afraid to talk, because no one else in the place was talking. And hadn't there been music before?

When the waitress came by again, Jenny insisted she was through, and Davis nodded that she should remove his plate as well.

"You know, all this time," Davis began, quietly, after the girl had gone again, "I have devoted myself to correcting for your mistakes, to making our lives bearable with Megan. That wasn't my idea of a good life, having such a child—and you knew there were going to be problems—but I studied up, I invented strategies, and I followed them, elaborate steps! All to make it work out for you, that impulsive, misguided choice."

"I'm sorry I made your life so rotten." She was boring into him, riveted.

"The thing is, we're almost through, now, with the rotten part. We can almost touch the other side!"

"Too much damage done, Davis."

"But not from each other, not damage from me or from you, but from Megan."

She shook her head. "I can't imagine you again as the man I knew before."

"Why? What is it, the lists? Where are you going?" She'd

stood and placed her napkin on the seat.

"Home," she said, and then walked out the door. Soon she passed on the other side of the dining room window, and he watched her march out to the roadside. It was a four-mile trek home, so he was certain she expected him to fetch her. He scanned for the waitress. While he waited to catch sight of her, he returned to the image of the necklace that had flashed at Jenny's throat when she'd stood. Could it really have been a bullet? Finally, the girl appeared from the kitchen with a plate, which she brought directly and set before him. The big cookie. "Oh, shoot," she said. "Is your wife in the little girls'?"

Happy Anniversary Jenny and Davis inside a red-icing heart.

"I'd like the check." Davis lifted his pleasantest face to hers.

# # #

Lindstrom looked surprised and uneasy after Davis flew in and perched on the guest chair.

"I have the results," Davis said, wanting to be proactive, slapping the envelope repeatedly against his open palm. "And you were dead wrong." They could hear men shouting and pounding on Davis's office door—the angry news crew missing their exclusive, which was supposed to have happened an hour ago.

Lindstrom screwed his lips and lifted his pen from the notebook. "We're not meeting for half an hour."

Squirming out of his suit coat, Davis continued. "I'm not going to reveal your misidentification, however. And I'm tearing up the evidence." Davis then ripped the envelope into four strips and let them float onto his lap.

"It wasn't a hyena, either, I take it."

"Two elite scientists, equally wrong." Davis nodded.

"Well, I didn't study the thing, for gosh sakes; I just went off the cuff."

"Likewise."

"Okay, so what was it?"

"Part chow, part beagle."

"I was righter than you." Lindstrom tossed his pen onto the desk and sat back.

"I know about Megan." Davis played his last card.

Lindstrom's eyes ponged side to side while he considered what to say. "Okay. What do you mean?"

"Your attentions toward her."

"Don't give me this bull, Davis. You've been at that girl since she was thirteen!" He slung himself back up, toward Davis. "In twenty minutes the police will be here. It's what I had planned for the meeting. I thought it'd be better if you were not arrested in front of your wife."

Davis slowly smiled. "Oh, this is—"

"Megan has an audio recording of you saying over and over that you were going to touch her and to get ready. I was skeptical until she played that. You're one big pervert, you know that?"

Loud cursing came from out in the hall, the video crew in full fury.

"You've been had. That audio is completely explainable," Davis said, surrendering fully to the wingback chair.

"Don't bother explaining to me. She's been bawling her eyes out in here, week after week, man."

"It was something she asked me to do when we were on an expedition." Davis looked up and to the right, trying to remember precisely what he'd said to her out in the woods.

"You're sitting there until the police arrive." Lindstrom strode to the door, opened it, and looked both ways into the hall.

"This meeting was never about tenure?"

"No! God, no! That was decided over a week ago. We put a letter in your box."

"You told me in a letter?"

"I wondered why you hadn't said anything." He returned and dropped onto his sofa, spreading his arms to rest along the back. "Don't you check your box?"

"I never check my box. What did it say?"

Lindstrom snorted. "What do you think?"

"I don't—"

Davis recognized the cameraman's voice passing by the door. "Fucking jerkoff! What a fucking jerkoff!"

"Fifteen more minutes," Lindstrom said after the quiet resumed. Then he had one more thought before the police came: "So it wasn't a hyena, though. What a surprise."

# # #

The courtroom was much less grand than Davis had imagined it would be, with a drop ceiling and fluorescent lights. It resembled a conference room at a midpriced hotel. And the judge also diminished the dignity of the court, with wadded-up tissues adrift on her desk and the slack posture of a sleepy drunk. This might be all for the better, given that Davis's lawyer had worn duck boots with his suit. Perhaps the man had forgotten to change them in the car, but then again, hadn't he gone on about his low pay just the day before? He was a man about Davis's age. He had come recommended by one of Davis's jailers. While they waited for their case to be called, the man kept patting Davis on the back, wafting up more cigarette smell from his jacket.

When they had first met face-to-face in the jail conference room the day before, Davis thought the guy looked limited— the thick eyeglasses and oily bangs and the way he walked in with his mouth open. They'd spoken briefly on the phone, and he'd sounded fine, but his appearance was expectations lowering. After the introductions, he'd set a briefcase and a well-worn paper bag on the table and pulled out the other chair. Then the open mouth turned up at the edges. "So you say she's done this before?" he'd asked, he eyes bulging behind the massive lenses.

"Once, yes. It was an art teacher a couple of years ago."

"And how'd that case come out?"

"He was found innocent."

"Did she have an audio recording of him, too?"

"No, that's new."

He unzipped his case and slid out a legal pad and pen, which he clicked and clicked and looked at like it was some newfangled thing. "And you say this recording was edited to make it sound like you said what you said?"

"No." Davis shook his head vehemently. Hadn't the man taken notes during the phone call? "No, I said what I said on her recording, but it was because she asked me to say it."

The man's pen hovered over the paper.

"She told me she was trying to get over the fear of being touched."

"So, okay, you were doing some kind of therapy for a known fear."

"Yes. Well, I hadn't known about the fear, and in fact she never had the fear. That's clear now."

"I have to think of how to frame this for the judge. Some of them aren't as bright as you'd think." He scribbled to test the pen on the paper, and it wouldn't write. "I have to pay for my own office supplies. Do you know what we're paid for court-appointed work? Most of what I do is for indigent clients."

Davis shook his head.

"Fifty dollars an hour. You heard right. Fifty fucking dollars. Barely keeps the lights on." The man dug again through his mottled, pulpy briefcase.

"Awful," Davis said.

The hairy hand emerged with another pen. "Less than your plumber! And it's been fifty fucking dollars for fifteen fucking years now! When you pay that little, you're getting ineffective counsel. You're encouraging it!"

"But I'll be getting competent counsel." Davis glared at him.

"'Course! You got me!"

"Good. So we'll have two people speak on my behalf at the arraignment." He double-patted the tabletop as though what he'd suggested was all that would be required.

"It's not done."

"I'd like you to call Peggy Sommers; my wife can get you her number. And my wife can also be a character witness, of course."

"Have you talked to her since you were arrested?"

"Not yet." Davis had made three calls to her cell, but she hadn't answered.

"I'll check in with her."

"Good," Davis said. "She knows this is false."

"The main question is why? What's Megan's motive?"

Davis stretched his legs beneath the table. "She doesn't want to be controlled. She wants to get rid of all outside control on her life. I'm the main controller. Ask Peggy, it's a thing with them."

"These Romanian orphans."

"The ones with RAD."

The man searched his scalp with the fingers of his nonwriting hand. "I think if we can confirm that diagnosis and the past false accusation, we are in a good position. What's Peggy's number?"

The lawyer dialed it on his cell and turned the speaker on.

Once Peggy got her bearings and understood who was calling and why, she started in: "Well, the problem with trying to figure out who is right in this scenario is that Megan is just as vulnerable as she is menacing. That's the problem. She comes on to men and seems to be asking for it. But she doesn't know what she's asking for. So you have to be careful not to assume she's lying."

"This is the father, Peggy," Davis said. "Did you know she was accusing me of this? Have you spoken with her about it?"

"Yes, yes, I did," she said. "And she was very upset, and I have to say, I heard the tape, which—I don't know what your lawyer thinks of it, but it doesn't sound good to me. And the mother also found—"

"Peggy," the attorney said, "if we want to know what the mother thinks, we'll ask her. Let's not get into your interpretation of what the mother thinks."

"It's not what she thinks, it's what she found!"

"What did she find?"

"The girl's underwear under his pillow."

Davis let his forehead drop dramatically onto the table.

"I see," the lawyer said, finally writing something down. "Did you know about the past false accusation?" he asked Peggy.

"Yes."

"So, it's a pattern. And was it also a pattern with your daughter who had the same disorder?"

"Yes."

"So it's a generally recognized symptom of the disorder. Thank you, Peggy." And he punched the red button on his phone.

# # #

Finally their case was called, and Davis's lawyer accompanied him to the front, where the judge ordered that he be released on personal recognizance, pending an order of protection for the daughter, given that naked pictures of her had been found on Davis's phone.

"No!" Davis brayed, until his lawyer clamped a hand over his mouth.

When they walked into the hall, Davis went wild. "She put pictures on my phone? It's unbelievable! And now I can't go home?"

"Not for a while."

"Where am I to go?" It was then that Davis recognized, most clearly, that he was a friendless man, because he couldn't think of one person who would take him in, or whom he could even ask to do so.

He drove around for an hour, then sat parked in a grocery store lot while shaking his head over the photos on his phone. She'd taken his cell from the charger when her friend Tara was visiting. That's what had happened. He pictured the friend snapping away under the direction of Megan, the porn queen. When he was finally completely exhausted, he thought of the Motor Inn, the concrete-walled U that he passed on the way to work, with a parking space in front of each door. *What sort might find that hole a welcome respite?* he'd often wondered.

# # #

When he placed his credit card on the counter, he worried that it was no longer his card, that he had somehow been removed from ownership. Why hadn't Jenny come to court? Or answered his calls from jail? He could only imagine it was another man, the one who had given her the silver bullet.

"How long will you be staying?" asked the clerk, an old

soldier with a long, whiffly beard.

"I have no idea," Davis replied. "Playing it by ear, I guess."

The room was no surprise. Bent blinds. Pressboard dresser. He had no suitcase, but his lawyer had promised to bring him some things from his home in an hour. He sank into the flabby bed in his Joseph Abboud navy suit and followed the fissures in the ceiling plaster. Was he to wait in this room for a month before trial? He would surely not be returning to his classes, not since he was now accused of such a horror. He felt as though he'd just awakened to a vast conspiracy against him by his department chair, his wife, his daughter, Dr. Peggy, and God knows who else. And what had he done? Only good work, only best practices derived from sound, rigorous research.

Through the window, he saw an old gold seventies Lincoln pull into the parking lot across the street. Two graying men in barn coats got out and headed for door of the Lobster Shanty. It was early for a drink.

# # #

Davis took a small sip of the top-shelf bourbon—what did price matter now?—and relaxed on the black pleather barstool with the rounded back. He tried to read the note taped up by the cash register: "Call Phil first if fridge craps out. Don't call for service!!" He thought about how he might discover whom his wife was seeing. Someone at her school, it had to be, or some kid's father. He could wait in the school parking lot and follow her, but then he might be seen as someone who liked to watch children. He could go to his home when neither she nor Megan was there and look around for evidence. And pick up more of his things at the same time.

The barn-coated men were at the other end of the bar. What did these guys do all day? he wondered. He should probably shout out some inane statement about the weather, buy them drinks and such, but he couldn't. He'd long been drained of all social lubricants. Rusted now. The beefier guy was pointing at the bartender, thrusting a finger at her as he talked. She was standing just in front of them, with her hands on the bar, seeming to both lean in and hold back at the same time. Davis tried to discern the big, bruisy tattoo on her shoulder, but the lines were too mushy. The talking man jabbed and jabbed, and when he ended his tale bellowing, "And they fucking shoulda seen it comin'!" the bartender turned away, laughing. "Doesn't surprise me," she said, and knelt down to crank up the music, which was a country song—nice little guitar picking.

He should have said no to the adoption. Everything would have been easier to take, to weather, without the weight of Megan. Then again, hell, maybe he should have said no to the BC football game! He'd have made more of himself. He would've had a circle of compatriots if he hadn't bothered to be a husband. He held his empty glass up for the girl to see. Husbands were imaginary creatures, anyway, he decided—men in disguise.

TIM

It looked like feeding time at North Shore Piano, with all of the baby grands open-mouthed. Showroom manager Chip deCarlo subsumed a stool behind the little glass counter, his sour expression telegraphing his poor opinion of Tim's crew, who wandered about, dirty fingers depressing keys, chunking awful chords in long succession while Tim carried in the blankets and removed the music rack from the piano that needed to be moved. DeCarlo finally made a loud series of coughs that tensed everyone and ceased all noodling.

"Get over here, guys," Tim called, as he deadened the piano strings with a blanket and closed the lid. Mike and Vinnie helped to drape more blankets over the case, and Tim walked around and around, snugging them to the instrument with plastic wrap from a big roll. "Get your ass over here," he said to Miles, who had moved on to screwing with an electronic keyboard. Soon the whole case was wrapped tight. Then Tim had Vinnie crawl under it and unbolt the pedals and one of the side legs while Mike and Miles held that side up. "Like a fucking bus," Miles groaned.

Tim viewed the scene from different angles. Then, after spreading another blanket on the floor, he said, "Let her down, slowly!" and they lowered the legless side to the floor and tipped the case up so they could remove the other two legs. Finally Tim bound the hulk with straps, like Houdini was inside. Together, they parked one corner onto a dolly and Mike wheeled the beast out the door with the other two steadying. "Very nice," deCarlo said. "Looks like that one's gonna make it."

Mike drove his Jeep to meet them at the buyer's house, while Miles and Vinnie rode in the cab of the piano store's truck with Tim, who played his Garbage CD again and insisted, "Listen to this one," before every song.

At one point, Vinnie, who sat in the middle, tried to stretch his arms around behind Tim's and Miles's shoulders, but they both leaned forward and wouldn't sit back again until he pulled his arms back.

"Hey, guys," Vinnie said, turning down the music, "we should talk about things. What are you reading on your phone?" He elbowed Miles.

"A book by my grandma."

"Are you kidding me with that?" Tim rocked up in his seat to look over at him.

"What's it about?" Vinnie tried to read the screen.

"I'm only on the first chapter, which is about how women are the rhythm setters." He looked at Vinnie. "You know how women have cycles and men don't? Well, Grandma says that women should be seen as the rhythm setters in life, and also, well, in bed—well, sex—and she tells women how."

"How does she say?" Vinnie asked.

Miles read from the screen: "If you like laughing, girls, you'll love panting, and keeping a regular beat with your breaths lets your lover know just how fast or slow—"

"No!" Tim pounded on the wheel. "Knock it off! Seriously, the end. No more reading Grandma's book." He tried to reach across Vinnie to grab the phone, but Vinnie blocked him.

Then came a sudden honking to his left—Mike's white Jeep in the lane for oncoming traffic. Idiot was leaning over and grinning up at them, widely mouthing some song.

"What the fuck's wrong with that guy?" Tim saw the approaching UPS truck and frantically fanned the air to move Mike back. "What the fuck's he doing?" The UPS guy laid on his horn.

Mike slipped back at the last second and tucked in behind them. Tim could see him laughing. "That man is completely unhinged," he told the others. "He's out of his basket."

# # #

Tim lay on his side on the couch like a sultan, having placed the whole six-pack on the floor for easy access. Winter Hill Lager. He was on his third, and it was still crisp and delightful, his gift to himself for clearing a hundred and fifty the night before. Halftime now in the Notre Dame game. He hated the know-it-all commentators regurgitating all the stats from the first half. Still, this was better than being forced to watch the real half-time show, the Notre Dame marching band. In Tim's opinion, sports were the ruination of bands. He pitied all those earnest marching-band kids—the toneless, friendless, commonly fat teens with polyester thigh rashes, drawing their lips tight as assholes to mewl out crappy arrangements of dated, unloved songs and marching around to form wobbly alien crop designs. They would never know real music, never unfurl a great Sousa march, blow it into glorious existence.

All the same, he kind of wished his son were in a marching band. It might be a step up in status for him. Miles was a musician's nightmare. His mother had purchased for him an expensive keyboard he'd fancied, but he refused to take a lesson. "I want to play it my own way," he'd said. But there are not multiple ideal ways to finger scales, Tim told him. Someone has already figured all of this out. Why reinvent the wheel? It was laziness. And Tim knew that the laziness was because of low self-esteem. This, finally, Miles hadn't had to learn on his own. He had a virtuoso in the house.

When his cell phone rang, he saw Sunny's number, which he was expecting.

"Hi, Sunny."

"I want these dogs out. Now!"

"Oh, is there a problem?" He stretched to set his beer on the coffee table, but it tipped and puddled the glass. Then he just listened.

"Miles!" Tim yelled after hanging up.

Vinnie leaned out of the kitchen. "He's out with Marie."

"Really?" Tim said.

Vinnie studied the toppled beer. "Do you need something?"

"I have to take Mum's dogs to the shelter."

Vinnie looked at his watch. "I'm sure they're closed by now."

"Yeah, but the lady needs them gone. I'm gonna have to leave them outside the shelter." Tim pushed himself upright. "I thought maybe they could sleep in the basement here tonight, but they'll bark nonstop and Mona won't sleep, and then hell will relocate to my bed."

"You get the dogs. I'll make them a nice bed in the basement, and I'll stay with them until Miles comes home. We're not telling Mona." He gathered up Tim's empties.

"You know what? That's a huge help, Vinnie." Tim had to admit, the man was helpful; he kept a small footprint in the house and he entertained Mona. And as long as the couch was already occupied, then they absolutely had no place to put Tim's mother when she was released from rehab.

# # #

In the truck, the dogs climbed him like a sausage lay in

wait at the top of his head. Sunny had been quite cold to him, had stood at the door with her arms tucked while he corralled the dogs out onto the lawn. Then she announced that her Klopotek was very well acclimated to her house, thank you very much. "Yes, I think it's ready," Tim agreed. "I'll check my appointment book and schedule a time with you." The dogs had scattered in the yard and Tim wanted to just let them make their way in the world, but he knew they would run for the truck when he opened the door, and so they did. On the way home, he stopped to purchase a dog crate that would hold all three.

Miles was on the stoop when Tim pulled up. The parking spot was again taken by the bar owners' van. "Your mum still out?" Tim asked, as he lifted the empty crate out of the truck bed and set it next to Miles.

"What's gonna happen while I'm eating dinner? They'll bark their heads off."

"You're gonna eat down there. I'll bring it. You'll turn off the lights and keep quiet."

"Dave told me to tell you he's looking for you."

"Who's Dave?"

"Dave." Miles nodded toward the bar.

Tim had his hand on the truck door handle. "How did he say it?"

"Sounded kinda mean."

Tim swung open the door, "Don't worry about it."

#

"Was Mona going to dinner with George?" Tim asked when he returned from the parking expedition.

Vinnie paused in his sit-ups. "I don't know," he said in his wide-eyed dramatic way.

"You want a turkey sandwich?" he asked Vinnie.

"Turkey, yes, but no bread."

In the kitchen, Tim pulled out the sliced turkey and ate half of it out of the package. He wouldn't have bread either. He'd lost eight pounds. He made Miles a big bready sandwich and wrapped it in a paper towel. When he opened the basement door, he saw his gangly son on a sleeping bag with three limp dogs atop him, one incessantly licking his neck.

"Here you go," Tim said and tossed down the sandwich bomb.

"If these dogs didn't pee or defecate, they would be awesome."

"Same goes for everyone."

Miles managed to prop himself up on his elbows without dislodging the dogs. "We never got a dog."

"You are our dog."

The boy happily nodded.

Then Tim closed the door and left the house, headed down the driveway, and took a left, walking backwards away from the bar. When he reached the big block of Section 8 housing, it was time to make the call. God, Blondie's voice was thrilling! Energy shot right up his spine. *Zot!* Rusty paraded down the centerline of the deserted street, fingering her silk underwear in his pants pocket, telling her more of what he'd discovered from Phyllis about the Mexican town they were both now dreaming of. He'd learned that it was so small they made public announcements over a loudspeaker, and that people rode their horses into town for certain delicacies sold right out of the casitas. Like there was a tortilla lady if you knew her door. There was a house for dried fruits that burst off your tongue. He stopped at one point, sat cross-legged on a lawn, and announced that she would determine the pace of their lives. She would be the rhythm setter, to which she gave a happy little cry of surprise.

"Hold on a second," he told her. Out of the corner of his eye, he'd seen, just at the next intersection, a silver BMW, now clearly with George and Mona in it and about to turn his way. "Hang on." He scrambled over to crouch behind a car, one cheek to the cold driver's door, until he heard it pass. "You okay?" Blondie whispered.

Sometimes they went to concerts together, George and Mona, and had a little dinner beforehand. George wanted her expert assessment of the singers, he told her. He was developing a real relationship with her. She mentioned him often, clearly thought about him on many occasions. Tim felt a familiar panic take hold of him, that sudden recognition of another obsessive desire that was all delusion—he was a fat, married man kneeling in dog shit. He stood up, and the one knee was smeared with it. He was the same as those stolen valor creeps who wear fake uniforms around shopping malls. Not Rusty. Not real. And, while he was at it, had he been such a great musician if he'd been turned down by twenty orchestras? It was bad enough to involve Blondie, but he was also a fraud to himself. He couldn't even satisfy *himself.* Of course George looked great by comparison.

"Do you need to go?" Blondie whispered.

"Something I gotta tell you." His heart was pounding, but he needed to get the ball rolling. "There's a mission coming up. It's a tricky one. Might be kinda like walking into the lion's mouth." When he tapped off the phone, he started to run.

# # #

Later that night when Mona came to bed, she lay in the dark for a long time and finally said, "He has nine sisters."

"What?" Tim tried to sound like he'd been startled awake.

"George does. What does that do to a boy to have nine sisters?"

"I'm not surprised."

"What do you mean?"

Tim knew she was imagining that having nine sisters would make a man the perfect companion because he would have been scolded and redirected enough to know very clearly what women do not want.

"Good concert?" he asked.

"Yes," she said and then turned away from him. "We both enjoyed it."

Tim imagined George kissing her in the car. Slipping his fingers into her hair. George's car hadn't been there when Tim made it home, but there'd been enough time for a kiss. He could see the shape of her now in the glow from the streetlight. Mona still had a fine body, and George would probably soon be rewarded with it for all of his help, for the banishment of her worries. Tim ran a finger down the back of her neck. After a moment, he did it again, which made her turn onto her back. "What?"

He took her hand in his and massaged her open palm with his thumb.

"Are we doing this?" she asked, finally looking at him.

"Yeah."

She turned the last half turn toward him and slipped her foot over his. He was catching a ride in George's wake.

# # #

"If there's a camera, I figure it's focused on the front," Tim said over the thumping of the wipers and the applause of the steady rain as he turned onto the street just beyond the shelter. Miles had the cage tilted into his lap, with the three dogs licking his bony fingers through the grill. Tim parked and shoved open his door. "Let's go."

Miles lugged the cage through someone's side yard and onto the animal shelter property, his posture defeated, more shepherd's crook than shepherd, while Tim swung his arms, fast-walking like he was approaching some longed-for confrontation. He looked back at the drowning boy, threw a finger toward the back door. "Hurry!" Then they settled the crate on the wet cement pad, the dogs' shudders showering them anew. Miles flashed Tim a look of disgust, took off his trench coat, and draped it over the cage. As they ducked back to the car, Miles shouted, "You're gonna call and let them know, right?"

Shut into the truck cab, they were sodden. "They'll be open in an hour," Tim assured him. Then, in a moment, the rain lightened up, and Tim took his hand off the key. "You know what? I'm gonna run, you drive."

"In the rain?"

"It's passing." Tim shucked his rain gear and dropped onto the road in his T-shirt. As he ran, the headlights reached beyond him into the gloom, and the blowing trees still let loose great whips of water. Seemed like he was leading the way to something bad, something recently discovered. A horrible thing.

# # #

Maniacal pumpkins lined the entrance ramp to the rehab center, their features seeming gouged out by unsteady hands. Tim knew these would add to Miles's depression. The boy sulked behind him. Tim gave his mother's name at the desk, and a shaggy young man loped ahead of them to her room and said "Ta-da!" when they arrived at the door to view Tim's mother, deflated in the far bed.

"Hey, Ma, how's it going?" Tim asked her.

She looked much older than before. She turned her head slowly toward them like a robot powering down and said softly, "Do they know I'm seventy-six?"

"Why?"

Then at normal volume: "They're pushing me to do things!"

"Seventy-six is not so old anymore, Ma. They know what you can do."

"I can *not* get up to go to the bathroom," she stated.

"What do you mean? Are you wearing diapers?"

"Does Miles have to hear this?"

"No," Miles said and evaporated.

"You're wearing diapers?" Tim shook her railing. "I don't think you're supposed to be here if you need diapers. You can't walk four steps to the bathroom?"

"I had hip surgery. I'm seventy-six!" Now she managed to lift her head.

"Fine." He settled into a chair and looked at the whiteboard with the current nurse's name on it. "Nurses nice?"

"Who's taking care of my dogs?"

"Don't worry about that."

"Of course, I worry." Then she turned her focus upon the flashing television. Tim looked to find where the tinny sounds were coming from and saw a small speaker lying beside her shoulder.

"How's the food here?"

She shook her head. "Can't eat it."

"No."

"It's like they're serving food they cooked days ago. Everything's gray. Congealed."

"Next time we'll bring you Kentucky Fried."

"That would be nice," she said, her glassy eyes not leaving the set.

"But we'll leave it in the bathroom so you have to go in

there to get it." This was disregarded.

"Is Miles coming back?" she gasped, as though asking about the brakes in a speeding car.

Tim looked out the window at Miles sitting in the truck. "I don't think he's coming back in. He has a girl now, you know."

"He told me. Could you ask her if she'd like some really cute dogs?"

Miles had the rearview mirror cranked toward him and was squeezing at his chin.

"He's not so bad. He's nice to people," Tim told her. He could hear her game show, like someone ringing a front desk bell, nonstop. "So, your son knocked a guy out the other night," Tim said.

"Miles?" she tried to sit up.

"No, your son, me. I protected a woman from rape. Knocked her attacker out cold."

"What? Where was this?"

"Outside the bar across the street. She was screaming for help, and I went down and took him out with a flashlight to the back of the head." Tim demoed his underhand swing and then made a *tock* sound for the impact. "I think he's gonna be fine, though."

"She must have been grateful."

"Asked me what she could do to thank me. Know what I said? Bring me a sandwich sometime." This is how it would have gone had the lady had any sense.

"Is that all you want, a sandwich? I'll make you a sandwich. That's all you want?" Applause from the pillowed speaker.

"If I'm still alive when you get out, you can make me one, Ma." He walked over and set his hand on her blanketed calf.

She half covered her face with her hands. "I just want to be home!"

"I know," he said, and looked up to see two Os flip into

place on a big game board. It was clear to him, immediately, that once the blank letters were in place, the phrase would be "Jump for joy."

# # #

Mona's father's living room still had the orange-sherbet walls on which hung giant framed photos of the grandchildren as dolled-up babies. And still on every flat surface stood the porcelain statuary his wife had collected: three Virgin Marys; the Infant Jesus of Prague; and St. Anthony, patron saint of lost items, carrying Jesus as though returning him after some mishap.

"The Beretta?" Mona's father looked pained.

"Just for a little while until things calm down with the brothers at the bar." They were crowded together inside the front door.

"You ever shot any gun?"

"I can take that Beretta apart and put it back together," Tim said, and nodded toward the man's bedroom. "Get it and see."

The guy went down the hall to his room, and Tim heard a drawer open and shut and then the shout. "I want all these bullets back!"

When he emerged, he said again, "I want all of the bullets back," and handed the clip to Tim. "How many are in there?"

Tim counted. "Ten. And you'll get ten back."

"Don't get cocky with this thing."

"I promise I'll only shoot it if it looks like I'm about to be killed."

"Or Mona. Or Miles."

"Goes without saying."

"Double-action trigger," he said, handing the gun over.

"That's a hell of a nice gun. You know where I got that?"

"Yeah," Tim told him. "I heard the story."

"So how about the parking space?" The man still blocked Tim from coming in further.

"Working on it."

"What do you mean? You got the price."

Tim slid the gun into the pocket of his anorak. "If the man will give the woman health insurance, and if she will sign his tax form, and if he will let her have all of the money from the sale, and if she finds a goddamn notary public in the middle of the Mexican desert, and if the full moon lines up with my left nipple, then we shall have our driveway."

The old man flapped a hand at him, like he was saying good riddance.

When Tim got back into the truck, he slammed the door angrily and pulled out his phone to call Mike, who answered quickly, saying, "That last piano tore my groin."

"Like hell," Tim answered.

"Seriously, I'm on fire."

"Listen, Mike," he said in the flat tone that everyone knows means disaster. "I gotta tell you something. Since you're in touch with Blondie and all, I need to get you in on this. I've decided to kill Rusty."

There was a sound like a hard candy clacking against teeth. "I don't know what you want me to say, but I think it's a good move."

Tim's father-in-law was peering at him through a fingered dent in the blinds. "I don't care what you think; I just need you to tell her I was killed. I already mentioned a big mission to her. It's like Ganjgal, so that's how you can describe it. I couldn't get out. It's happening in a couple of days."

After a sigh, Mike said, "Sorry, man."

Tim looked away from the old man's slotted eyes, over at

his own reflection in the rearview. What a blotchy, knobby face. It did credit to no one. Just as well his dad didn't have to see it.

DAVIS

After sliding his coelacanth into the back seat, Davis reentered his house and moved on to the kitchen, where he riffled through her personal bills. He knew she'd been paying on their mutual accounts because he still had access online, and in fact their savings was quite robust at the moment, since she'd deposited his inheritance check. He was hoping to find her personal credit-card bill, which might have incriminating charges on it, but it wasn't among the stack. Then he mounted the stairs to their room and heard her voice. She must have parked in the garage, he realized. Wait—on a school day? He nearly ran back down and out the door, but then he stopped. Was that her laughing? As he closed in, he recognized the *zizzing* sound of the exercise bicycle, so he knew he could open the bedroom door a bit, and she wouldn't see him, since the bike faced the far wall. When he cracked the door, he could hear a man on speakerphone: "So if you want, we could go there, take a walk along the beach."

"I'd love it!" she said in this odd, breathy voice.

"All right. I'll tell you, though, my mom isn't going to be too thrilled that I'm heading out of here so quick after getting home."

"Well, don't make your mom mad!" She sounded like one of his ninny students!

"I just think, you know, we need to meet."

"I do, too!"

"When you get off the bus in Portland, I'll be outside in a white Jeep. I don't know if I can drive right up or if I'll have to park, but it's a white Jeep Wrangler."

"And I know what you look like."

"Only with my shirt off! Hey, bring an overnight bag if you want to stay over down there. There's plenty of room and all at my friend's place in Kennebunkport. I know your family's kinda messed up, so if you need a break. I'll be staying there anyway."

"I'll think about it."

"Okay, well, guess I'll see you at two twenty-five on Saturday!"

"Can't wait!"

Internet dating. He wouldn't have guessed that. And choosing a man with a shirtless photo, that wouldn't have been his guess either. He wanted to confront her, but the fact that she was on the bicycle stopped him. She hadn't used it in ten years. She was going hard and seemed to be doing her best to speed away from him. He almost expected her to look back to see if she was in the clear. He clicked the door closed. During the call, a bowling ball had dropped into his stomach, and it seemed to sink further as he crept back down to his study.

Flipping the light switch started all of the display-case lights buzzing. He glanced over the contents, moving quickly. There wasn't anything in them that he treasured any longer. Truth be told, some he didn't really believe in, like the Fouke Monster. But he did want his gun and, of course, the skull of the *Ebu gogo*, which fit easily into his other pocket.

TIM

In the middle of the night, Tim's phone dinged. He picked it up, expecting an insane Phyllis communiqué, but it was Blondie.

So happy about Mike but wish it was you.

"Who is it?" Mona asked.
"Phyllis," he told her, then typed back:

Sorry?

On leave!

Right. Lucky bastard. We can't all go at same time.

Will be nice to meet him.

"What?" Tim asked his phone.
"What?" Mona repeated in high alarm, whipping over to see, but Tim held the phone away.
"Don't worry about it, Mona. I'm taking care of this." He got out of bed, still naked, and walked into the hall to type:

I want to think of you guys meeting. When?

Saturday! 2:25 if my bus isn't late.

# # #

"Four weeks until the big day!" The Publisher reminded Tim. Then she popped a load of M&M's into her maw and swished them around.

Tim sighed himself deeper into her guest chair. "Got your questions lined up?"

She sucked and nodded.

"Great."

"Guess where the party's going to be?" *Bells Up* always hosted a party during the convention.

"Hmm."

"Isabella Stewart Gardner Museum. The one that was robbed of all those paintings."

"That's nice."

"Rita fixed it. Very dress-up." She scolded him with a finger.

"Yeah, okay."

"Bring Mona. Maybe she could sing something."

"She's never turned down a request before, but unfortunately, she's got a gig that night."

"It's going to be lovely." The Publisher set her chin upon her clasped hands and got dreamy-eyed. "I may have to retire after this. How would I top it?"

"Hey, how about doing something in Angela's honor this year?"

"Yes!" She bolted upright. "What?"

"We should invite her family and offer a toast to her and have a large photo there with her name and some sentiment on it."

"Rita!" The Publisher yelled. "Rita, please come in here!" And then she instructed her to make all of this happen and said that Tim would write the sentiment.

As Rita started to leave, Tim said, "Hang on a minute, why don't you present Angela's family with an oversize check, like they do for lottery winners. It'd be for her final earnings, plus maybe you round up." He'd wanted Rita to be there when he proposed this, because The Publisher was all about saving face.

"Isn't it too crass?" The Publisher made sour lips.

"Not for the people who get the check," Rita said.

"Picture the room when this check appears, which is for quite a bit more than anyone is expecting. This is the sort of thing that makes everyone cry. It's munificent." Tim nodded.

She ran her thumb around the face of the phone she was holding, like a worry stone, and shifted her pupils from Tim to Rita to Tim to Rita without moving her head. She appeared cornered.

# # #

Once Tim and Rita were on the other side of The Publisher's closed door, Rita said, "Hang on a minute," and she took a small sheaf of pages off her desk and held them out. "People who want to be in your band. I'm getting five a day. They all have a lot of questions. Maybe we should put an FAQ on the website.

He sorted through the stack. He'd known they would come. This was only the beginning.

# # #

Portland, that's where the Concord bus from Greenstown arrived at 2:25 on a Saturday, and from there it would be a quick drive for Mike to drag Blondie to all of The Publisher's empty beds in Kennebunkport after telling her Rusty was dead. Tim set his cell phone showing the bus schedule back down on his desk. Now he would patiently await one of the big dolt's daily office visits, and when the guy appeared, the door to the photo archive room would close and lock for the very first time. Tim would come at him from both directions, blowing the head side to side against his wall of cement. He couldn't be Rusty, but like hell this sicko was going to be his driver, or hers.

# # #

When Tim opened his front door, George's ass was in his face. Mona had him doing the breathing exercise, touching the toes of his tassel-topped slip-ons while she stood to the side, counting. Between his knees, George's purple face pleaded. Then came the wet rush of his exhale.

In the kitchen Tim grabbed a glass and filled it from the tap. His hand trembled as he raised it. "That's as long as you can go?" Mona chided George.

Mike had promised he wouldn't meet Blondie when Tim caught up with him in the parking lot. He said he'd call the whole thing off, but his eyes darted around the whole time, so of course he was going. It was Blondie, after all. And this was what Tim had playing in his head all the way home. Of course, the guy would be there to pick her up, take her out to the beach, tell her her man was dead.

When Vinnie came into the kitchen, they looked at each other like they'd each been insulted.

"What's your problem?" Tim asked.

"The police came to the Cheesecake Factory. That's what *he* did."

"What happened?"

"Everyone was watching, and I told them, 'I did not steal that car. You think I need to steal a car from a man?' Tim, I taught that man how to dress, how to be. And when his mama died, I fed him."

"Where's the Miata now?"

"Well"—he worked off his tie—"they don't know where I'm living. So they aren't looking here."

Tim pulled a chair out with his foot and landed in it.

Vinnie sat across from him. "You know what? He can have his car. It's a gay man's car, everyone knows that, so he can be out to everyone now."

"What's his name in case he shows up here?"

"Devlin. D-E-V-I-L-in."

George was attempting some impossible vocalization in the living room, low to high in unwieldy leaps.

"That guy has a sad dream." Vinnie pointed toward the sound.

"If you think the dream is singing, then yes," Tim said. "If you think the dream is spending time with Mona, then he's a big success."

"When they told me someone was there to see me, at work, I thought it was the man I used to—"

"Dad!" Miles blasted in, holding his open laptop high like he was saving it from small savages. "Look at this. The dogs are at the kill shelter. You can see them online."

"Calm down, Miles."

Miles tripped, rushing over, and tossed the laptop onto the table. "It's absolutely them."

Tim pushed the laptop away from himself, but Miles turned it back to face him. "And I don't see a picture of Sophie, just the other two. Look."

"Okay." Tim put his palms up. "Relax. They are probably fixing her teeth. Then they all get adopted." He shoved the computer away again.

"Dad, they're not gonna fix her teeth at the kill shelter. We need to go get them!"

"We are not getting those dogs, Miles. Get over it."

"But I'll stay with them in the basement till Grandma's home." Miles slid into a chair and stretched his prayer-clutched hands across the table toward Tim.

"Are you deaf? Huh? The dogs are staying where they are."

Miles's jaw went slack, and his eyes hardened. Then he drove his fists down onto the Formica, making the laptop jump. "God! You suck! You're such an evil bastard!"

Tim stood so fast, his chair fell. "Go to your room! Now!"

"A Fucking. Evil. Bastard!" the boy said again, as he loped out and smacked open the door.

"Can someone explain?" Mona asked as she reopened the swinging door.

"If you want three defecating dogs living here, then please get involved," Tim told her. "Please."

"I'm giving a lesson," she said slowly, as though teaching him to speak.

When she left, Tim righted the chair. He and Vinnie avoided eye contact as they sat waiting for George to run out of time.

# # #

"So I spoke with my accountant," Andy began. Tim listened while looking out his bedroom window, checking on his truck and the Miata in the driveway. Andy sounded down. "And since Phyllis took out her whole IRA and never rolled it over, she has a huge tax liability, so having her sign my tax forms is a bad idea."

"Oh, yeah? Well, would you consider putting her on your health insurance anyway, Andy? I know you care about her health."

"I can't! We're no longer married! They don't let you put

anyone you want on your health insurance."

"Right."

"Can't she get Medicaid?" Andy asked.

"She doesn't have a U.S. address."

"Oh, boy. That's right."

"Yeah."

After a moment, Andy said, "Hey, could she use your address?"

"No. My address? No. But, okay, you'll still give her all of the money from the sale, right?"

"Well, the problem with that, my lawyer explained, is that all of that money will be taken by the court because of the foreclosure. We owe creditors money, so they'll take all of the proceeds. Doesn't bother me, but Phyllis won't want to sign the property over if she's getting nothing."

Tim let the curtain fall back. "You didn't know this? No one mentioned this to you?"

"No. I just talked with my lawyer today."

Tim could not believe the man hadn't known this all along. He'd been fucking with them. "You're some kind of a shitbag, Andy. You know that? You acted like you wanted to help her, but you never did, did you? I should have called the police on you that day I heard her screaming bloody hell."

"Now, Tim—"

"You should get a dick punch every day for the rest of your life." Tim hung up the phone and threw it onto the bed. The *Fire Team Missions* had all been aborted.

#

Out in courtyrd of casita swaddled in blankets. A million stars rain down while dogs and roosters, last of the night, call to each other cross the lanes.

Occurs to me here you cn fall and fall lk stars, never hitting ground. Did you call Andy? Leaving messge not enough!

# # #

They waited a few minutes after the throbbing had started up, because maybe it was a passing car with the sound jacked. Then Mona bolted upright in the bed. "Go out with the meter." She hopped out and slid the sound meter's case off the bookshelf. The last time they called the police about the bar music, the cops had told them the city decibel limit was 55, but they didn't have a sound meter, so there was nothing they could do.

"Maybe we let this one go." Tim held the sheet up to his chin.

"Then why did I even buy a meter? You don't have to talk to those guys, just hold it over by their wall."

"You're the one who knows how to use it."

"You want your wife out there in the pitch dark?" She slipped the foam ball over the microphone and brought the contraption to Tim in bed. "See this green button, you press this. Hold the meter right up to their wall and press the green button. Then press the Max/Hold button, and that will tell you the maximum level that's detected. Stay down there till you get a number above fifty-five."

There was no one in the street when he cracked the door, so he ran across in his pajamas and pressed the mic against the throbbing building.

"Max/Hold!" Mona shouted from their bedroom window.

The meter showed 60, then 66, then 71. He looked up at her and shouted, "Seventy-one!"

"I'm calling the police." She shut the window.

That was when the cargo van turned onto the street and lit Tim up. "Hey!" one brother shouted from the passenger side as he opened the door of the moving vehicle. The other then stopped the van short, and they were both on him before Tim could get back across the street. One shoved him into the other, who grabbed his shoulders. "What're you doing? Jacking off on our bar?" *Bam!* He punched Tim in the belly while the other one hooked Tim's elbows and held fast. Tim tried to kick the one in front, but the guy hopped back. Then he came in again hard at the ribs, three shots. Tim bawled like a calf. His feet were kicked out from under him by the guy in back, and as he crashed to his knees, he was bricked again in the face. Pain shot into the ends of his hair. He let loose a horse's scream.

"Belt him," the guy behind grunted, and the puncher unbuckled his belt and yanked it out. He whipped it behind him, and then it came whizzing back, so the buckle thwacked Tim's right upper arm. The guy thrashed in a frenzy, pulping Tim's arms, which shrieked and burned like in a branding. Then the beast threw the belt aside and walked back toward the van— for a bat, maybe, or a two-by-four. Tim sucked in as much air as he could and shoved out a wet bray. The guy stopped then and turned, rocked himself to gather momentum like a long jumper about to launch. How could this be continuing? Tim wondered. Where was everyone else in the world? The bull finally propelled himself in four bounds toward Tim and blasted him in the crotch with a boot. It was like being hot-knifed and cannonballed at the same time. Finally, Tim was living only in the moment, sensing only ringing pain and nausea.

Footfalls came, finally, down Tim's porch stairs, and he watched Vinnie fly onto the monster, take him down sideways, pin him and knee his groin with shuddering constancy. When at last the other guy released Tim's arms, Tim fell sideways. He watched Miles kick at the guy's back, his long hair flouncing, arms winging, until the boy's boot was snatched up and he was pulled off balance, his head cracking onto the road. It was only after three rounds of gunfire that everyone finally flopped and rolled apart.

"I have called the police!" Mona shouted from the window, her father's gun pointed skyward.

JENNY

In the Good Behavior Game, a teacher divides her students into four teams. Jenny had named the teams by colors, which the children wore on their wrists—colored rubber bands. Several times a day, she would announce that a game was to begin, and she would remind them what good behavior looked and sounded like during whatever lesson or activity they were about to do, and also what some of the unwanted behaviors looked and sounded like. No leaving your seat, for instance. No talking over others. After the brief review, she would set the timer for twenty-five minutes (that was the amount of time they were up to now) and go about the lesson. When Jenny witnessed a distracting behavior, she would say which team the perpetrator was on and make a tally mark on the board for that team. But no child was named personally. No one got individual attention for acting out. Then, when the buzzer rang, any team with three or fewer tallies could participate in the prize, which was always just some quick release of energy, like thirty seconds of dancing. The game had worked wonders for her students, and for her! She had moved from crying throughout the day to feeling like she actually taught a few things of value. She had grown to like some of the kids she had once thoroughly hated. Bullying and tattling had all but ended in her classroom.

It was the idea of not letting the team down that was the key to this game. People might not care about the prize for themselves, but very few could feel apathetic about hurting others' chances at the prize. Jenny wondered what might have happened had Megan's early teachers known about this game. Maybe it would have changed her. Jenny herself felt she had been playing this game all her life, adjusting her behavior to fit expectations, especially in church. The rules had been clearer at the church; it was easier there. But now those rules were melting. Dogs could go to heaven. The day before, the Pope had said it wasn't even necessary to go to church, or to give the church money! So the rules were fluid, and besides that, she had come to realize that the prizes were no longer motivating at home or in church. In fact, she didn't know what the prizes had ever been. And the great success of this game in her classroom—how easy and how profound the changes had been—made her feel bitter about all of the years of unnecessary anguish. Cheated.

As she applied lipstick, she caught sight of the white Jeep with its soft top on, pulling past her in the bus station lot and parking in front and to the right of her car. Heavy rock music punched out of the Wrangler and she could see his drumming thumbs on the steering wheel.

Now that she knew what her early life choices had led to, she wanted a redo. On all of them. On Davis, on teaching, on Catholicism, on Megan. And for some reason, the biggest drive within her in these past months had been for a redo on her life as a young, sexual being, as someone who was seen, craved. She would like to give in, this time, to all temptations.

She rolled her lipstick into its tube and popped the cap back on, picturing herself beside that young brute in the Jeep's woolly interior, crossing dunes, ending at the sea. Then, as though hearing her cue, she snapped her purse closed and stepped out of the Nissan, walked right past his open window, bold as you please, through a fog of his musky cologne, his rugged face there in the side-view mirror. And just at that moment, he sang out with the chorus, startling her into a stagger. "And you've stayed too long. That fire has jumped the break." She put a hand to his hot hood to steady herself. "There's not a car that can outrun my [something]. It's going to overtake!" The brazen voice of a man ready to seize her.

She would go into the station and come back out for another pass, she decided. Inside, she bought water from the vending machine and pretended to browse the brochures. She'd no intention of speaking to him. That's not why she had come. She wanted a glimpse down the rabbit hole at the life that was her truer life, the one she had denied herself. Envisioning that life had required real actors, and she owed them the courtesy of taking it as far as she could. She pushed open the door to the outside and smiled right at him as she approached this time, made a beeline for his passenger side like she would if she really was Blondie, then let her fingertips slide along the length of the Jeep as she passed.

When she shut herself into her sedan again and set her purse back on the passenger seat, it was 2:15. She wondered how long Mike would wait for her after the Greenstown bus arrived. How soon after would he text to ask where she was?

Then a fat man caught her attention as he hobbled down the lane between the rows of cars, his face bruised and hard set under a reddish brush of hair. With one sleeve empty of a hand, he came around the back of Mike's car and then that sleeve went right into Mike's window as the man began to bark. She couldn't hear what he was saying, but his near eye was swollen shut and his head thrust with each spitting word. When he pulled the arm back out there was a gun at the end of it, which he kept trained on Mike as he stepped back enough to let him out of the car. She was witnessing a carjacking! Jenny pulled her purse onto her lap to find her cell, but Mike then took a ring of keys from the armed man, and he just ambled down the row, looking back a few times, while the fat guy climbed into the Jeep. She watched Mike enter a red truck, which then screamed out of its spot, down the row, ripping through the drop-off area and onto the road.

What had she witnessed? That redheaded man looked familiar to her in some way, and she finally hit on the idea that it was Rusty he resembled, an older Rusty—Rusty's father! She hadn't seen a picture of the father, but she was now certain of it. Was Rusty's father now waiting for her? Had something happened to Rusty?

She had just grabbed her purse and reached for the door handle when an older, red Volvo sedan like Davis's crept by, PG 433 on the license plate. Dear God, it *was* Davis. How was this possible? she thought. What was occurring? Did her car have a tracking device? She started her engine. Then she noticed that he'd pulled around to the front of the white Jeep and stopped, right in the lane. He left his car door ajar and dinging as he walked to the driver's side of the Jeep and spoke with Rusty's father. Jenny slid down so only her eyes were above the wheel.

There he was, lecturing the poor man about what? She knew that expression well. Davis was the warner-in-chief. A great crusty mess marked his jacket sleeve; his flat hair was unwashed; his eyes had sunk into dark hollows. He was at sea without her. This was why she had avoided him. She didn't want to come upon this wreckage and be lured away from her Mexico plans.

It was quite a long conversation for two complete strangers. Davis did a lot of insistent nodding and shaking of his head *yes* and then *no*, disgusted. Then he turned to look beyond her, at the bus that was coming down the road, the 2:25, which made its way around to the back of the station. He pushed off from the door of the Jeep, slapped the hood, and returned to his car. Then the Jeep backed out, circled around to the road, and left.

She watched Davis park and hurry into the station. He'd come for her, knowing he had rivals.

DAVIS

After zippering his pistol back into its case on the motel bureau, he stood back from it. By the time he had driven halfway down there, he knew he wasn't going to shoot the man. But he'd wanted to see him. And her. Together. What a strange scene it had been. The man was overweight (he'd sent her a shirtless photo?). When Davis told him Jenny was his wife, the tub said he'd only known her as Blondie, and wasn't Davis a bit old? "Me? What about you?" Davis had said, "How old do you think she is, anyway?" Then he learned that she'd claimed to be eighteen. "God, no. Forty-five."

"I've seen her volleyball videos," Bellyroll had argued. "She's no forty-five."

"That's our daughter!" Davis shouted at him. "Volleyball? That's my daughter you think you're meeting! Well, joke's on you, buddy, because the woman you spoke to on the phone was my wife. I heard her talking to you."

The man looked pained as he started the Jeep. "It was going to end today anyway."

"I want to see your driver's license," Davis had said. "I want to know who you are."

"Tough."

"I've got a gun in my waistband." Davis looked about the lot. Then he untucked his shirt to display the handle of the gun. "Three-fifty-seven."

The porker actually gave it some thought before hoisting

himself up to get his wallet out. Then he held it open with his driver's license in a see-through slot. Timothy Turner, Malden, Mass.

"You stay away from my daughter, Timothy Turner, or you will be dealt with. You hear me?" He pushed away from the window.

After all that, she never even got off the bus! Jenny hadn't come to meet the guy. But then how could she if she was playing eighteen? She never intended to meet him. She was trying to turn back time, he knew, while he himself was forever slogging forward.

#

While he stood at the motel room window and watched the Lobster Shanty bartender hoist a trash bag up into a bin, Davis used his newly returned phone to call his lawyer. He told the guy about the pervert at the bus station and about the videos his wife had clearly sent this man of their daughter playing volleyball. "Can't you use that to get her to convince Megan to knock this off?"

"Do you need something else I can get for you from the house? That might be a good time to mention it."

"Get me my Fouke Monster castings. And remind my wife of Aletta Van Der Hooft, will you? Mention the coffee-and-a-cigarette lady that I never got to know, which was my great sacrifice. Now it's time for hers."

He pressed the button to hang up and walked out across the parking lot, cold in his shirtsleeves, toward the pulsing red lobster sign. He thought he'd have a Tanqueray this time. Perhaps he'd tell the bartender the story of the "extinct" catamount. He still had a video of it on his phone. Long tail switching in the grass. Impossible to fake.

VINNIE

D evlin's dead mother's house—the one that should now be his and Vinnie's—was a bit squat and had vinyl siding that Vinnie would have scrapped, but since Devlin was living here with Mia now, that didn't matter. Still, Vinnie pictured himself replanting the gardens, wearing some old, soft chinos, and painting the front door aquamarine as the sun now rose to illuminate it all.

"Miles"—Vinnie woke the kid, who'd been sleeping a few hours now in the truck—"it's her." A woman's face had appeared in one of the windows, and because she kept moving away and then back into place, Vinnie figured it for the window above the kitchen sink. She had a pinched look, he thought. A malcontent. She was probably critical of Devlin, whereas Vinnie had always been overly encouraging and supportive, to a fault probably. "Wait till she sees the car."

As if on cue, the sun off the silver Miata must have flashed in her eyes, because she leaned toward the window and her jaw dropped. There it was, in her driveway, at last.

"Here she comes." Vinnie elbowed Miles, again.

She wrapped a sweater around herself as she stepped off the porch and floated across the frosty lawn in her pink slippers and pajama pants. The newly washed and waxed car looked straight off the assembly line, and the headlights—Vinnie had spent a whole day wet-sanding them—like crystals. Now she's thinking about how great she will look in it, he figured. Her hair would have to be carefully managed, but this car would likely be the best dress she'd ever owned.

"Here we go." Vinnie wasn't trying to hide from her. He didn't duck in the truck cab. He hadn't parked down the street, because she wouldn't be looking at anything but the dream car.

They watched her lift the passenger door handle and crack open her present. Then nothing. "Where are they?" asked Miles as they both leaned toward the scene.

The men had shut the three dogs in for five hours with marrow bones littering the interior like in a mass grave. Marrow, Vinnie learned, gave dogs the runs.

At last, the dogs shot from the car, bouncing off of the frozen woman and shaking off foamy loads of saliva with each leap upon her pink legs.

"Devlin!" Mia flung her arms into the air and scrambled back to the house while the wet mutts whirled around her. "Dogs have shit up my whole fucking wedding car!"

Once she was shut inside, the guys opened the truck doors, stepped out, and whistled for the trio. Miles loaded them into the crate, and Vinnie then had to wedge the cage onto the kid's lap after he was back in place. When they pulled off, Vinnie said, "Did you look in that car? Did you see it? Don't fuck with us, people."

"I think they need water," Miles said while the dogs licked his face through the wire.

"Sure. We'll get water. And when we get back, I'll leave them out in your grandma's yard for a while to get everything out of their system."

"Guys, guys," Miles protested, giggling. "They're gonna be happy to get home. Her oven doesn't work, by the way."

"That's fine, I'm only there six months. I can eat salad. I need to lose weight for the part anyway."

Miles kept moving his squinting face up against the cage

for tongue flashes and then pulling away again.

"It's the lead role." Vinnie waited for a question. "I don't know if I told you, but this theater is the best in Boston. Of course, they wouldn't cast me for a deaf mute before. Oh, yeah! True story! But now that I've been in New York, everything's different. And that's how it goes."

"That sucks."

"Well, it makes sense, though, because if you make it in New York, then you are at the very top. No denying it. Hey, read me some more of your grandma's book," he said to Miles, who then managed to reach around the crate and pull his phone off the dash.

"We're on chapter ten, The Power of the Bush."

"'The Power of the Bush,'" Vinnie repeated, like announcing a fighter in the ring. "That's a best seller right there, Miles. Get ready for a very famous grandma."

TIM

Sunny stopped on her way through the living room, her arms loaded with used books from a sale. She looked weary. "I feel sorry for you, Tim."

"Well, I feel sorry for you. What's it been? Three weeks?" A mover's blanket had been covering her floor the whole time, to contain all of his pegs and tools, but it was now nearly Thanksgiving and he was still at that Klopotek. It was the making of the jig that offset his drill press to the precise angle of the peg holes that had been the biggest bear; now it was just the slow process of repositioning the jig precisely for every hole, clamping it down and drilling. "I'll try to finish up, but you may be making me a plate of turkey on the day," he said, as he tap-tapped the jig with the wooden mallet, microshifting it into position.

That afternoon, Tim and company were to move another piano; it had become his main business again since he'd been fired from *Bells Up*. They moved pianos in the evenings and on weekends when Mike was available, since he was the strongest among them. It couldn't happen without Mike, so he'd been forgiven.

"Are you going to Sheena's party tonight?" he called out in the direction of the library.

"Hadn't heard of it," she said, reappearing in the doorway.

"Oh, I'm sure it's just for singers, then. One of those things."

"I give more than I'd care to say to that organization."

"Aw, you don't want to go to this thing, Sunny. It's a party in name only. The woman should be a funeral director." He was going only because Mona had seen the invitation from the Opera's artistic director as a sure sign she was back in favor, that she maybe had a chance at Rosina. "I'm telling you a week in advance so you can get pants that fit," she'd told Tim, and when she learned he was going to move a piano that afternoon, she panicked about time, so Tim told her if he was not back by six-thirty, he would meet her there. "I have to take this job," he'd said. "The piano store guy is the don."

Tim rolled down the drill bit to test his position and then made a few more taps and tried again. Precision work was not his thing.

"Will you tell me if there are other donors there?" She'd come back to the doorway.

"I certainly will," he said, and then switched on the drill and cranked the bit into the hole, where it sent shreds streaming out like frightened, skinny worms.

# # #

The Bösendorfer Model 225 Semi Concert Grand has four extra bass keys and weighs in at a whopping 924 pounds. This one was going into a condo in what was once a Back Bay town house. Tim knew it was on the third floor, but he hadn't shared this with the guys. They double-parked the piano store's truck on Commonwealth Ave., and Vinnie looked up at the elegant buildings with their mansard roofs. "What floor?"

"Think of your tip," Tim said as he swung out.

When Mike arrived, they rolled the piano into the foyer, and Tim covered the first flight of marble stairs with blankets. The side of the beast that would rest on the stairs had a board strapped to it that would allow it to slide. Tim and Miles, it was decided, would control the upstairs end, yanking on straps, so they got into position, and then the other two tipped the piano until its long end rested on the blanketed treads. "Mike," Tim instructed, "put the top of your head right up against the case, just above the fallboard. Vinnie, you'll walk up behind him with your hands pushing up higher. Now it'll be one, two, push, then hold. Okay, ready? One, two, push!"

"Arghh!" Mike groaned. A small movement occurred. Six inches.

"And one, two, push!"

They roared.

"Kick the lower blankets out as you go." Tim would make $250 for this move. The others would get $100 each, plus dividing the tip. If he lucked out, Tim would score tuning work, too.

"One, two, push!"

# # #

Joe Masotta had fixed this life for him. Joe, who had sat beside The Publisher on stage and exchanged pleasantries with her over their handheld mics, and when he'd answered all of her questions and she asked if there was anything else he'd like to touch on, Joe had smiled another moment and then begun, "Pain retains. That's a Marine saying." And The Publisher had looked out to the audience with an ecstatic expression. "We were told that a lot in boot camp," he continued. "When the sergeant wanted you to remember something for a very long time, he'd make sure it hurt. We'd say it during relentless push-ups with our muscles on fire. Pain retains. We'd say it when we were forced to hold our heavy racks off the floor for an eternity. And while I was in agony, every single night, I also had to contend with obsessive thoughts of my best friend, Tim

Turner, screwing the only girl I ever loved. You know Tim?" he turned to ask The Publisher, whose smile could not be relaxed.

"Senior editor for *Bells Up,* I believe," the man said. "Tim, would you like to stand?" But Tim held fast. "He's sitting in among all of you wonderful band leaders who should also know that this journal that you imagine celebrates you actually looks at you with disdain, sees you, in fact, as liars and thieves. Weren't those your words?" He'd turned again to The Publisher. Then he went on to say that this woman also despised her staff. And had, in fact, refused to give a breast cancer victim's family her final paycheck.

"That's a lie!" The Publisher hauled herself up, her metal chair teetering. "Her check is to be presented tonight! In a special ceremony! Bring out the check, Rita!" She called into the wings. And then, after hearing someone knocking about backstage, the audience saw a slight woman in an outmoded long dress struggling to cross with the oversize check. "Is Angela's family here?" The Publisher called out.

Rita rapidly shook her head. "They were only invited to the party," she whispered loudly.

"It's for quite a bit more than she'd earned," announced The Publisher in her most majestic voice.

# # #

By the time they got the Bösendorfer safely onto the first half-flight landing, their heads had purpled and their breaths were as loud as bellows. Miles rubbed his hands on his pants. "It's slipping on me, Dad. I can't do this."

"Are you saying we have to do what we just did five more times?" Mike agreed.

"No. We don't have to do it five more times. No. We only have to do it one more time. Get to there." Tim nodded up to the next landing.

"Yeah, each time, one more time," said Miles.

"You know, we might get a thousand-dollar tip on this one, guys? It's possible." Tim patted Vinnie on the back. "Take a rest," Tim told them. "We're not working by the hour." He would be happy to miss Mona's opera party, where she would likely hear that someone else got Rosina, after all of her believing. He put his forehead against the landing window, looked down at a Mercedes parked in the alleyway. "Mercedes-Benz. Look at that. I ever tell you guys about the time I dropped a gallon of white primer out a fourth-floor window onto a black Mercedes-Benz? Oh, God, this is a good one."

# # #

Before Joe Masotta dropped his payload at the convention, before the interview of sorrows, one hundred and six men and women in black trousers and dark jackets discovered their kin on Boylston Street in downtown Boston and were arranged into rows by a chubby man with a clipboard as they held aloft their glimmering treasures, recently unearthed and oiled— music having weeks before been laid on a kitchen table where their breath began, again, to turn into sound, no, a song.

"You got a lyre?" Tim asked one flutist about her music clip, but she shook her head and said she didn't need one; she had the music memorized. "You're my idol," he told her.

They hadn't practiced any of the three pieces together even once, and this made them all nervous, being the taskmasters their jobs had required.

"How long's it been?" they asked their neighbors, some with ranks-collapsing comebacks.

The mix was lopsided, too few clarinets and way too many tenor saxes. Drummers evidently did not often go into music education; they had only three snares. "Twenty trombones!"

Tim cried, putting the last one in line. They all turned to high-five. Tim had brought in ringers from his old playing days, a guy on cymbals, two bass drums.

Those who lived locally were waving off their families to go find places along the route. The players were nearly all over forty and many well past that. They were instantly in love with each other and laughed too loudly and pretended they couldn't see the tiny music and were liable to trip in the effort. One man shouted out, "Six to five? Eight to five? Some of us have a limited stride," and they all hooted.

"Twenty to five!" one woman decided.

Tim gave the order of the pieces: "The Washington Post," "Hands Across the Sea," and "Our Director" (for obvious reasons). He hoped they'd be playing "Hands Across the Sea" as they began circling the Common, where most of the people were. It was a grand piece with some big tuba statements, and he knew these players would have it down.

Soon they got the signal to start, and Tim lifted his sousaphone over his head and joined the other five of his kind. He'd borrowed their enormous instruments from a local high school along with the bass drums.

They were silent in anticipation. Then the snares played the cadence that precedes a march and the band stepped off. They'd only gone a block before the drums changed their rhythm to signal the start of first piece, and all bells rose. Sousa's "The Washington Post" begins with a little windup—everyone playing the same notes in different octaves, a climb and a descent, a climb and a descent, a climb and final descent to a complete, full stop. *Kshhhh!* A cymbal crash. And now they're off and running, with alternating soft and loud proclamations of the vast superiority of everyone playing and hearing this music over everyone else on the earth.

EPILOGUE

Dear Rusty, I'm not trying to start up again, just a note to say that I bought the land in Pozos that your friend was selling, and now that we've settled our daughter in California (where she seems to have a quality that many movie directors love!), we're down here putting up a casita. Your friend Phyllis, the realtor, has introduced us around, to all the other ex-pats. The common denominator is that we all believe in signs. You must believe in signs to decide that this is the place. Davis is out dawn to dusk, hunting the chupacabra, the "goatsucker." He will be voted in as mayor if he finds it, as it eats a lot of livestock. He is also planning a museum in the town, which God knows could use some kind of a draw. When I first imagined myself in this place, you were here with me and we were wild and young, our hair ropy with dust, our bodies strong, and for some reason I saw you playing the guitar while strolling the mountainside. And I don't even know if you're musical at all!

I'm happy to have known you, Rusty. It's like we invented a new piece of the past that we can now remember beside all of the other pieces: the time when you were a gunner on a fire team at war, when I was such a man's desire.

ACKNOWLEDGMENTS

This novel had a great number of contributors, not least were the friends and family who read it at early stages and made wonderful suggestions: Renee Bender, Margaret J. Broucek, Sharon Rousseau Brown, Brock Clarke, Joan Dempsey, Anne Dubuisson, Larry Mondi, Kate Montgomery, Bill Roorbach, Leigh St. Pierre, and Karen Smith.

Thanks also to my muse, the great Chicago storyteller Jack Zimmerman, who told me stories over beers that inspired some of the better scenes in this book.

Hewnoaks Artist Colony provided me time away to write (and surrounded me with introverts so I was forced to).

Unending gratitude goes to Tim Schaffner, my adventuresome publisher, and Sean Murphy, my comedy-loving editor, who have brought this novel into the light of day with great care and passion.

Brian McMullen created the arresting cover design.

Pamela Marshall was the novel's sharp-eyed copyeditor, a real language maven.

And finally, big thanks to my family and friends for celebrating and commiserating with this lucky writer.

Two books, in particular, helped me write about foreign territory: *Into the Fire: A Firsthand Account of the Most Extraordinary Battle in the Afghan War* by Dakota Meyer and Bing West and *Cryptozoology A to Z: The Encyclopedia of Loch Monsters, Sasquatch, Chupacabras, and Other Authentic Mysteries of Nature* by Loren Coleman and Jerome Clark

Most of Davis's cryptid trophy collection can and should be seen in person at the wonderful International Cryptozoology Museum in Portland, Maine.

ABOUT THE AUTHOR

Margaret Broucek is a filmmaker and playwright whose works have appeared Off-Broadway and in festivals in the U.S. and Europe. She has had short stories published in the anthologies *Sudden Fiction, Continued* (W.W. Norton) and *Best of TriQuarterly*, and also in *Alaska Quarterly Review*. She holds an MFA in Writing from Sarah Lawrence College.

PUBLISHER'S NOTE

THE NICHOLAS SCHAFFNER AWARD FOR MUSIC IN LITERATURE celebrates the life of the publisher's brother, Nicholas: poet, musician, esteemed music critic, and author of several books, including *THE BEATLES FOREVER, THE BRITISH INVASION, and SAUCERFUL OF SECRETS: The Pink Floyd Odyssey*. Nicholas, who devoted his life to music and literature about music, died in 1991 at the age of thirty-eight. This award has been created to celebrate his legacy and to encourage emerging writers whose lives and writing have been profoundly influenced by music.

For submission guidelines, please visit
www.schaffnerpress.com

Bateus)